MW01034539

"*War in the Wastela...* known for many years ... storyteller. Indeed, this .... of a can't-put-it-down thriller with the intellectual tensions of a historical drama: taut plotting, strong characters, and soaring backdrop. Put this one on the top of your must-read list."
GEORGE GRANT, author, teacher, pastor at Parish Presbyterian Church

"*War in the Wasteland* is a gripping, informative, adrenalin-producing picture of World War I. Bond captures on every page the awful moments of fear and the reflective conversations of men who don't know if they'll survive the day."
DOUGLAS E. LEE, Brigadier General, USA (Ret), President, Chaplain Alliance for Religious Liberty

"Douglas Bond is a historian with unusual insight."
RUSS PULLIAM, *Indianapolis Star*

"*War in the Wasteland* gives a back story of the pre-Christian Lewis, a literate atheist arguing against God in the trenches of the Great War. A non-nostalgic glimpse of war, Bond's characters bring historical life and color to the human costs in WWI, without romanticizing its brutality."
MIKE T. SUGIMOTO, Professor of Asian Studies and Great Books, Pepperdine University

"Douglas Bond is one of my family's favorite authors. A new Bond book produces a thrill of anticipation around our table. His latest, *War in the Wasteland*—a compelling, emotive story—lives up to this reputation."
RAY VAN NESTE, Chair of Biblical Studies, Union University

WAR IN THE WASTELAND

Also by Douglas Bond

Mr. Pipes and the British Hymn Makers
Mr. Pipes and Psalms and Hymns of the Reformation
Mr. Pipes Comes to America
The Accidental Voyage

Duncan's War
King's Arrow
Rebel's Keep

Guns of Thunder
Guns of the Lion
Guns of Providence

Hostage Lands
Hand of Vengeance
Hammer of the Huguenots
The Revolt, a novel in Wycliffe's England

STAND FAST In the Way of Truth
HOLD FAST In a Broken World

The Betrayal: A Novel on John Calvin
The Thunder: A Novel on John Knox

The Mighty Weakness of John Knox
The Poetic Wonder of Isaac Watts

Augustus Toplady: Debtor to Mercy Alone
Girolamo Savonarola: Heart Aflame

Grace Works! (And Ways We Think It Doesn't)
God's Servant Job

WAR IN THE WASTELAND

DOUGLAS BOND

IBP
INKBLOTS
PRESS

ISBN-13: 978-1-945062-00-1 (pbk)
ISBN-13: 978-1-945062-01-8 (ePub)

Cover: Photograph by James Francis Hurley, taken October 5, 1917. Original held at the National Media Museum, UK; there are "no known copyright restrictions."
Cover designed by Robert Treskillard.
Printed in the United States of America
Library of Congress Cataloging-in-Publication Data
Bond, Douglas, 1958-
War in the Wasteland / Douglas Bond.
pages cm
Summary: Nigel Hopkins finds himself in the trenches of World War I under the command of teenage atheist 2/Lt C.S. Lewis. Nigel and his war dog must learn the source of true courage while facing a desperate enemy in No Man's Land in the final offensive of the war. Meanwhile, underage WAAC Elsie Fleming, working at the field hospital in Étaples, will have her idealism about war challenged by the brutal realities she sees in the broken men who return from the Front—and the many who never return.

ISBN: 978-1-945062-00-1 (pbk.)
1. C.S. Lewis--Juvenile fiction. 2. World War I--History--20th century--Fiction. [1. World War I--Fiction. 2. France--History--20th century--Fiction. 3. Courage in wartime--Fiction. 4. Animals in World War I--Fiction. 5. Christian apologetics--History--20th century--Fiction. 6. Christian life--Fiction.] I. Title.
PZ7.B63665War 2016
[Fic]--dc23
2015001268

For
Gillian, Giles; Desmond and Shauna;
Cedric and Ashley;
Rhodric, Tori, Gwenna, and Amelia;
Brittany and Jesse

With gratitude to my mother

In memory of
the combined dead and wounded of World War I
37,000,000 souls

In acknowledgement of
50,000 dogs who served in World War I

"The first bullet I heard 'whined' like a journalist's or a peacetime poet's bullet. At that moment there was something not exactly like fear… a little quavering signal that said, 'This is War. This is what Homer wrote about.'"

C. S. Lewis, November 29, 1917

"Patriotism is not enough; I must have no hatred or bitterness towards anyone."

Edith Cavell, facing a German firing squad in 1915

"One has indeed personally to come under the shadow of war to feel fully its oppression; …to be caught in youth by 1914 was no less hideous… By 1918, all but one of my close friends were dead."

J. R. R. Tolkien

CONTENTS

1.	Birthday Conscription	11
2.	Sauerkraut Spy	19
3.	Blood on the Pier	25
4.	Torpedo	32
5.	Bayonet	42
6.	The Advocate	50
7.	Bacon	54
8.	French Boots	66
9.	Trench Billet	73
10.	Nowhere Safe	80
11.	Bullet and Barbed Wire	89
12.	Night Raid	97
13.	Latrine Duty	102
14.	Wrong Duty	109
15.	Prisoner	115
16.	Morning Hate	126
17.	Captains of Our Fate	133
18.	Quarrelling	143
19.	Cosmic Sadist	149
20.	Trench Foot	159
21.	Whispers in the Night	163
22.	Villains by Necessity	170
23.	Backs to the Wall	177
24.	Conscience Round	185
25.	Vickers Machine Gun	193
26.	Fusillading	199
27.	Don't Shoot	207
28.	Sniper	213
29.	The Quick and the Dead	220

30.	Meaningless	226
31.	Creeping Barrage	236
32.	This is War	242
33.	No Man's Land	248
34.	Flesh Wounds	257
35.	Extraordinary Destiny	265

Glossary of World War I Terms	274
Timeline of World War I	278
Acknowledgments	279

1

BIRTHDAY CONSCRIPTION

Standing at attention on the crowded pier in Dover, Nigel Hopkins could not ignore the war of emotions gnawing inside his chest like rats at a rubbish heap. Hooking his thumbs in the straps of his rucksack, he tried easing the weight. On tip-toe, he strained to get a better look over the broad shoulders in front of him. The gangplank seemed miles away, and the column of khaki-uniformed soldiers waiting to board the troopship seemed endless. Back on his heels, Nigel adjusted the strap on his Tin hat, and swallowed hard at the lump that had lodged in his throat three weeks ago.

"Ayres! Wallace! Spike! Perrett! Hopkins!" Barking in a penetrating monotone, as easy to ignore as an air-raid siren, a sergeant read off names of platoons and squads, and shouted orders—always shouting.

Crammed together like kippered herring in a tin, there was little space for the men to move. The back of the soldier ahead of Nigel was so close to his nose he could smell the bacon and buttered toast the fellow had eaten for breakfast—and the minty scent of his shave cream. His khaki shoulders did not move. Nobody moved. In three weeks of training, he'd learned at least one thing about soldiering: hurry up and wait. Or was that two things?

Rising like the cold walls of a prison, the topsides of a troop carrier towered above the pier. Nigel scowled. How were all these men going to fit in that boat? The pier was enshrouded with a vast sea of British wool and Tin hats containing men waiting to board one-time merchant ship RMS *Amazon*. Like the men, it too had been conscripted to serve the British Expeditionary Force. Thousands of men, not hundreds. Crammed inside its iron confines, off to France, and war. As if finger painted by Gulliver's children, the troopship had been splotched with white, gray, and charcoal paint, apparently to create a camouflage that would be harder for German reconnaissance biplanes to spot from the air, or U-boats to pick off as the floating coffin rose and fell with the roiling swell of the English Channel.

Turbulent as the sea swell, the war of emotions heaved in Nigel's insides. For three years he had read the news reports of the war to end all wars. He had been fifteen years old August 4, 1914 when the Kaiser mobilized his troops, in defiance of international treaty, to invade neutral Belgium. Fifteen when King George V and his Prime Minister Herbert Henry Asquith declared war on Germany and the Central Powers and threw in the lot of all Britain with France and Russia in the Triple Entente.

Along with everyone else in England, Nigel had been thrilled with the prospect of war—at first. He could think of little else. Lying awake at night, he would imagine his exploits, his skill in marksmanship, his valor in the teeth of danger, his prowess in killing Germans, his rapid climbing up the ranks, a battlefield commission, a company command—giving instead of taking orders.

Nigel would imagine the king pinning the Victoria Cross over his heart, the swelling adulation of all Britain gathered in the streets to welcome her courageous son home from war. A speedy war, a decisive victory, a glorious triumph. Newspapers had been filled with little else. Fueling the initial euphoria, poets had sharpened their quills, enflaming the young men of Britain to volunteer and drive back the enemy.

For all we have and are,
For all our children's fate,
Stand up and take the war,
The Hun is at the gate!

So Rudyard Kipling had urged all young men in England. The tabloids had reported that the beloved author was so eager to see his own son in uniform against the Hun, Kipling had petitioned every government official he knew to get his son John enlisted. "If you can keep your wits about you while all others are losing theirs, and blaming you," Kipling reportedly had written to his son, "the world will be yours and everything in it; what's more, you'll be a man, my son."

The world and everything in it. It was intoxicating. "War might teach you a bit about taking orders," Nigel's father had commented, eyeing his son over the morning newspaper. "But at such a price." For reasons that had both frustrated and worried Nigel, his father had been more tentative about the extent to which this war would make boys into men. "May do for some. But the rest? War like this war? It'll make 'em dead men." Murmuring the words, Nigel's father had then tossed the newspaper onto the floor and returned to his tea and toast.

The recruiting posters seemed to agree with the poets. Nigel had felt more than a twinge of guilt in 1914 while on a visit to his aunt's for Guy Fawke's Day in London. At the base of one of the giant bronze lions in Trafalgar Square, smartly uniformed cavalry officers invited men to enlist. Amidst the blaring of horns, the puttering engines of motor taxis, and the clattering of horses' hooves on the cobblestones, the wide bell of a phonograph rang out the call to arms, and hundreds of men queued up to heed the call, the line trailing for blocks beyond the entrance to the closest underground rail station.

"How old do you want to be?" called one of the officers. The man was looking directly at Nigel. "Strong young lad like you, not a day under eighteen, I should think."

As he studied the other young men in that long queue, many of them looked fifteen, so it seemed to Nigel; later, in his sleep, they would all be fifteen, fifteen and sneering, and pointing an accusing finger at his chest. From a poster, Secretary of State for War, Lord Kitchener stared with dispassionate though penetrating eyes, pointing his index finger directly at Nigel's chest.

At that moment, he had wanted to wrench himself from his aunt's side and take his place in the queue, for England, for the free world. Nothing would be more glorious. But there was the matter of his age. He had cajoled all he had dared; his father would never approve of his enlisting, not until his eighteenth birthday.

Nigel smiled ruefully with recollection. Three years ago, he had been bitterly certain the war would be long over before he ever turned eighteen. So had his mother—at the first. "Surely, it will soon be at an end, surely, it will be," so she often declared, first with smiling confidence. But as the war ground on, the same words faltered into a tremulous question. Ineligible, Nigel feared fighting was beyond his reach; he had felt bitterly cheated by this war. Why couldn't he be older? Why couldn't the war last? He had even prayed that it would last, though he had done it in secret. In a war, he could do his bit for England, and war could do its bit for him—make a man of him.

That had been three years ago. During which Nigel had celebrated his sixteenth birthday, the war still roaring on; Kipling's son John killed in a gas attack at Loos in 1915. And then his seventeenth birthday, war still raging on. That was 1916 and the Battle of the Somme, with more casualties in a single day of fighting than in any other in British history. Thirty-six grinding months of war, each month producing more facial hair, and with each new whisker, bringing Nigel closer and closer to his eighteenth birthday party. Each month also brought new reports of death and dismemberment from the Front, the initial euphoria of volunteers dwindling proportionately.

The numbers were staggering. So immense, with effort Nigel found it possible to simply ignore them, to imagine that each number did not actually represent a human being, a young man, like himself, made of flesh and blood, hopes and dreams—and fears. When he read in the *London Times* of 250,000 casualties in but four days at the first Battle of the Marne, or of 60,000 on the first day alone of the Battle of the Somme, with average daily casualties in that five-month battle over 5,000, a body count of 750,000 lives, he refused to think of them as men, individual human beings with mothers and fathers, sisters and brothers, sons and daughters, best girls and wives. They were just numbers, pawns on the chessboard of a continent, but not real flesh-and-blood men—young men, many only months older than Nigel.

Though he attempted to ignore the over-burdening reality, Nigel found his enthusiasm for war plummeting with every new casualty report. It seemed that the human race had outdone itself. By creating a war technology so cataclysmically ingenious in killing, then turning those weapons on itself, they were annihilating the very human ingenuity that had invented the weapons in the first place. German artillery and machine guns, capable of cutting down large quantities of men in an instant of time, had so reduced the British Army at the Front, it was feared that by attrition alone, simply too few men left to resist, the Central Powers would overrun the free world. Britain would be no more.

Hence, the daily carnage had created a numerical imperative. To replace the ranks left vacant by death, more men were urgently needed, vastly more. The recruiting poster with the Secretary of State for War pointing at the viewer had taken on a tragic significance. Torpedoed by a German U-boat in 1916, Lord Kitchener had perished at sea, himself a casualty of the war into which his guilt-inflicting eyes and pointed finger had cajoled so many men.

And then it arrived. Nigel's birthday. His eighteenth birthday. And it had not taken a blaring phonograph calling him voluntarily to arms, or the guilt and shame induced by recruiting posters. It was life or death. His country needed him. The war needed him. But now it was no longer a matter of patriotic choice.

Nigel would never forget that birthday. Old Billy the postman had shuffled up to the barn just as Nigel had finished measuring out feed for the pigeons. It was a gray, drizzly morning in October. "And many happy returns of the day," Billy had murmured, diverting his eyes as he handed Nigel the envelope. Not just any envelope. It was perfumed with *eau de bureaucrat*, aromas of carbon type-writer ink, odors of tobacco smoke, with hints of floral-scented hand soap. An official communique from the War Office—stuffed, stamped, and sealed with Nigel's conscription order.

Nigel's eighteenth birthday dinner, mutton and boiled potatoes, had been a meagre and solemn affair, his mother often turning and dabbing her eyes with the corner of her apron. Angrily, he blinked back the hot moisture that wanted to whelm up in his own eyes as he took leave of his family. Gripping his father's work-hardened hand, Nigel had felt a sick emptiness taking cold possession of his heart, and no amount of blinking had kept back his own tears as he kissed his mother good-bye. But there was one family member he had determined not to part with.

He'd known it was coming, and he'd been planning it for weeks. When his birthday arrived, and his conscription papers on the same day, he would smuggle Chips with him. Impossible as it seemed, he'd read in the papers about other men—dozens of them—smuggling their dogs to war and getting away with it. Dogs had proven themselves to be extraordinarily useful in this war, so said the newspapers. The Germans used them, and so did the British—tens of thousands of dogs combined.

But Chips was like no other dog; Nigel was convinced. "Training dogs all my life," so said his father. "I've never seen his equal. A good animal obeys his master. But Chips, here—he has an uncanny ability, one in a million, is he. He knows what his master's thinking almost before his master does."

After two grueling weeks of training in Somerset, during which Chips had become fast friends with the camp cook, here they were, at the base of the gangway, awaiting their turn to board ship, cross the narrow sea, and enter the fray. Reaching down and scratching Chip's ears, Nigel tried to quell his inner turmoil. He scanned the grim faces all around him, the vast sea of khaki and Tin hats, the human faces.

Try as he might, Nigel could not avoid the question looming in his mind, perhaps in all of their minds: Who among these thousands would make the return voyage?

Would he?

2

SAUERKRAUT SPY

H alt!" barked a sergeant. "What, in the name of the god of war, do we have here?"

Clutching tighter to Chips' lead, Nigel felt his mouth go dry. "A-a dog, Sir," he managed.

The sergeant sneered. "A dog? And might I make so bold as to enquire—" he shouted, waggling his head, his face reddening, "*What are you doing bringing a dog on my boat?*"

It was the moment Nigel had dreaded. For three weeks he had managed to keep Chips concealed. It had been easier than he had feared. It turned out that other Tommies liked dogs too—especially the camp cook— and had helped keep the dog from discovery. But he knew it couldn't last forever.

"He's keen, Sir, quite keen," said Nigel.

"Keen, is he?" His face twisted with revulsion, the sergeant narrowed his eyes at the scruffy terrier. "That's as may be. But keen compared to what? A rat? If that flop-eared cur happens to be smarter than it looks— which I doubt—it may be keen at herding sheep, chasing rabbits, at working the farm. But this here is war, boy!"

A low growl rumbled in Chips' throat. With a glance from Nigel, the dog sat on his haunches and was silent. Staring through a wiry, unruly mop of coarse gray hair, the dog fixed his eyes unblinking on the sergeant. At rigid attention, not another sound came from the animal.

"This here is war, my boy," repeated the sergeant, lowering his voice and feigning a paternal tone. "You're not embarking on a holiday in Flanders' fields. On this little outing, pets stay home—*in England! Am I making myself perfectly clear?*" He was shouting again. Shouting seemed to come naturally to the man.

"H-he's not only keen, Sir," stammered Nigel. "He's well-tutored."

"Well-tutored, is it! My great aunt was well-tutored, but do you see her on a lead, tail wagging, marching up the gangplank to war? *No you don't, now, do you! Well-tutored, bah!*"

The broad shoulders and back of Wallace, the man in front of Nigel, had not moved. At this rate Nigel wondered if he would ever get to the gangplank and board the ship. Clearly, something had stalled in the loading of troops, and nobody was moving. The sergeant was killing time. Nigel knew that if he didn't do something, and fast, Chips would be taken from him, and he would be off to France without him. He had to do something, but what?

Looking down the long line of Tin hats, the sergeant shouted at the recruits. "Any more pets? Which of you Tommies brought along your pussy? Any hedgehogs? Canaries? Any goldfish coming along to do their bit?"

Men who thought it prudent to do so, laughed. Perrett behind him, and Wallace in front, did not. Nigel had an idea.

"Sir, might I demonstrate for you, that Chips is no ordinary dog? He would be very useful, might even save lives, our boys' lives, and kill Germans? Might I demonstrate?"

"You've got your work cut out for you, laddie," said the sergeant. "Little rat mongrel like that? The line's about to advance. I'm nearly out of patience."

Nigel knelt down beside Chips and fingered the dog's floppy left ear. Looking up at the sergeant, Nigel asked, "What would you like him to find, Sir?"

The sergeant scowled at the mass of soldiers that fanned out from the gangway onto the pier. "Find me a Hun."

"Sir?"

"Ain't you read the papers? England's crawling with Bosch spies. Now then, you say he's keen." A sneer of triumph on his features, the sergeant continued, "Go on, then. That mongrel finds me a Hun, we'll swear him in. Give him a commission, even!"

"How 'bout a knighthood?" scoffed a fellow Nigel knew from training camp who went by the name of Spike. Nigel had yet to figure out if it was his real name.

"Sir Chips of Mutt Manor," another chimed in. "It's got a ring to it, now, don't it?"

"Or you could make 'im a bishop," said a man named Lloyd. "Bishop Chips of All Hallows Barking—you know, barking like dogs do, and like they calls that church in London."

21

"We get it, we get it," sneered Spike, narrowing his eyes at Chips appraisingly.

"Go on, then," said the sergeant, looking levelly at Nigel. "Find me a Bosch spy in this lot. Be quick about it."

Nigel was about to explain how it worked with dogs. They couldn't sniff out nationality or family genealogy. He looked at the sergeant. No, it was clearly not the time for a jest about Anglo-Saxon origins, go back far enough in history and all English people had been of German descent. The sergeant looked like a man who would not appreciate anything that smacked of a jest.

Bored with standing idle on the pier, more men took an interest in the diversion. The whispered voice of Perrett came from behind him, "C-can he do it?" Dozens of eyes were on Nigel and his dog. It was now or never. Dropping to his knees beside Chips, Nigel looked into the brown intelligent eyes and said, "Sauerkraut."

Uproarious laughter broke from the ranks. "Shell shocked already," scoffed Spike, swirling his index finger around his ear, "and 'e ain't even got in the trenches. Step up, lads. I lay you five to one the dog can't do it. "

Folding his thick arms across his chest, the sergeant didn't stop the banter or the betting. "Go on, then. I'm waiting for my spy."

Nigel repeated the word slowly to Chips, "Sau-er-kraut." He unclipped the dog's lead and said, "Find it!"

Nostrils twitching, Chips hesitated for only an instant. Turning with a leap, the dog raced down the line of men, tail beating against the puttee-wrapped shins of the men as he laced in between and through the forest of legs and boots. Passing dozens of men at a run, near the outer rim of the press of men, the dog halted abruptly. Chips squared off in front of a soldier and let out a sharp bark followed by a menacing growl.

"Pardon me. Excuse me, please. Terribly sorry." Nigel made his way through the dense mass of humanity as quickly as he could until he caught up. "Good dog." Nigel studied the young man Chips had cornered. The rim of the man's helmet was pulled down low over his eyes, concealing most of his features in shadow.

"What the devil!" said the sergeant, breathing heavily as he came up alongside Nigel and his dog. "What's that blasted mongrel think it's doing?"

"Sir, with respect," said Nigel. "Chips has discovered a man who eats sauerkraut, perhaps has some in his kit. It likely means nothing; the only fact that is clear is that this man has eaten sauerkraut sometime very recently. And my dog knows it."

"You there!" shouted the sergeant. "Drop your kit and let's have us a look." Turning to Nigel, the sergeant said, "If your flop-eared, runt of a dog's right about this." He broke off without finishing. "I say, you there! Drop your rucksack! On the double!"

The soldiers on either side of the man cornered by Chips grabbed hold of him, roughly helping him off with his gear. "Sergeant, he do smell of Bosch cabbage. Where is it, you blighter?" One of them knocked the man's washbasin helmet off. It clattered onto the pier. "Hey, that's Bosch hair, and look at them Arian eyes. Sergeant, Sir, this dog's gone and sniffed us out one of the Kaiser's boys—bleedin' spy, ain't you!"

Nigel turned to the sergeant. "It's just cabbage, 'Liberty Cabbage' the Americans call it, and many Yanks still eat it, so I'm told. It doesn't mean, Sir, that he's a real German. There's English folks that eat—"

The sergeant cut him off with a growl. "Who made you the prime minister? I'll decide what it means."

What transpired next Nigel never could have anticipated, neither could he ever forget it. Clenching his fists, the blond-haired recruit unleashed a well-aimed punch first at the soldier on his right and then at the other. Both soldiers lay flat on the pier, howling in pain, blood oozing from their noses. Breaking rank, the man bolted. Free of his rucksack and kit, he ran like his life depended on it, leaving the densely packed company of men behind him.

"Stop him!" shouted the sergeant, shoving his way through the men. "He's a Bosch spy or I'm Mata Hari! Stop him!"

3

BLOOD ON THE PIER

S top him!" shouted the sergeant again.

Others took up the cry. Nigel heard an officer call out from the rail of the ship, "Do not let that man escape!"

Afraid Chips might get trampled in the fray, Nigel snatched the dog up in his arms. "Well done, Chips." While the dog licked his face, Nigel scratched the wiry hair between the dog's ears pensively and added, "That is, I hope it was well done."

Every soldier on the pier was encumbered with half again their weight in equipment, and though several men had dropped their kit as fast as they were able and taken up the chase, the fair-haired man had a substantial lead, and, with every stride, was nearing a row of dock warehouses. In an instant he would be out of sight.

Nigel heard an officer's voice. A clipped command. "Five rounds in the breach!" Another command. The metallic *chink-chinking* of a round being chambered. Another command. An instant of silence.

Pee-ooh!

The British Lee Enfield rifle has a distinctive sound when fired. Nigel had grown accustomed to it during his weeks of training. The .303 bullet makes a unique noise upon discharge, a sort of *pee-oohing* as it erupts from the barrel toward its intended target. Nigel was hearing that sound at the moment, as was every other man on the pier.

And with that rifle shot, the running man faltered, stiffened, then crumpled onto the pier. He lay motionless.

The mass of men had surged after the fleeing soldier, Nigel and Chips with them. Nearing the place where the man had collapsed, Nigel stared at the scene. The fair-haired man, dressed in British khaki, lay in a grotesque sprawl on the pier. He did not move. There was a complete absence of life, rivulets of blood radiating into a crimson pool around his head and shoulders, filling the worn depressions in the planking of the pier. His features looked even fairer in death.

Though he knew it was war, and in theory he knew that men are killed in war, Nigel was numb. So full of life and vigor one moment, and now dead. Worse yet, the thought pressed hard on Nigel's conscience: This man's death, had it been his fault? Rarely a day went by without *The Times* reporting on spies. Of course, there were German spies in England, and had been for years.

Nigel's own father had been forced to turn in another pigeon handler, a foreigner, a man who, as it turned out, had for some time been bringing carrier pigeons into England. The man had lived in England for several years, and though he spoke English with precision, almost too much precision, he had been a German. The Kaiser had been planning ahead.

Nigel's father had learned that, brazen and impossible as it then had seemed, the German had been sent to establish a pigeon loft for sending information gathered by German spies operating in London back to the Kaiser in Berlin—nearly 600 miles away, the distance a good carrier pigeon could travel in sixteen hours of flying. By raising up new pigeons hatched and trained in England, Germany could exploit the homing instincts of their feathered army for conveying critical and sensitive intelligence to and from her operatives and saboteurs working in England.

Staring numbly at the still form of the dead German on the pier, Nigel was torn. Just as there were English people who liked to eat Bavarian Bratwurst and drink Rhineland wine, so there were English people who liked to eat German sauerkraut. Taste in food doesn't make one a spy.

Perrett, his face the color of the green sea water sloshing against the peer, stood rigid and speechless at Nigel's side. With a heaving sound, Perrett fell to his hands and knees, his back arched, his whole body convulsing—and emptied the contents of his stomach on the pier.

Patting him on his trembling shoulders, Nigel tried to work it out. The dead young man, had he been one of them, a German spy? It seemed too fantastic. What if his dog's instincts had been wrong? What if the man had merely been fond of cats and Chips had halted in front of the poor fellow because he had gotten a whiff of cat, nothing more—if so, an innocent man just died, his life snuffed out before he ever got to the trenches in France and faced off with the German Army? What if it was all a tragic mistake, made still worse by this man's life being ended by an English bullet?

Wallace, shouldering his Enfield, strode up and stopped beside Nigel. Eyes cold and hard, seemingly devoid of emotion, he stared down at the dead man.

At the training camp in Somerset, Wallace never missed the target; he rarely missed the bulls-eye. Nigel had never met anyone as sober as Wallace. Grim and methodical, Wallace approached every military training exercise with purposeful determination. Eating and sleeping didn't seem to matter to Wallace, and neither did talking.

"Did—did you?" Nigel could barely get his mind around what had just happened. "Shoot him?"

Eyeing Nigel, his jaw set, Wallace gave a nod—a single, terse, unfeeling jerk of his head. He turned and strode back to his place in the queue.

Stroking Chips' coarse fur, Nigel listened numbly to the voices. "Stand clear. Back in your ranks. We'll get this tidied up in a jiffy. Country's crawling with this lot. His taking off will save hundreds of our boys. There's a war on, after all, isn't there?"

Ten minutes passed, during which Nigel watched as stretcher bearers carried the dead man's body away, and men with buckets of sea water sloshed fresh blood—and Perrett's breakfast—off the pier.

"On your legs! Back in your ranks!" shouted the sergeant.

As men fell back in line for boarding the troopship, some were sober, others laughed it off. "Single bullet to the heart?" sneered Spike, "it were too easy, too quick, too painless for a Hun."

"You're just sore 'cause you lost a fiver," said Lloyd.

"Shut your mouth," snarled Spike, slapping Lloyd's helmet.

Halting in front of Nigel, the sergeant wore not exactly a smile, but a satisfied expression on his features. "They found damning evidence on him, all right," he said. "In code. Likely dispatches. Our cipher boys'll go to work and learn all." Squatting down, the sergeant extended a hand toward Chips. "Now there's a good fellow. I believe I may a misjudged you." Turning to Nigel, he added, "Keen, you said he was. And keen he is. I'll grant you that. It's beyond me. How'd you teach him to do it?"

Now would not be the time to admit that he had not been entirely sure that Chips could do that, not with just a word. "On our farm, it's what my father does," said Nigel. "Trains animals: dogs, mostly."

"For herding sheep?" asked the sergeant.

"Yes, but more for other things," said Nigel. "Sentry dogs, guide dogs for the blind, rescue dogs, even attack dogs."

"You said he trains *mostly* dogs," said the sergeant. "Anything else?"

Nigel nodded. "Pigeons," he said.

"Pigeon—O, I do like a good pigeon pie," said the sergeant licking his lips. "Now, my missus, she do make the best pies and pasties. But it being illegal, what with the fighting, the War Office has gone and slapped huge fines, even prison, for shooting down pigeon. There's

been no pigeon pie on my table for—what's it been?—
nigh on two-and-half years."

Nigel suppressed a grin. "We don't eat our pigeons,
Sir."

"Don't eat 'em?" said the sergeant. "Ah, it's them
other kind, then, is it?"

"Yes, Sir," said Nigel. "My father breeds and trains
carrier pigeons, for homing and carrying messages and
the like."

The sergeant stroked his chin, appraising Nigel
critically. "I don't have the final say about much that
goes on in this war—things would be different if I did,
and no mistake—but after what your dog done today,
it's safe to say, your dog's in His Majesty's army now."

A shout from the rail of the ship interrupted his
words. "Up and Out! On your legs!" And then a long,
shrill blast on a whistle followed. Chips rubbed a paw
over his ears. It was a sound, in the months that lay
ahead, that Nigel would come to know all too well. It
would pierce into his imagination in his sleep and
penetrate with dread into his dreams.

"I'll do what I can!" shouted the sergeant over his
shoulder to Nigel. Then he turned and bellowed, "Make
a hole!" his words reverberating like a shock wave
against the steel wall of the ship rising above the pier.

Nigel watched the sea of helmeted khaki part as the
sergeant plowed his way through the mass of troops
back to his post. It was nearly ten minutes before Nigel's
part of the line began inching forward. Inching forward
two steps, then wait. Another tread, then wait. Half an
hour later, Nigel heard the clunking of his own boots on

the gangplank, Chips at his heels, Wallace ahead of him, Perrett gripping the gangplank rail behind him.

Nigel felt his heart thudding faster under his khaki tunic with every tread. It was really happening. He was boarding ship for France. This was war.

4

TORPEDO

Three and half weeks later, from the quarterdeck of the same troopship *RMS Amazon*, carrying another load of soldiers, Elsie Fleming watched waves crash on the outer breakwater of the port of Dover, growing rapidly smaller behind the ship's wake. Gray-on-white seagulls cavorted behind the ship, muscular wings arched, screeching at each other as if it were all a frolic. With a quick tilt and nod of her head, Elsie chose to imagine that, instead of scrounging for rubbish jettisoned from the ship's galley, they were her own personal feathered escorts wishing her farewell, a speedy war, and a happy return. Twirling a thick lock of auburn hair around her index finger, she tried to smile, but her lips refused to cooperate.

Though her father had tried to warn her, Elsie was unprepared for the intensity of the emotions she felt as she watched the jagged coastline diminish. The white cliffs rose precipitously above the gray-green of the English Channel, shrinking in size and becoming more opaque with every turn of the troopship's massive screw.

Exhilarated with the adventurous prospects of war, Elsie had barely been able to contain herself when she had read the newspaper report in January, 1917. The War Department had established a new corps, the Women's Axillary Army Corps, called the WAAC for convenience. But ten months later, November 18, 1917, on board a troopship, in convoy with destroyers and armored cruisers, heading into the U-boat-infested waters of the English Channel, she found that a good deal of her exhilaration had given way to giddy uneasiness.

Breathing in the damp salty air, Elsie was grateful for the sea spray and mist tugging at her hair and bringing the water to her eyes. It helped conceal the tears of another kind she knew were there. It had been different ten months earlier; she had been all enthusiasm, begging her father to let her enlist.

"Aye, lass, that's all good and well, I'm sure, but you have but eighteen years to your name," he had observed. "And the WAAC requires, and most properly does it do so, a young woman to have not a day fewer than one and twenty years. Now I know that you've never fancied yourself good at mathematics, but even you can work it out, my dear, that eighteen is nae the same thing as twenty-one."

"There's only a wee difference, really. And I'm tall for my age." She had tried every argument she could think of to persuade him. "The Germans are planning another big offensive—everyone says they'll be doing it. And the War Department has made it clear that we need more of our boys at the Front, doing the actual fighting. Father, don't you see, that means that every woman who enlists in the WAAC frees up a man to fight in the trenches. Father, this could be the difference between winning the war or losing it!"

When Elsie had paused for breath, her father had smiled. "You ken I think the world of you, my Elsie, but even I donnae think that you can do that."

"Do what?"

"Win the war, my precious," he said.

"O Father, you're infuriating!" she said, battering playfully at his broad chest as she said it.

As the transport vessel began rolling with the channel swell, Elsie wiped the sea spray from her face and eyes. "This will never do," she murmured. Being here, going off to do her bit in the war, it was everything for which she had begged and cajoled her father. For months she had persisted. Every article she saw in the paper about women doing their part for the war effort, she had read aloud to him. "And here's one about women being ambulance drivers and helping save the lives of our boys near the Front."

"I'll nae have my Elsie so near the fighting as the Front," he had said, shaking his head with decision.

"There's another about typists—but that wouldnae do for me," she had said. "I'm a wee bit deficient at the spelling."

"Elsie, my love, you're an abysmal speller."

"But wait!" she said, pretending not to hear. "Here's another: 'Nurses needed.' Father, that's it!" Elsie had jumped to her feet with excitement, holding the advertisement so he could see it. "That's it! You've taught me everything about surgery and your practice. I could do nursing."

"Perhaps you could, dearest," he said gently, "if you were doing it on a horse, or a dog, or a heifer. Elsie, my dear, I am a veterinary surgeon, not a people one. You ken that."

"It can't be that different," she had said with a quick bob of her head. "Besides, there are thousands of horses and dogs doing their bit. I could help with them. O, Father, please?"

"I ken you want to do your part," he had said. "And a most commendable quality it is in you, dearest. Truly it is." He broke off, his brow furrowed in thought.

"If, on the other hand, you had brothers," he continued, "though it would break my heart to lose them—and your dear mother's, God rest her soul—your brothers, if you had brothers, to be sure, they would enlist and fight. It would be our duty as a family for them to do so."

"Aye, Father, like Uncle Kincaid, and Uncle Edgar, and all my cousins, there's Ralph, Jamie, Charles, Roland, Warren, Clive—Father, how is it that I have all boy cousins, even the distant ones? Well, it doesnae matter; they're all of them doing their bit."

Gazing with vacant eyes into the coal fire on the grate, her father had passed a hand slowly across his brow. Elsie had not intended to hurt him. There was nothing she would ever intentionally do to hurt her father.

"Aye, and my youngest brother, your Uncle Kincaid is in hospital," he had replied.

Elsie remembered her father's voice when he spoke of his brother; it had been like the low moaning of the wind in the standing rigging of the ensign on the *Amazon*.

Her father had continued. "Wheezing out his final days, his lungs forever ruined in a gas attack at the Marne." He hesitated. "And poor Ralph, a mere eighteen years old himself, you ken he's been missing for more than three months and presumed dead."

Bringing Elsie back to the present with a start, the ship lurched, heeling abruptly to starboard, and then fell into the trough of a wave with a shudder felt from stem to stern of the vessel. The Union Jack snapped irritably from its spar. Several of the WAAC's squealed. Elsie gripped the rail until her knuckles were white.

"What happened?" cried Trudy. "Were we struck?"

"Zig-zagging course," said the forewoman in charge of Elsie's unit, her voice a steady monotone. "Standard naval procedure in time of war."

"Why a z-zig-zagging course?" stammered another, the girl's voice higher pitched than Elsie had remembered it being in their training.

"Quite simple, really," said the forewoman, droning like a bored professor. "German U-boats find it more challenging to fire torpedoes accurately at zig-zagging convoys. Not impossible, mind you. Simply more challenging. The same for German aircraft. Whilst we make sudden and unpredictable alterations in our course, the difficulties encountered by enemy airplanes attempting to strafe our decks are considerably augmented."

"'Strafe our decks,'" repeated a timid female voice to Elsie's left. "P-perhaps we ought to go below."

Even the thought of going below made Elsie's stomach rumble and heave. Trying to ignore the convulsing in her throat, she looked out across the gray swells, whitecaps thrashing in the heavy seas. Less than a cricket pitch away steamed a British destroyer, and visible astern of them, an armored cruiser. There were at least three troopships, she couldn't be sure of the exact number, encircled by heavily armed vessels of the Royal Navy, all white and black and gray blotched for concealment. For an instant, Elsie toyed with the notion of seeing an enemy U-boat, and how glamorous it might be if it did its best to launch a torpedo at them. With all these ships of war, surely it would be a losing proposition for the enemy. Surely it would be.

Dampening her enthusiasm against her will, a shudder passed throughout her body, and it was not from the soggy November weather. She would never forget the reports of the *Lusitania* in 1915; her father and she had huddled around the radio. *Lusitania* had been a passenger vessel, not a troopship carrying combatants. It had been filled with women and children, hundreds of them, mercilessly torpedoed by a German U-boat, nearly 1,200 perishing beneath the frigid sea, including more than thirty infants. She scanned the iron-gray horizon, wrapping a lock of hair around her finger and pulling till it hurt; she had read in the newspaper that U-boats usually surfaced for better accuracy before firing on their target.

With these reflections, Elsie took a moment to indulge herself in a reverie of mental Hun-loathing, calling down imprecatory curses, like a Hebrew prophet, on the German race. She was forced to admit that she seldom found this activity as satisfying as she hoped it would be. Most often, when the fit passed, she found herself feeling empty, cold, and far more ashamed than gratified.

Another lurching of the troopship *Amazon* interrupted her thoughts. But this time something was different. Clutching the ship's rail with her fingers, Elsie felt a trembling through every rivet in the hull of the vessel, a trembling that reverberated through her whole body. Suddenly from the ship's bridge, the steam siren blared. *"Whoop-whoop!"*

More sirens peeled from the other ships in the convoy. Elsie's heart beat faster. Surely it was only a training exercise. The *Amazon* burst instantly into a flurry of activity. Officers shouted orders. "Battle stations! To your battle stations!" Sailors ran past, their shoes ominously rumbling on the iron decking like drum sticks on a giant kettle drum.

"What is it?" cried the forewoman to anyone who would listen. She had dropped her monotone; her words sounded more like a shriek.

"U-boat detected!" shouted a sailor running past. "Get below!"

His voice was drowned out by the ship's siren. *"Whoop-whoop!"*

Below? Elsie wondered just how much safer going below could be. If they were struck by a torpedo, she felt she would be far safer on deck nearer the lifeboats. Leaning over the rail, Elsie stared wide-eyed at the oily gray water: hissing and rolling like a fury in the wind and swell. Feeling like a draft horse had planted a massive hoof on her chest, for an instant, Elsie was afraid her heart had stopped working. This must be fear—raw, unregulated fear. Her father had done his level best to shield her from coarser realities, ones that induced the kind of fear she felt at the moment. Her mother had died when she was too young to remember, so, by the oblivion of childhood, she had been spared the anguish of grief and its twin: all-engulfing fear.

There it was again, the maddening steam siren. *"Whoop-whoop!"*

But if death was to occur in the briny depths swirling about the troopship, this kind of death would be different. It would be her death, imminent and horrific. Another shudder ran the length of the ship, unnerving Elsie further. And she hadn't even been able to do her bit. She fantasized the headlines: Lost at sea before ever setting foot in France. Another young life wasted in this war. Running the back of a hand across her forehead, she suddenly felt a wave of guilt. Her father had not wanted her to join the WAAC, and he would be inconsolable at the news—that is, at least, she hoped he would be.

"Torpedo in the water!"

At those spine-chilling words, Elsie felt like the draft horse had now placed both front hooves on her chest, the breath now completely gone from her lungs. Could this really be happening?

"Torpedo in the water!" an officer shouted. The ship's siren and its relentless wailing followed, *"Whoop-whoop!"*

Following the excited gestures of the seaman on the control bridge above, Elsie looked out to sea. Appearing as a thin black line a half mile away—it was difficult to judge distance at sea—was the deck and gunwale of a German U-boat. So low appearing in the water, it looked to Elsie like a sinking ship in its last gasp before slipping fully beneath the waves.

Sailors on the bridge shouted. Several of the WAAC girls screamed. The siren wailed.

Elsie had never in her life felt more helpless. She had never seen a torpedo before, didn't really understand how they worked, but at that moment, it did not seem to matter.

"W-what's that!" cried Trudy, pointing with a quavering finger.

So this was a torpedo. Elsie had seen a picture of one once—a gigantic bullet, loaded with high explosives, sheathed in iron. But this was not a picture of one in the newspaper. This was a real torpedo, in the water—armed and coming relentlessly toward them, a white streak cutting through the choppy sea--directly toward the hull of the troopship *Amazon*.

"Are we going to die?" screamed Trudy, her words were caught by the wind and flung back in her face.

Elsie placed her arm around the other girl's shoulders. Trudy was also supposed to be twenty one. Like Elsie, she was not. Age, or the lack thereof, was more obvious in some than in others. Too terrified to speak herself, Elsie wished she could find some words of comfort. She was about to say, "Everything will be all right. Don't be afraid," but caught herself. Trudy had not proven to be the brightest girl in the WAAC training camp, but it was doubtful that even she could be fooled by such hollow comfort.

"I do not want to die," murmured Trudy. Her voice faint and slurred, she seemed to be slipping into a stupor. "I do not want to die."

Afraid she might scream if she opened her mouth, Elsie tried to swallow but said nothing. Unblinking she watched the white streak of death slicing its way through the frigid water of the Channel. It came on at terrifying speed, bearing down closer, closer. Bracing herself for impact, Elsie clung to the rail of the ship and to Trudy.

"Whoop-whoop! Whoop!"

Suddenly, the ship lurched and heeled abruptly to port. An unhinging tremor convulsed throughout the vessel. Hemmed in by the assaulting chaos of the ship's siren, the shouting, and the screaming; Elsie bit her lower lip, trying desperately not to join in the latter. At her side, Trudy collapsed in a limp pile of wet wool skirt and tunic. Gripping the rail for her life, Elsie felt the *RMS Amazon* moaning and hogging into a roll, now to starboard. Falling into a deep trough, frigid green spray drenching the decks, the troopship gave a shudder.

5

BAYONET

W-what's it like?"

Nigel glanced at the huddle of khaki wool uniform crouched in the mud immediately to his right. It was Perrett's voice. In his short time in the army, Nigel had learned that most men attempted to feign courage—even when they didn't feel it. Most men did their best to steady their voices, by iron resolve, determined to keep a stiff upper lip, to be a man, to do their duty, or at least to appear to be doing it. Perrett was different. Like his voice, Perrett was trembling, his fingers clutching his Enfield rifle so tightly his knuckles were bone white. It was as if Perrett either didn't know he ought to pretend to be courageous, or he was just entirely incapable of doing so.

What *was* it like? How was Nigel to know? He was just as green as Perrett, that is, he'd had no more training, and certainly hadn't been in the army any longer.

When Nigel had met Perrett at the Somerset training camp there was something immediately familiar about him. Then it struck: They had been at school together, but that had been years ago, when they were boys. Perrett seemed very much still to be a boy.

Nearly a month ago, they had boarded the troopship *RMS Amazon* en route to Étaples and training camp in France, the over-loaded merchant vessel hogging in the troughs as the ship lurched and plunged in heavy seas. Perrett had never been on a boat before in his life, not so much as on a lake in a rowboat. The English Channel in late October was no lake, and the top-heavy troopship was no rowboat.

Down in the hold, diesel fumes combined with human sweat and urine created a stench more than sufficient to make the sturdiest of stomachs queasy. Perrett's had already proven not to be one of the sturdiest. Youngest child with four older sisters, Perrett's father had died before he had any memory of him. He had been raised by his mother and sisters, and had turned eighteen two weeks before Nigel. When the ranks had been so drastically depleted by casualties, the void left by their taking off the government filled by conscription of any and all men, eighteen to fifty, men who could stand on two legs, including men like Perrett.

Few men Nigel had met during his weeks of training were more ill-suited to warfare. Timorous and scrawny—Nigel was fully a head taller—Perrett was handed a trenching tool, a Lee Enfield rifle, kitted out with a Tommy helmet and khaki uniform, and dubbed a soldier.

Most of the men shunned Perrett, as if his honesty about his fears might be a virus, catchy like a cold or, worse yet, catchy like the influenza. They ignored him, afraid that their fears would be awakened and given vent by Perrett's candor about his own.

Worse yet, there were others like Spike and Lloyd who found a release for their own hidden fears by tormenting Perrett for his. Nigel even overheard Spike taking bets on how long Perrett would last; every situation was a gamble for men like Spike. Though embarrassed and frustrated with him, on the whole, Nigel felt sorry for Perrett and sometimes came to his defense. Desperate for someone to carry his fears for him, Perrett had latched onto Nigel like a stray puppy.

"Stay close," whispered Nigel to the trembling form at his side. Nodding toward their new sergeant, he continued, "Don't think about anything but his voice."

Perrett tried to nod in acknowledgement, but it looked more like a convulsion of the neck and head.

"Up and out! Up and out!"

There was his voice. Nigel breathed more easily at the command. He knew what it meant: "Come out of your dugouts; take your place in the trench; ready your weapons for action." It meant it was time to be a soldier, time to earn your pay—one shilling a day—time to face off with the enemy. There was no getting around it in Nigel's mind. He knew that for some these words would mean it was time to be wounded, time to be dismembered, time to die. So why did this sergeant's words make him feel so at ease? Try as he might, Nigel had not worked it out, but when their new sergeant gave the order—any order—he felt that he wanted to obey the man, that, come what may, following this man was the right thing to do.

"On your legs! On your legs!"

There it was again. Nigel couldn't explain it; neither did he feel that he needed to. It was as if Sergeant Ayres's words lifted something from his shoulders, made things align themselves in proper order in his mind. The man's words made him feel relieved of the responsibility to cower at danger; it was as if his commands suspended the obligation to fear the outcome.

"On your legs! On your legs!"

Sergeant Ayres's all-business monotone was gone. Unlike other sergeants Nigel had encountered, Sergeant Ayres didn't shout, not like the others. It wasn't that he lacked the necessary volume in his voice when it was needed. But his voice carried more like the baritone voice he had heard at Westminster Abbey singing the part of Jesus in Bach's St. John's Passion—not shouting, but loud, clear, and somehow penetrating into the deepest regions of the affections.

No private could excuse his disobedience for lack of clarity or volume from Sergeant Ayres's lungs. But it wasn't the same bullying shouting of other non-commissioned officers Nigel had experienced. The sound of Ayres's words had the effect of quickening the blood; it conveyed utter urgency, and roused the mind to action. It also somehow assuaged the cold chill that began skittering down the back of Nigel's neck only moments before.

"Fixed bayonets." This instruction came from the proper Oxford English voice of a junior officer, a youthful voice, slightly arrogant, with a hint of Irish influence, doing its best to sound confident, authoritative, bold, but convincing few in the effort.

No one moved. After a slight pause, Sergeant Ayres's voice resonated down the column of men in the trench, "Fi-xed!" Led by Wallace on Nigel's other side, there followed a coordinated metallic clicking and snapping sound. Then another instant of silence as men readied themselves for the rest of the order. "Bayonets!"

It is difficult to describe the combined shying and shearing sound of hundreds of eighteen-inch steel bayonets as they are drawn from their iron sheaths and affixed to the barrels of hundreds of Enfield rifles, all at once, all on the command, "Bayonets!"

Combined and coordinated, that is, for all but Perrett. At the command, he managed to drop his bayonet with a sploosh in the mud. With a whimper, Perrett fell to his knees, groping for it in the foul slurry with his bare hands.

"Careful, you'll slice a finger off!" hissed Nigel. Glancing toward Sergeant Ayres, Nigel propped his rifle against the wall of the trench, bent over, and retrieved Perrett's bayonet.

"Th-thanks," murmured Perrett, attempting a smile as he wiped a streak of mud across his forehead.

And then nothing. Nothing but waiting, and more waiting.

"W-what's it like?" asked Perrett again. His voice cracked.

Nigel nodded toward Sergeant Ayres. "Perrett, don't think about anything else," he said. "Just do what he says." He nodded again. "Do what he does."

Nigel's words were cut short. The second lieutenant's trench whistle, shrill and penetrating, sounded through the trench. Vaulting over the top, Sergeant Ayres led the way. Like a racehorse at the start, Wallace vaulted up next. Nigel scrambled up the ladder after them. Something about Sergeant Ayres made Nigel never want to be far away from him.

Behind him, Nigel heard pushers yelling at the men hanging back, Perrett among them. "Out! Out! Up and out! Face the Bosch or face a firing squad of our boys. Up and out with the lot of you!"

Over the top, a wasteland of shattered trees, mud, and artillery craters lay before Nigel. On every side there was a chaos of noise, shouting, rumbling, pounding feet. The man to his left stumbled—Spike, it was, he couldn't be sure—then collapsed face down with a splat in the mud. Another man foundered in the mud—Lloyd it appeared to be. Leaping to clear the man, Nigel hurtled forward toward the enemy. Narrowing his eyes, his head low, he ran harder, rehearsing the maneuvers that had been pounded into him in his training.

"Left jab, right cross, feint low." Boots pummeling the mud and turf, knees bent, rifle at the ready, Nigel had nearly caught up with Wallace and Sergeant Ayres. His mind raced with the intricacies of bayonet training. "Thrust-and-lunge-attack: crouch position, knees bent, rifle held close to body; thrust bayonet forward, lowering left hand to line up blade with the chest and vitals of the enemy; step forward with right foot whilst driving right hand and rifle forward."

Suddenly in front of him was a gray-clad soldier wearing a Stahlhelm, the coal-scuttle helmet now used by German infantry. More of them, crouching at the ready, awaiting the charge. Wallace and Ayres were upon them, bayonets flashing. Nigel felt his heart pounding in his tunic, in his ears, echoing in his Tin hat. And another sound, yelling voices, his own voice, involuntary yelling, not words, just yelling as if his life depended on yelling.

"Plunge the cold steel into the chest," so the drill trainer had said just that morning, "or the eyes, or the kidneys. It will go in as easy as butter."

And then he was upon them. "Left jab, right cross, feint low." With a vicious lunge, Nigel rammed his bayonet into the mid-torso of the enemy. There was a rending sound as the German wool tunic split open with his blade. Withdrawing his blade, he swung the butt of his rifle into the face and head, the Stahlhelm gonging with the blow. Another thrust with the bayonet, following with a skull-shattering blow with the butt.

"Halt!" The shout of the officer in charge intruded on Nigel's frenzy. "Halt, I say!"

Blinking at the shredded uniform, the dented helmet, the scattered straw stuffing littering the training ground, Nigel slowly lowered his Enfield and bayonet.

"Commendations to Sergeant Ayres and *some* of his squad," continued the officer in charge of training. "Several of your men entered the fray with uncommon vigor. To them, I say, jolly good show; well done, indeed. As for the rest of you, study well the carnage of these Bosch dummies. Fight like school girls as you have today, and it will not be mere straw rubbish and cotton wool spread about the battlefield. Neither will it be the Bosch's. It'll be your own bleeding entrails!"

It had felt so real, the trench, the mud, the commands, real bayonets, even the uniforms and helmets of the dummy enemy. Nigel suddenly felt exhausted. The physical and emotional energy of the first genuine enactment of battle in his training at Étaples had sapped his strength, made his legs feel like paste, as if they were made of his mother's lemon curd. Maybe Perrett was on to something. If it was not like this, what *would* real battle be like?

The training officer growled on. "It's back to the fencing musket for most of you, strictly school-girl stuff. What you hold in your hands at present, the real bayonet mounted on the business end of a real Lee Enfield rifle, is designed to do the maximum damage to the internal organs of the enemy. Precious little of that done today. So, as you wish, it's back to the retractable bayonet with the blunt end, back to the toy musket designed *not* to hurt your sparring partner. You slackers have demonstrated most eloquently that toy guns are the thing for you. You are in the Bull Pen now. Here you learn to kill or be killed. Face off with real Bosch like you did today, and most of you lot would be like that lot over there!"

With a riding crop, the training officer pointed at the nearest of several cemeteries, rows of wooden grave markers; officers buried alone, enlisted men buried two beneath one marker. Nigel could feel Perrett trembling at his side at the man's words.

"Now, look sharp!" continued the officer. "Report for duty one hour earlier tomorrow morning! Dismissed!"

6

THE ADVOCATE

Sergeant Ayres, unlike most sergeants Nigel had encountered, was a quiet man, not given to speaking unless it was necessary to speak, and then he did so with clarity and utility. He was a man Nigel both feared and respected. So it was, when they were dismissed to their quarters, and Sergeant Ayres strode directly toward Wallace and Nigel, his heart skipped a beat.

"Well done, men," he said, nodding at Wallace. He met Nigel's eye and locked there.

Wallace brought his knuckles to his Tin hat in acknowledgement.

Nigel saluted. Though his airway felt constricted, he said, "Thank you, Sir."

Chips, who had taken up a position on a hillock overlooking the training field during the mock battle, chose this moment to rejoin his master; he looked up at Nigel with a tongue-lolling grin and sat down to heel at Nigel's side.

"I read a brief report about your dog," continued Sergeant Ayres, nodding at Chips. "If what I have heard is true, he and you may be useful to the Somerset Light Infantry—and to your country."

"We hope to be so, Sir," said Nigel.

Sergeant Ayres paused, appraising Nigel. Not certain what to make of the man's scrutiny of him, Nigel decided to seize the moment. "Sir, if I may," he continued.

Ayres hesitated, a slight flush of irritation, or was it shyness, came to his cheek.

"It's about Perrett, Sir," continued Nigel, "Private Perrett, my mate." Nigel broke off. It suddenly occurred to him that his speaking to a superior could go against Perrett, make things worse for him.

"What about him?" asked Sergeant Ayres.

Lowering his voice, Nigel continued, "Perhaps, Sir, you have observed that he is not... that war does not bring out the best in him. What I mean to say is, I think he may be able to be useful in ways that are more suited to his... to his abilities." Gnawing on his lower lip, he broke off.

"And what are his abilities?"

Nigel cleared his throat. Now that he was actually attempting to do it, to speak up for Perrett, it all sounded so ridiculous. "He plays chess like no one I have ever seen. He's always been like that. At Malvern, as a boy, when we were at school together, he never loses, Sir." Nigel broke off.

"Chess?" said Sergeant Ayres.

"Yes, Sir. I have personally lost to him more times than I can count; most of the time he wins in fewer moves than I can count on both hands. Wallace doesn't play chess, but Perrett does the same to the others. No one else in the platoon will now venture to play chess with him."

"From Private Perrett's ability to win at chess," said Sergeant Ayres, measuring his words slowly, "what is it you have concluded?"

"Well, Sir, someone who can do that," continued Nigel, "I believe he has special abilities that may be invaluable in some other duty, away from all this."

"Is that all?"

"Yes. I mean, no," said Nigel. "In the barracks, of an evening, now that few will venture to play chess with him, Perrett does puzzles. He loves doing puzzles. He can put a puzzle together—one made for adults, Sir, not a child's puzzle—in minutes. It is astonishing to observe, Sir."

"Puzzles? Puzzles and chess, you say?"

Nigel blinked rapidly. "Yes, and crosswords and riddles. Don't you see, Sir? Might this not mean he has special aptitude, Sir?"

"For?"

"Well, I'm not absolutely certain, but surely something other than infantry soldiering, Sir. May I speak bluntly, Sir?"

"You may continue," said Sergeant Ayres, lifting an eyebrow and drawing air through his front teeth.

"Might not someone with his unusual ability with chess and puzzles," Nigel leaned closer to him and lowered his voice. "Might not this skill be useful in codes, Sir, in the breaking of them, Sir?"

"It is commendable of you, Private," said Sergeant Ayres. "But things don't work that way in the military. I am under command, as are you and Wallace, as is Private

Perrett. Where and in what capacity Private Perrett serves King and country in this conflict is entirely beyond my control—or yours."

"Entirely, Sir?"

The hint of a smile played on Sergeant Ayres's lips. "You are importunate, Private Hopkins, like Abraham pleading for Lot. But I am a man under authority. Nevertheless, I will speak to my superior. Beyond that, there is nothing more I can do."

"Thank you, Sir," said Nigel.

"There is one other matter," continued Ayres.

"Sir?"

"Word of your dog has come to the attention of several of the officers in the regiment. You are to appear at the officers' quarters tomorrow morning, with your dog."

Nigel felt like he had taken a rifle butt in the abdomen during hand-to-hand combat training. "What will they do with him, Sir, with my dog?"

"I have my orders," said Sergeant Ayres. "Beyond that, it is not my duty to speculate. Now you have yours. Tomorrow morning promptly after roll call."

7

BACON

Nigel's heart was heavy as he neared the appointed billet of his second lieutenant, as if he were marching to his own execution. Along with the churning in his stomach, there was a crawling sensation on his skin—but that could just be the lice. Sensing that his master was ill at ease, Chips whined, walking to heel closer to Nigel's side than usual.

Engrossed in smoking and throwing dice, neither of the two privates on duty at the officers' billet seemed in any hurry to announce Nigel's arrival. Sitting on a mounting block in front of the wooden barracks, Nigel inhaled the pinching odor of thousands of men and horses encamped in close quarters and surveyed the camp as he waited. "It's no good fretting about it," he murmured, fiddling idly with Chips' floppy ear. "There's a war on, and as Sergeant Ayres put it, 'We're men under authority,' men and dog, that is." Nigel smiled. Chips tilted his head to one side, and he gazed up at his master with the look of unrelenting devotion so enviably peculiar to his species. "Well, at least for one of us," said

Nigel, cradling the dog's chin in his palm, "being under authority comes without chafing."

The officers' quarters for the Somerset Light Infantry stood on the east end of the camp, nearest the Front. From where he stood, Nigel could look down rows and rows of wooden barracks; if he squinted his eyes they looked like dozens of identical wooden crates arranged in perfect formation. Behind him radiated rows of white tents, the temporary billet of the enlisted men. If he let his imagination go just a bit, Nigel imagined them as hundreds of licked ice cream cones. Narrowing his eyes, he could just make out his tent, his and Perrett's, and three others, including the taciturn, stern-jawed Wallace.

It was a mild day for November, and off-duty soldiers loitered about the camp, some playing checkers, some writing letters, some washing their clothes, some cleaning their rifles. A few were laughing and singing. But it was the nearest sounds that caught and held his attention.

While he waited, Nigel could not help overhearing through an open window the voices of two young men talking—wooden barracks were little better than tents for privacy. It was impossible not to overhear their words. Though summoned to report and arrived as instructed, he must have arrived early. As the speakers made no effort to conceal their conversation, there was little else Nigel could do but listen in.

"Of course, it is detestable," said the first.

Nigel recognized the voice as the second lieutenant with the hint of an Irish brogue, only on certain words, and only the merest hint; otherwise he spoke Oxford English, refined and sophisticated.

"The war, you mean, Jack?" came the reply. "My good fellow, you are profundity itself this morning. Of course war is detestable. So why bother saying it?"

"That's just it," said the one called Jack. "One expects war to be nothing but detestable. No sane man thinks one ought to like it. The whole thing is an odious necessity, a ghastly interruption of rational life. Your scholarship at Queens, for example, idling itself away whilst you play at soldiering."

"There are times, Jack, when you are incomprehensible—maddeningly so," replied Johnson with a laugh. "Perhaps you need to sharpen your quill and divert your musings into more scribbling of your poetry. Here, have another cup of tea."

"But you see, that's just it," continued Jack. "When a thing advertises itself as pleasure—which, of course, a war makes no such effort at declaring about itself, though journalists, politicians, and peace-time poets labor to make it seem so. But when a thing advertises itself as pleasure but in the end is nothing but tribulation, such falsified hopes make tribulation far more difficult to bear. Take one of my grammar school experiences, for example. Wyvern Purgatory, so we called it, was a diabolical place, the headmaster finally removed and committed to an asylum."

"You're jesting?" said Johnson.

"I am doing no such thing. I am attempting to make a point. Tribulations without pretense, for example, straight tribulation, as in this war, is far easier to bear. In fact, war breeds camaraderie, even something akin to a kind of love between fellow-sufferers. Don't you agree?"

Idly ruffling the scruff on Chips' forehead, Nigel leaned close to his dog's ear and said under his breath, "I wonder if they'd say that if they were billeted like sardines in a tin?"

"Well, Jack, you have yet to find yourself in combat," said Johnson, his voice sober. "Combat changes a man, changes him forever—that is, if he survives."

"O company commander, who knows of what he speaks," said Jack. It sounded to Nigel as if the young man was having to work at keeping up a tone of jocularity; that hint of an Irish brogue had surfaced slightly more noticeably. "Speak, for your servant is listening," he continued.

"In the trench, Jack, facing off with the Bosch," continued Johnson, "you will find out just how odious, detestable, and ghastly war truly is. You will have no illusory notions of it as a tribulation devoutly to be wished for. However, when trench warfare has given you a clearer grasp of the tribulation of war—which it most surely will do—you will also find the camaraderie proportionately augmented. Without the camaraderie, that bond of brotherly love forged between fellow sufferers, the tribulation of war would be apocalyptically hellish. Believe me, there will be times when it will seem so even with the camaraderie."

The two junior officers chatted on for a few more minutes.

"I do not know where I would be," continued the one called Jack, "without Sergeant Ayres. Nearly of an age to be my father, a seasoned military man in His Majesty's army, an 'Old Sweat' if ever there was one, but never so much as a flicker of condescension at being ordered about by a second lieutenant not yet nineteen, with eight weeks of Oxford under his belt, and absolutely no military experience." He laughed. "Do you realize that before cadet training at Keble all I knew of warfare I had learned from Homer?"

"From the literature of the ancient Greeks!" laughed Johnson. "Has it come to this? The future of England lies in the hands of a neophyte bookworm?"

Nigel heard teacups clinking together as the men laughed. "Our cause would be doomed for sure," continued Johnson, "but attrition has forced the Bosch to the same extremity; like us, they're sending younger and younger men to fill their ranks—and their officer corps."

"Let's just hope theirs know nothing about the Trojan War," said Lewis. "Now then, where is the fellow with the dog? Sergeant Ayres has told me some rather tall tales about this animal."

"You there, Roberts," said Johnson, "call in the private with the dog, if you please."

"Private Hopkins, reporting for duty, Sir," said Nigel, saluting. Standing before them, his back and shoulders grew tense and rigid. Though the youngest could scarcely be more than a few months older than Nigel, these men had the power to dismiss his dog, to send Chips back to England—or to employ a yet more immediate and efficient method of being rid of him. "Sergeant Ayres said you asked for me, Sir."

"Indeed, we did," said the older-looking of the two, Lieutenant Johnson. "You and your dog. We've heard stories, haven't we, Jack?"

"Indeed, we have."

"If he's been a nuisance, Sir," began Nigel. "I-I'll see to it that it never happens again, Sir."

"Relax, my good man," said Johnson with a laugh.

"Indeed, we have heard fantastic stories," said the one called Jack, "almost too fantastic. Though we have every intention of reserving judgment until we have seen for ourselves."

Nigel looked around the junior officers' billet. The enlisted men in the Somerset Light Infantry slept in canvas tents, rows of military issue cots lining the thin walls, with just enough room to come alongside the cot for getting in and getting out of bed, little more. So narrow was the space that to avoid clamoring into each other, Nigel, Wallace, Perrett, and the rest of the men in their tent had all agreed to rise on the left side of their cots, left, that is, when lying on their backs. Living in such close quarters, required a sort of coordinated dance in order to get on peacefully with one another.

The junior officers' quarters, on the other hand, were far more spacious. The billet included a small private bedroom for each man, a commons room with a desk and chair, a table and two chairs for dining, a mirror for shaving and washing up, a stovetop and tea kettle, cups, plates, several bottles of French wine and one or two of German hock, a pantry with ample rations—Nigel could not help noticing the blue packages of chocolate—and they had a phonograph.

"The story is," said Johnson, "that your dog is remarkably keen, able to sniff out a Bosch spy on the pier, like nobody's business, so the story goes."

"Yes, and if it proves true," said Jack, "Sergeant Ayres tells me there may be a highly specialized duty in store for you and your dog—if it is so."

"What we mean to say," continued Johnson, "is that we would very much like to see of what stuff your dog is made."

"May we propose a demonstration?" said Jack, tilting back in his chair and crossing his arms.

Though he had feared the worst, Nigel had hoped it might come to this, and that Chips would not fail him. "What, Sir, would you like to have him do?"

"Well, another Bosch spy unearthed and exposed to the light would be a delight to behold," said Jack.

"Short of that," said Johnson, "might you have him fetch something for us?"

"What would you like him to fetch, Sir?"

"Any old thing will do," said Johnson. "Why don't you surprise us?"

Chips, who had been lying with his fore paws crossed throughout the conversation, sat up on his haunches, intelligent eyes fixed on Nigel, muscles twitching with anticipation. Nigel knelt beside him, fingering the wiry fur between the dog's ears absently. They would expect a stick or a ball—or a rat, but a rat wouldn't do; there were too many rats around the camp; any dog might fetch a rat—a dozen of them.

"Take your time," said Jack, a hint of sarcasm in his tone.

What would they least expect? Nigel mused. It had to be something a dog would be most unlikely to find and carry back—all in one piece. That's it.

"How about my Testament?" said Nigel. "Meaning no disrespect to its sacred pages, that is?"

"Not quite on a par with sniffing out the enemy," said Lewis. "Or is it?" he added with a short laugh.

"I despair of you, Jack," said Johnson. "I think it is a marvelous idea. But can he do it? My experience with dogs and books, though memorable, has never been a good one. Once our old spaniel got hold of my algebra book. He slavered and gnawed away on it till there was nothing but a mound of shredded goo left. The headmaster caned me so badly next morning, I could not sit down for the remainder of the day."

"Algebra—devil take it!" said Jack. "I believe yours was a very smart dog. Now if he had chewed his way through Chaucer or masticated Milton—that would have been a high crime indeed. Do you realize, I failed the mathematics portion of the entrance examinations for University College? If it wasn't for the Bosch creating a shortage of males to fill the halls of learning, I may never have been accepted to university in the first place. I say, therein lies another benefit in tribulation."

Nigel, having his own doubts, began taking mental inventory of other objects he could use to demonstrate what his dog was capable of doing.

"Only if you think he can do it," said Johnson.

"Perhaps first we ought to make inquiries with the regimental chaplain," said Lewis, "you know, find out what the penalty is for feeding the Word of God to a dog."

"Which reminds me of Bacon," said Johnson.

"Bacon? As in breakfast meat?"

"No, no, as in Francis," said Johnson.

"Oh, *that* Bacon. You had me salivating myself."

"How did Francis Bacon put it about books and digestion?" asked Johnson.

"'Some books are to be tasted,'" recited Jack, "'others to be swallowed, and some few to be chewed and digested,' so Bacon put it."

"A meaty axiom, that," said Johnson. He slapped his thigh, and both young men burst into laughter.

"Well, perhaps we should enquire of the dog," said Johnson, dropping to one knee and patting Chips on the head. "What is your pleasure, old boy?"

"Poor fellow knows what bacon is," said Jack. "He's having more than a bit of trouble with excessive salivation himself."

"It's a good long way back to your tent, Private," said Johnson, "through a labyrinth of men and equipment, not to mention horses, other dogs, the rats, even the pigeons could get him off the scent. I wonder if it might simply be asking a bit much of any dog."

"He can do it," said Nigel, "Sir."

"Mind you, it's no shame if it can't," said Jack. "It's only a dog."

Pointing back in the direction of his tent, Nigel looked steadily at his dog and said, "Test-a-ment." Chips sat at quavering attention, eyes fixed on his master.

At Nigel's command, "Find it!" Chips launched himself off the top step of the quarters. Paws churning the mud, the dog bolted down the track toward Nigel's tent.

"At that rate," said Johnson, "it can't take him long."

"Not long, Sir," agreed Nigel, hoping he was correct.

Feigning unconcern, Nigel stole a glance at the mud road Chips had taken to his tent. The thoroughfare was a chaos of soldiers, horses, motor bicycles, other dogs. There was no sign of Chips. Nigel cleared his throat. Lewis pulled out his watch, studied it, eyed Nigel, then snapped it closed, and returned it to his pocket.

"It was a tall order," said Johnson, "asking a dog to fetch a Testament."

"Perhaps he is a canine atheist," said Lewis, "and cannot abide close proximity to a Testament."

"I really do despair of you," said Johnson. "No dog is an atheist. Dogs accept things as they are. It is people—some people, that is—who attempt to construct a world for themselves without God." He laughed. "I once heard a fellow observe, 'If there was no God there would be no atheists.'"

Lewis rolled his eyes. "That's meaningless rot."

"Is it?" replied Johnson. "'Meaningless,' you say? Curious, is it not, for you to use a word with its negative suffix, a word that depends rather heavily on its root. One who uses the word 'meaningless' has inadvertently implied that they feel the world ought to have meaning."

"You're being a deplorable milksop," said Jack. "Better there not be a God than that there be one who made a world so shot through with evil."

"But, there it is. You're about to do it again," said Johnson. "How is it that, when the world doesn't seem to make sense, you're so quick to blame the God you say is not there? Such dizzying illogic sounds more like meaningless rot to me."

Nigel realized he hadn't taken a breath for what seemed like minutes. What if Chips didn't return, wasn't capable of being a war dog? With the stroke of a pen, with a mere word, one of these junior officers could send his dog home. Deep down, Nigel knew that no officer in His Majesty's army would bother to send an unfit dog home. They would simply have it shot. Nigel eyed the Webley Mk VI revolver protruding from the leather holster at Johnson's hip. A single bullet to the head, and there's an end of Chips.

Just when Nigel was afraid he was about to be sick on the floor of the officers' quarters, he heard it: the scratchy pattering of a dog's paws on the wooden steps. Nigel expelled a deep, long sigh of relief. Tail swishing the air, Chips bounded into the officers' quarters. Clamped in his mouth was Nigel's leather New Testament. "Good boy," said Nigel. "*Good* boy." Wiping saliva off the leather binding with the back of his sleeve, he held it out to the junior officers.

"I say, not even teeth marks!" Johnson turned the little book over in his hands. "Now, I'd be truly impressed if he could read it to us, as well."

"Taking the military oath on it is one thing," said Jack, with a short laugh, "but that's no call for reading it—dog or man."

"Am I intruding?" It was a commanding voice. The doorway was filled with the silhouetted figure of an officer. Springing to their feet, the two second lieutenants stood at attention and saluted smartly. "Captain, Sir!" they said in unison.

Nigel, too, had risen to his feet and saluted. He had learned that much in the army. When anyone of higher rank comes in view, privates step to attention and salute.

64

Since every other rank in the army was above private, he had plenty of practice at saluting.

Without fanfare, the captain entered the room. "At ease." Shuffling through a sheaf of papers, he murmured, "Such a pile. Now, then, let me see. Ah, yes, Second Lieutenants Johnson, Lewis. Gentlemen, your orders." The captain thrust the brown envelopes toward them as if they contained the influenza virus. Briskly, he turned on his heel and left.

"What's yours say?" said Johnson, looking over Jack's shoulder.

There could have been a slight cross breeze in the barracks, though Nigel hadn't noticed any wind that morning; but he couldn't help noticing a tremor in the paper dispatch the young officer held in his hand.

"It's our orders," said Lewis, measuring each word. "The Front."

"Same as mine," said Johnson with studied nonchalance. "When is it for you and your platoon?"

"Tomorrow," said Lewis, "up and out at first light."

Stroking his chin in thought, Johnson calculated, "Two-day march to the Front." Slapping Lewis on the back, he said, "That'll put you there on your birthday. *Bon courage, mon ami.*"

8

FRENCH BOOTS

As a boy, Nigel used to like going on long hikes with his family. One summer they climbed Old Man Coniston in the Lakes District, and another he and his father hiked Hadrian's Wall, from the Solway to the mouth of the Tyne, all eighty-four ancient miles of it across northern England. Though he had been deliciously weary at the end of a long day of hill walking, those hikes had been great adventures, memorable fun.

The march to the Front, though intensely memorable, was anything but fun. While horses and donkeys strained at their traces, pulling dozens of carts loaded with tons of ammunition and supplies for the Front, Nigel and the rest of the soldiers of the Somerset Light Infantry did what infantry does, has always done: marched on their own two feet. One hundred kilometers, eleven hours of marching each day, for two long and grinding days.

At the training camp in Étaples, many miles from the Front, the vague *ploomp-ah* of artillery had sounded soft and benign, almost playful, the sound of teammates kicking the rugby ball in a scrum. With each weary tread, the sound changed, became louder, more visceral, more crushingly harsh, more penetratingly impossible to ignore. With each whistling launch, Nigel felt his pulse quicken, then came a breathless interval of suspended waiting, followed by a gut-pounding eruption of exploding heavy ordnance. The closer they came to the Front, another sound arose. Intertwined in each barrage of artillery was the mowing staccato of machine gun fire, serving as an irritable descant above the grinding basso continuo of the far bigger guns.

There were times in that two-day march when Nigel felt he had fallen asleep marching, only to be jerked to alertness by the next artillery barrage, forced to remember that it was nothing so tame as a nightmare. This was foot-blisteringly real. This was war.

"W-what is that awful smell?" It was Perrett at Nigel's heel.

"That'd be your tea," growled Spike, clearing his throat loudly and *pa-too-ing* a glob of phlegm at Perrett's boots.

It was the most putrid stench Nigel had inhaled into his lungs in all his life. Chips' nostrils twitched, but he trotted onward at his master's side. The source of the stench Nigel would all too soon discover.

As they neared the support trench north and west of Arras, Nigel nearly collapsed. Welcoming them to the trenches, the November sky darkened, and a steady drizzle now fell. Droplets of chill rainwater dribbled off the back rim of Nigel's Tin hat and down his neck, seeping into the seams of his uniform.

Surveying the battlefield for the first time, Nigel shuddered. Nothing he had been told could have prepared him for this. The Front: a muddy, barren, wasteland as far as his eyes could see. Not only had men been killed in this war, many men, the very land seemed dead. It was the complete absence of green, of anything living, shrouded by a rending web of barbed wire obstacles. Where plane trees had once lined pastoral country lanes and bordered lush fields of wheat and sunflowers, in their place were shattered stumps and grotesque branches, clawing heavenward as if in futile supplication.

"My feet," moaned Perrett, "they're killing me."

"Shut up!" growled Spike, giving Perrett a shove that almost knocked him into the mud. "Be glad you've still got feet."

"Yeah, look at those blighters," said Lloyd.

"Leave him be," said Nigel. Chips glared at Spike and gave a low growl, wiry hair on the back of his neck stiffening.

"You keep that mongrel off a me," said Lloyd, a tremor in his voice.

Narrowing his eyes, Spike looked appraisingly at Chips. Nigel had seen that look before and it troubled him, but only a bit. Chips, more than any dog he knew, could take care of himself.

Stretcher bearers struggled toward them, picking their way cautiously in the mud, carrying the wounded, several men with sodden, bloodied bandages on their feet—or what had been their feet. There were a dozen like that, maybe more, and some with once-white bandages across their eyes and faces, being led by their comrades.

Nigel stared numbly, doing his best to quell the urge to turn about face. After the stretcher bearers, came a column of silent men plodding toward them, shoulders slumped, staggering, weary, staring with vacant eyes at nothing, stupefying shock etched in their countenance. These were the lucky ones, the survivors, the yet-living men they had come to relieve. Nigel clamped his eyes shut and wiped a hand across his face. It was insanity, a world gone mad. They were marching to where these men had just come from; they were plodding to the place where these men had been mangled and crushed. One man did for an instant meet Nigel's eye as he passed. He was about Sergeant Ayres's age, and the numb anguish in his eyes filled Nigel with dread.

"Men, we have a task to do." Speaking to the forty men in the platoon, it was Lieutenant Lewis's words, strained and weary, coming to Nigel's consciousness like the hollow voice in a poor telephone connection. "Tonight we move into our new billet, cozy dugouts in a sector near *Riez du Vinage*, just there." He pointed to the east and north. "Squad sergeants will give you instructions and your duty assignments."

"We will march single file through a series of support trenches," said Sergeant Ayres to his squad. "Then along communication trenches that will take us to the fire trenches, our dugouts, and the Front. Once at the Front, Fritz is but a grenade toss away. All commands will be issued in silence, passed from man to man." He paused. "We have a task to do. Stay alert, keep your head down, and may God be with you."

There it was again. Nigel's anxieties seemed to melt away with Sergeant Ayres's words, or at least to diminish so that his stomach did not feel hard like bone instead of flesh.

"Safety catches on!" The order was passed man-to-man through the squad. "Ten rounds in the magazine!" There was an orchestra of metallic clicking as men loaded their Enfield rifles. "The weapon is now loaded!"

At Sergeant Ayres's command, "Advance!" the squad began slowly to move forward, Wallace in front of Nigel, Perrett behind. "Watch your step, and keep you heads down!"

Lined with sandbags, the support trench they entered was reinforced by rough-sawn timbers, covered by a patchwork of corrugated iron sheets. Walking in the trench was like walking in a fetid river of mud, forcing the men to spread their legs wide as they tried to find better footing along the edges of the trench pathway.

Along the walls on either side of the trench were men from the same regiment, some on duty, rifles at the ready, but most idle in their dugouts and alcoves—idle, for the moment.

Nigel shivered as the cold water seeped into his boots and socks, the mud sucking at his aching feet with each tread. It was late afternoon, darkness approaching, and the artillery barrages seemed to have settled into only an irritated grumble, the machine guns erratic, as if the Germans were not certain about this war, at least not this soggy November evening.

Nigel could not help observing the strange transformation that came over Wallace as they neared the front line. Glancing over his shoulder at Nigel, he grinned, the eerie evening light flashing on two jagged rows of teeth; he was smiling as if they were setting out for a summer afternoon picnic at St. James Park. In hushed whispers, Wallace became almost voluble. "At last," he hissed over his shoulder to Nigel.

"At last, what?"

"War," said Wallace. "The real kind. Being here, so close to the Bosch, the real ones, not them overstuffed dummies. These ones is real, real flesh and blood Bosch. Them's the best kind."

Shivering, Nigel made no reply. Wallace had not said this many words in all the weeks of their training.

"It's what I signed on for," continued Wallace. "Killing Bosch—it's what I've dreamed of for these three years. And here we are, at last."

"Stand down!" came the order, passed down from man to man as darkness fell.

"At last, here we are," said Perrett, releasing the straps of his rucksack, the burden squelching into the mud. "I've never been so tired in my whole life."

Whistling and blasting of artillery had fallen off to a distant rumbling, as if the Germans, just for the moment, were too busy making their dinner to carry on with the war. As evening fell, all was quiet, at least in the sector of the Western Front near *Riez du Vinage*.

The men of the Somerset Light Infantry dropped their kit and began settling into their regimental billet at the Front, a series of dugouts radiating behind and beneath the fire trenches, a labyrinth entwining a labyrinth. Here Nigel and his platoon had been ordered to stand down for the night.

An old sweat sergeant acting the role of a traffic bobby directed them to their billet. "Straight away," he said in a husky whisper, "then take a left at that coil of barbed wire, just there; then sharp right at the French boots."

Nigel blinked rapidly. "French boots, Sir?"

"Our boys took over this sector after the French," explained the sergeant. "Some slacker Frenchie didn't do a very good job of burying his mate, now, did he?"

"H-he's in them?" stammered Perrett.

"The boots? What's left of him is," said the sergeant.

Dread pressed down on Nigel like a steamroller on a roadway. He halted, a trickle of water seeping into his boots. "Why wasn't he buried, proper like?"

The sergeant turned slowly, narrowing his eyes at Nigel. "You're new around here, aren't you? Let me tell you why. We're a tad bit busy in my neighborhood. 'Let the dead bury their own dead,' as the good books says, don't you know? No, you don't know." Stroking his chin, he eyed Nigel appraisingly. "Not yet. But soon enough, you'll know."

9

TRENCH BILLET

Covering his nostrils with the back of a hand at the stench, Nigel squinted into the dimness of their new home. There was mud, mud everywhere, mud and barbed wire, mud and mangled tin panels. Unlike the comparatively tidy ditches used for training in Étaples, there was nothing tidy about these.

"Battlefields—not the most conducive to hygiene," said their old sweat escort apologetically. "I know what you're thinking. The most derelict flat in East London beats this, and it do—by heaps."

Breathing into the sleeve of his tunic, Nigel nodded slowly. He'd never been to a flat of any kind in East London. But he could not imagine any habitation meant for human beings that would be worse than this. There were timbers encrusted with mud, corrugated aluminum panels smeared with mud, niches and alcoves for sleeping formed from the walls of mud.

Yet there was something intriguing about it all. For an instant Nigel imagined himself a boy again, discovering a vast and intricate system of underground passages, how frantic with elation he and his mates would have been at the discovery. If it weren't for the war and an enemy a stone's toss away hell-bent on killing you, this would be the ultimate playground for boys. What is more, the labyrinth of trenches were a sort of a vast subterranean monument to human ingenuity and the will to make something useful out of the most primal of materials; in this case, fractured timbers, barbed wire, corrugated tin, and the ever-present mud.

It was almost like art. But while a sculptor fashioned from earth and clay a work of fine art, a triumph of the human imagination, this sixty-mile excavation of the once-beautiful garden of France was a grotesque sculpture commemorative of the erosion of human civilization. It suddenly struck Nigel. His father, if he were here gazing at the desolation that was the Front, he would see it as a metaphor of biblical proportion, a reenactment of the Fall, rebel man excoriating the primal garden of the world into a deformed wasteland.

"It ain't the Ritz, but it'll do," said Wallace, bending low as he ducked under the timber header over the entryway and looked about the cramped quarters of the dugout. "It'll do just fine. What could be better? This here's the Front, and them there's Germans—within spitting distance."

While Nigel and Perrett attended to their boots, rations, and blankets, Wallace cleaned his Enfield rifle, wiping it carefully with oil, then bringing it up into firing position, one eye squinted tight shut. "*Pa-kew!* Got me another one," he would murmur.

Ducking low, Sergeant Ayres entered the dugout. Nigel scrambled to his feet, wincing as his bare head clonked into a low timber holding up the earthen roof of the dugout. "At ease," said Ayres. "Looks like we're short on quarters. I'll be bunking here with you men, that is, if you have no objections?"

"No, Sir," said Nigel. "You're most welcome."

"Though we're sorry about the cleaning lady," said Lloyd. "She called in sick today, as you can see."

Ayres smiled briefly. "Long march it's been," he said, rolling out his bedding.

"Yes, Sir."

"Mind the fleas," he continued, "and the lice. Odd how such tiny creatures can cause such great discomfort. It's what the Keating's Powder's for. Bullets for the Boche, Keating's for the bugs. Without it you'll be dancing the Highland Fling before morning."

From a square tin, Sergeant Ayres sprinkled generous amounts of Keating's on each of their bunks. Stepping gingerly on stockinged feet, Lloyd moved to one side to give him room to douse his bunk. Lloyd had his trousers off and was holding a lit match along the inseam. Little popping sounds came as the flame came in contact with another flea. "Does that bug powder work in the trousers?"

Sergeant Ayres nodded and handed him the tin of pesticide. "You men look hungry," he said. "It being your first meal at the Front, I'll be cook."

Each man inventoried his food ration. Humming softly under his breath, Sergeant Ayres proceeded to chop up potatoes, carrots, and an onion and set them to boiling in a pot. "Maconochie Stew," he explained. "Named derived from the Scots regiment that came up with the concoction. Top it off with House of

Parliament sauce, and it's the best trench meal you'll eat."

The stench of mud, ordnance, and human filth that stubbornly held sway over everything, reluctantly began giving way to the comforting aroma of the sergeant's stew. When the ingredients came to a boil, Ayres buttered a pan, added beans and stirred in a tin of bully beef. Nigel's stomach growled audibly. Licking his chops, Chips sat patiently at his side. Filled with the pleasant aromas of the kitchen—and with Sergeant Ayres—the atmosphere of the dugout began to be transformed.

"Stir in a bit of flour and water," explained Sergeant Ayres, "and, *Voilà*, Maconochie Stew."

"I've never smelled anything so good, Sir," said Nigel, "well, excepting my mother's cooking, that is."

"Neither have I," agreed Perrett.

"It ain't steak and ale pie," grumbled Spike. He lowered his voice and added, "How they expect us to win this bleeding war fueled on that slop's beyond me."

"Well, it's better than nothing. I'll take a 'eap, Sir," said Lloyd, "with my compliments to the chef."

"Pass the HP sauce," growled Spike.

After eating his portion of the stew, Nigel fought to keep his eyes open. The regiment had marched one hundred kilometers in two days; he had barely slept last night in their exposed bivouac. As his young metabolism went to work on the stew, all other systems in his body wanted to shut down, his digestion absorbing the nutrients from Sergeant Ayres's meal like a blast furnace consumes scrap wood fuel. After cleaning up the leftovers, Chips planted himself at the doorway of the dugout on self-appointed sentry duty.

"I'll just make myself comfortable here, Sir," said Wallace, "me and the dog." In the darkness, Nigel heard the scraping of an ammo box on packed earth as Wallace positioned it for his pillow. A metallic *clink-clinking* came from his direction as Wallace checked the rounds in the magazine of his Enfield rifle, followed by an exhalation of satisfaction.

Though Nigel was lying down to sleep in a fire trench, a muddy hole in the ground, well within range of the enemy's artillery, machine guns, and Mausers, he felt an inexorable wave of weariness come over him. Heavy breathing came from Spike, Lloyd, and Perrett. It was not possible to resist it.

"Do you hear them?" It was Sergeant Ayres's voice—hushed and steady—coming from the darkness.

Nigel, jolted back from the brink of sleep by his words, strained to listen.

"*Ich hasse diesen verdammten Krieg.*" He could make out the sounds of the words, though he did not understand their meaning.

"Aye, hear 'em and smell 'em," said Wallace. "Bratwurst and sauerkraut—yes, Sir. I hear 'em and I smell 'em."

"How close are they, Sir?" asked Nigel into the darkness.

"Close. A few dozen yards. No more."

Though it was November, sweat broke on Nigel's forehead. Weariness momentarily abated by fear, he wondered how it was possible to sleep in such proximity to men who were sworn enemies, soldiers trained to kill, their fingers on the trigger, their imaginations ablaze with zeal for the Fatherland. He reached down and patted Chips' head and felt the soft nuzzling of his dog's nose in his palm.

"Sir?"

"Yes, Private?"

"Do they, Sir—they don't ever—?" Nigel broke off with a cough. Clearing his throat, he began again, this time attempting to make his voice sound as if he were asking what was on the menu for breakfast. "Do they ever attack, Sir, in the middle of the night?"

There was an instant of hesitation before Sergeant Ayres replied. "We don't call them attacks when they come in the dark. We call them raids, night raids."

Nigel mused on what the finer points of difference might be between an attack and a raid.

"It's why we have sentry duty," said Sergeant Ayres. "You'll have your turn. And when you do," he paused, "never fall asleep. Falling asleep on sentry duty, dereliction of duty, it's a most serious offense, an offense against the other men in your platoon, leaving them to the mercy of the Boche—that is, if they had a German word for mercy, which you'll find reasons to doubt. Fall asleep on sentry duty and you leave your mates to get their throats cut in a night raid, without mercy or warning. A most serious offense, indeed."

Nigel's fingers strayed to his neck; he felt the quickening rhythm of his pulse. "What is the penalty— besides getting your own throat cut along with the rest?"

"The penalty? Go to sleep on sentry duty and it's court-martial. Court martial for dereliction of duty means you'll face off with your own mates one last time—at the business end of a firing squad. It's that serious—everything in this war is serious—and make no mistake."

"Yes, Sir," murmured Nigel.

"That's also why we use wire," continued Sergeant Ayres. "Barbed wire pickets, well-maintained ones. They make things pretty nasty for any Bosch trying to make his way in the dark into our trenches."

"Maintained?" said Nigel. "How do you maintain barbed wire? It's up there, isn't it? In No Man's Land? I mean, can't the Boche see us?"

"Stealth, Private Hopkins," said the sergeant. "Remember your training. But all in good time. For now, get some sleep."

10

NOWHERE SAFE

E lsie shuddered, imagining what it would be like when the torpedo struck the hull of the troopship—the rending explosion, the roiling flames as the ship's fuel caught fire, the hogging of the vessel, groaning as it filled with water and began sinking, the screams of terror, fire lapping at the oily surface of the waves, the heat and cold, the darkness and choking of the last moments before the troopship and the thousands of men it contained—and the three dozen young women—sank to oblivion, Elsie with it. So many would have died, and such a horrific death.

If it had not been for the skill of the captain of the *RMS Amazon*, Elsie and everyone on board the troopship would have been at great risk. A split second before the torpedo would have hit, the skipper ordered the helmsman to steer hard to starboard. That diversion, combined with the roll of the ship in the heavy swell, sent the torpedo shooting past, where it spent itself, sinking harmlessly to the bottom of the Channel. *RMS Amazon* and all on board had been spared.

Though cold and squally, the remainder of the voyage to France was uneventful. Once on the pier in Étaples, the WAAC forewoman scurried her young women, like a nervous cattle dog, to their billet near the hospital.

They had been briefed about Étaples. Once a charming French coastal town, it had been subsumed by a vast military staging ground where at any one time 100,000 British and Commonwealth troops had their last days of training before heading to the Front, and where some of them returned from the Front to recover from wounds, trench foot, and other wartime maladies—or where they failed to recover. The landscape of Étaples, a sprawling clutter of hastily erected wooden barracks, and row-upon-row of tents, was surrounded by a vast patchwork of military cemeteries sprouting wooden grave markers faster than poppies spring up alongside wheat fields in June.

The latest WAACs had been briefed. Elsie knew it would not be easy. She had readied herself for hardship; she even welcomed it, or thought she did. The war had cost so many so much, her hardships would allow her to join in their sacrifices. Though she was far from the front lines, there was a real war on. Her father had done his best to prepare her.

Elsie, his daughter, would be most likely quartered in the crudest of accommodations, without the comforts of home. What is more, she would be a young woman— to her father, more beautiful in form and character than any man's daughter—and as such, the object of the attention of tens of thousands of Tommies, men whom the war had separated from the fairer sex for long months, even years. Her father had taken great pains to prepare her for this. She was soon to learn just how important his pains were.

Trundled into the back of a diesel lorry and jostled through potholes on the muddy network of narrow roads that crisscrossed the camp, Elsie had peeked out the flap hung over the tailgate of the truck at the dingy sprawl of the camp: rows of makeshift wooden structures, rows of tents, and rows and rows of grave markers.

"And 'ere we are, ladies!" called the driver as the truck lurched to a halt.

"We're stopping here?" said Trudy.

Elsie's mouth fell open in amazement. She had not prepared herself for this. "It's a palace."

"Far from it, ladies," said their driver. "In its day, it were a lovely seaside resort 'otel; that would be before the war." Following their gaze up at its gables and dormers, its stonework and tall narrow windows looking out on the sea, he shrugged. "She's a tad bit run down—not derelict, mind you—but a tad worn down by the war, as are we all." Eyeing the young women in his charge, he added in a philosophical tone, "War does that, you know, wears things down."

Had it looked the way it did now in peacetime, it would have been a resort to disappoint, lacking as it was in the finer amenities. As a billet in time of war, though dozens of its many window panes had been shattered and were covered over with boards, Elsie decided it was a palace, her own palace.

"Trudy, have you ever seen ceilings so high?" said Elsie moments later as she pirouetted in their new room. "Sure, it's a tad bit dingy; it could use a coat of fresh paint. But there is a war on, after all, isn't there? I never expected to be billeted in such finery!"

"I was afraid we would be sleeping in a tent," said Trudy, flopping onto one of the single beds, its springs creaking and pinging under her weight.

Elsie pulled back the drapes and gazed out the window. "It faces the sea, toward home," she said. "Standing right here, it's almost as if there was no war on behind us."

Trudy joined her. "Maybe if you squint your eyes and ignore the harbor just there with the troopships, cruisers, and destroyers, oh, and the barbed wire along the beach, and that company of soldiers hurtling themselves at that line of German dummies with their bayonets along over there, and the hundreds of tents and shacks on the far left. Indeed, precisely as if there was no war on."

"I said, 'almost,' didn't I?" Elsie laughed. "If you make a wee hole with your fingers and thumb, and sight through it, like a telescope." She made a cylinder with her fingers. "And just peer at the parts you fancy, you can remove whatever bits you don't fancy. And you always have it with you. Simple, really."

"Simple? I'd call it silly," said Trudy, eyebrow arched at her new roommate. "Worse than silly. Certifiably blighty, and you've only just arrived!"

After dinner with forty or fifty other WAACs in the hotel's dining room, their forewoman rose, clanged a spoon on her glass, and said, "Welcome to France. Welcome to the war. Allow me to introduce the matron of the hospital. You shall call her 'Matron.'"

Elsie admired the tall woman, whose shoulders were made to look broader by the purple capelet she wore over her ankle-length gray dress.

"Rules." The matron intoned the word as if it were the most important word ever spoken. "Rules, ladies, are there for a purpose." Scanning their faces, she narrowed her eyes. "There are 100,000 Tommies outside that door. Men who have been away from their homes, their wives, their sweethearts for a very long time. You are here to heal their wounds, not to inflict greater wounds, wounds of the heart. Therefore, there shall be no scent, no lipstick, no hose, no high heels, no provocative clothing whatsoever. You shall wear, at all times, the uniform of your calling: the blue dress, white smock, white cuffs, white Red Cross arm band—fitted, thusly—the white collar, your hair discretely covered by the white cap and trailing veil, worn strictly as prescribed. There will be no provocative behavior, nothing that invites male attention, from any one of you. Do I make myself perfectly clear?" She paused, again scanning the young upturned female faces, their heads nodding. "Best foot forward, ladies. And remember: Rules are there for a purpose."

The matron nodded and left the platform. After a brief applause, the forewoman resumed her place.

"Tomorrow you begin your duties for King and country," she said. "Your several duty assignments have been posted on the bulletin board in the front hall. Do check them and consult the map so you are able to find the ward where you begin your service promptly in the morning. Then get some rest. Remember, no lights after dark, and don't forget to close your black-out curtains.

Roll call is at half past five, breakfast at six. Do not be late. Dis-missed!"

Elsie was too excited for sleep that first night in France. There was a full moon, bluish-white beams streaking across the floorboards. Glancing at Trudy curled up on the twin bed beside hers, Elsie grabbed a blanket off her own bed, took out her journal, pen and ink, and crept to the window. She pulled back the black-out curtains. The walls of the hotel were nearly as thick as the length of Elsie's arm, making the sills into spacious window seats. Elsie curled up on the window sill; with a shiver, more of excitement than with cold, she looked out in wonder at the beach and sparkling English Channel. Creasing back a page in her journal, she began her account.

"It was as clear as daylight, that first night in France. I really am here, in the war at last." She paused, biting her pen. "Well, not in the war, not like our boys are in the war. Truth be told, I am far from the Front, as Father wished it. But I can hear the war. Far away, I hear the grumbling of the big guns, or is that thunder? Perhaps I will learn names of all the guns and know which ones are firing when I hear them. I am sitting here in the moonlight shivering with anticipation, eager to begin doing my part, eager for the thrill and excitement of being in some small way in a real war. Tomorrow, for me, my duty begins."

Biting her pen, Elsie smiled. "I am forced to confess to a mad fancy lurking in my imagination. What if I was to pinch a Tommy's uniform, tie back my hair, walk with my legs wide apart like a boy, speak low? March out with a combat unit and see what war is really like? I know it is a school girl's fantasy and like most fantasies, ridiculous and absurd. Then again, I am little more than a school girl, officially three years too young even to be in the WAAC.

"Nevertheless, I imagine myself taking up the mantle of a worthy heroine like Edith Cavell, doing memorable things for the war effort as she did. Glamorous though she seemed when I first heard of her back in Scotland, however, I would rather not face a German firing squad as Miss Cavell did, and die for my country. I would much prefer to live for my country than to die for it."

Elsie's father had encouraged her to write the more complete account of her time in France in her journal and send him shorter dispatches from it back home to him in letters. Closing her journal, she took out a piece of stationery, tapped her pen on the window in thought, then, dipping it in the ink, she wrote the date, the place, "Étaples, France," and, "Dearest Father." She hesitated. Ought she to tell him about the torpedo? It would be exciting to tell, and would show that she was not entirely tucked away in some safe billet far from danger; it would demonstrate that she was truly in the war. But it would most surely worry him to distraction.

The exploding of artillery miles away at the Front rumbled on, unceasing. But as Elsie sat musing and listening, another sound caught her attention. Faint at first, it had gradually grown louder, clearer. An engine, and though Elsie had little experience with airplanes— she had only seen one a few times in her whole life—she knew this was not a motor lorry. It was a smoother and higher-pitched engine sound than made by lorries. Pressing her face against the cold glass of a window pane, she searched the sky. With this much moonlight, surely she would be able to spot it in the night sky. When first she did catch sight of it, the plane looked like a phantom, moonlight catching on its upper wing as it banked, descending lower over the vast encampment, lining up over a row of tents, the billet of soldiers training to march inland.

"What is it?" came Trudy's voice, creaky with sleep.

"Come see!" said Elsie. "It appears to be an airplane with two layers of wings, flying low over the encampment. Do you see it?"

Rubbing her eyes, Trudy nodded. "Do tell me it's one of ours?"

Elsie laughed. "Of course it is. It has to be. They use them for reconnaissance—that means gathering information. Imagine the view from high up in the sky—it must be magnificent. I think I would like to fly one someday. Listen to the thrumming of its engine; it's getting closer. Hey, Trudy, perhaps we can go along as a passenger in a real airplane. Wouldn't that be marvelous?"

"No thanks," said Trudy. "Both feet on the ground for me. And they use them," she added, "for more than reconnaissance now, you know."

"I've heard that," said Elsie. She squinted at the low-flying biplane. "What color do Germans paint their planes?"

"I don't know," said Trudy. "Why?"

"And the insignia? I've never seen a German plane before," said Elsie, her face pressed hard against the window pane, her voice a hoarse whisper. "What's on its wings?"

"A cross, an iron cross," said Trudy. "Why?"

"O Trudy—!" Elsie's words were cut off

Bursts of machine gun fire from the biplane rent the night sky. *Dat-dat-dat-dat-dat!*

"What's that!" screamed Trudy, her eyes wide with horror. "This isn't the Front. We're meant to be safe here!"

"Someone forgot to tell the Germans!" cried Elsie.

The biplane's engine whined in the night air as it maneuvered over another sector of the training camp. Again its machine guns began firing. *Dat-dat-dat-dat-dat!*

Engine accelerating, the biplane pulled up, climbing steeply into the night sky. It banked hard to its right.

"Is it going away?" screamed Trudy, her hands clamped on her ears, tears streaming down her cheeks.

"I-I don't know," cried Elsie. "I'm afraid he's coming back!"

"Straight toward us!" screamed Trudy.

"Get down!" yelled Elsie, grabbing Trudy and diving away from the window. "Under the beds!"

Dat-dat-dat! Louder it came on, deafeningly closer. *Dat-dat-dat-dat!*

Suddenly, the windows shattered, glass shards bursting into the room. Then all went silent and dark.

11

BULLET AND BARBED WIRE

As near as Nigel could calculate, it was sometime just before midnight of his first night at the Front when he heard it. A single rifle shot, the bullet whining through the black night.

While Nigel lay on his back staring at the darkness, trying to get his brain to compute what it meant, Sergeant Ayres was fully awake and on his feet. Outside the dugout, Nigel heard a cry of alarm, then the scuffling sounds of someone falling, and a squelching splash as a body fell into the muddy slurry of the trench.

"Are you hit, Sir?" It was Sergeant Ayres's urgent, whispered inquiry.

There were other voices, and the sounds of men in the platoon snatching up boots, Tin hats, weapons, and stumbling in the darkness. Chips' low growling was perceptible only to his master. Nigel was fully awake and on his feet. He made his way from their dugout into the fire trench to where he had heard Sergeant Ayres's inquiry.

"No, I-I believe I am unhurt."

Nigel recognized the voice. It was the young second lieutenant in command of their platoon, his voice strained, shocked; though somehow devoid of what Nigel would actually call fear. More like awe than fear.

"What happened, Sir?" asked Ayres.

"I was merely surveying our position," said the junior officer. "And there was a shot, a bullet."

"As you were!" ordered Sergeant Ayres. "Back in your bunks, the lot of you!"

Ayres was the only man Nigel had ever heard who could give an order in a whisper that not only everyone in the platoon could hear, but in a tone that resulted in instant obedience. Nigel, like the rest, returned to his dugout. But it wasn't far to go. If he strained his ears, he could just make out the sergeant and the second lieutenant's conversation.

"Right past my left ear," continued the second lieutenant, his voice a monotone of whispered astonishment. "The bullet whined like a journalist." He broke off in a laugh that was no more than a single breathy exhaling of air through the nostrils. "Or a peacetime poet's whining. Right past my ear."

"Well, you've been spared, Sir," said Sergeant Ayres. "That's a good sign."

"What is today?" asked the young man.

"Today, Sir?"

"The date, the month and day?"

"Well, as it's not yet midnight," said Ayres, "it'd still be the twenty-ninth day of November, I should think."

"My birthday," continued the young officer. "My nineteenth birthday."

"And many happy returns of the day, Sir," said Ayres.

"This is war," murmured the young man, his words meandering and barely audible. "This is what Homer wrote about."

Back in the dugout, Wallace would not let anyone in the squad go back to sleep. "I ain't about to lie down and let Fritz take pot shots at Lieutenant Lewis like that! Filthy Bosch. I say we give him what for, that's what I say."

"Private Wallace," said Sergeant Ayres, "your zeal is commendable. Make no mistake, you will have your chance. But charging halfcocked into No Man's Land after the Bosch would be fool's courage." He paused, narrowing his eyes at the strained expressions on the faces of the men under his charge. "All right, then, there's no time like the present. Being as how we're all wide awake, let's us up and out for a patrol of the wire."

Sergeant Ayres began, in whispered tones, to rehearse with his men the training they had received for patrolling the barbed wire in the dark. As he spoke, Ayres held a wine cork over the candle, black smoke rising as the burning cork swelled out in sooty nodules.

"Smells like burning tires," said Perrett.

"Smells better than the rest of this hole," murmured Spike.

"Now smear it on your white cheeks," said Ayres, demonstrating on his own face. "Like this."

Blackening his own features, Nigel looked at the muddy faces of the men huddled around the candle—there was little means in a fire trench for having a proper wash—he wondered how much need there really was for more concealment.

"Help each other," continued Sergeant Ayres, "and don't miss any bits. Blackened up like this you'll be invisible to a Bosch sniper searching for a white face in the dark."

When every face in the dugout was blackened, Sergeant Ayres gave each of them an assignment. "You've done it all in training. This here's the real thing. Wallace, you take up a position, just there, and Private Perrett, you with him, at the ready, up and over, behind the first row of sandbags. Ten rounds in the magazine, but mind you only shoot if you must. Remember, when we give them something, they give us something back. Our goal tonight is to repair the barbed wire guarding our trenches, not to start a fire fight with the Bosch. Privates Lloyd and Spike you carry the coil of wire and the pickets—but no clanging of them. Mum's the word. Not a sound from any of you."

"Ah, Sir," said Nigel, clearing his throat. "What about me, Sir, and my dog?"

Sergeant Ayres glanced down at Chips before replying. "Best not risk it. One stray bark from the dog and Fritz'll turn his guns on us all."

"Chips won't do that, Sir," said Nigel.

"But you can't be sure, now can you?" said Sergeant Ayres. "It's all new to him, is the Front, the fire trenches, the mud, the smells, the real enemy. It's all new. You can't be sure just how a dog'll react. Nobody can be."

Nigel knew it was true. He hoped that Chips would help them, do his bit for England, but he knew Sergeant Ayres was right. He didn't really know how Chips would react to war. With effort, Nigel swallowed the hard knot in his throat. He didn't really know how *he* would react to war, let alone his dog.

"Perrett, Sir," continued Nigel, "permission to exchange places with Perrett, Sir? Perrett could stay with Chips, if you please. I could go with Wallace."

Sergeant Ayres turned slowly around and faced Nigel. Surrounded by his sooty blackened features, the sergeant's eyes were white and penetrating. "Private, stay with your dog. Perrett comes with me."

"Yes, Sir," murmured Nigel.

"Stay low, and keep a tight leash on him." With that the sergeant signaled the other men to follow.

Nigel held his breath as he watched Wallace and Perrett mount the ladders. Wallace went up the ladder like someone was clanging the dinner bell and there wasn't enough to go around. One after the other, his boots never resting on the rungs for more than a split second. After an instant of assessment as Wallace scanned the barren wastes of No Man's Land, the soles of his boots disappeared into the dark. Nigel could see the man in his mind's eye, eagerly low-crawling into position toward the enemy trench line.

Perrett's boots were different. One boot shuffling up on a rung, then, after a timorous positioning and repositioning, it was joined by the other; after that, a lifting of the heels as he tested each rung, weighing himself cautiously before daring to venture the next step. At the point where Perrett's head must be rising, wide-eyed, to view, the wasteland that separated the opposing fire trenches of the enemies, the boots froze eloquently. There was a tremor in the knees that reminded Nigel of his mother's sewing machine. At last, toes scuffling in

93

the mud, the soles of Perrett's boots disappeared reluctantly over the edge of the trench.

It was painful to watch. Nigel felt certain that Perrett could not survive this war, not without somebody watching over him. For reasons he never fully understood, Perrett had latched onto him, depended on him. Nigel shuddered to think what might happen to him out there without him.

"And here we are," said Nigel, wrapping Chips' velvety flop ear around his finger. "Doing nothing." Chips licked his hand. "'They also serve who only stand and wait,' so Milton put it. It's a raw deal, waiting. If only I knew what was going on up there." Placing his fore paws on Nigel's lap. Chips began licking the black soot off his master's face.

Deep down, something bothered Nigel. He knew that Chips had to prove himself in combat—or else. That troubled him.

"That's enough, old boy," he said, wiping the sleeve of his tunic across his face. Then there was Perrett. Watching helplessly as his boots disappeared over the lip of the trench terrified Nigel. He was certain Perrett could never prove himself in combat; the only thing combat would prove is that a fellow like Perrett was not supposed to be fighting in this war in the first place. At first, Nigel had to confess, he'd tried avoiding Perrett like most everyone else in the platoon, hardening himself against him, leaving him to brace himself like a man, to do or die, but it had never worked. It seemed like Perrett needed him, and if something happened to Perrett, Nigel would feel that it was his fault for not being there to help him. If only he could convince Sergeant Ayres to transfer Perrett to code breaking. Perrett would be a genius at code breaking. But not this. Sure, he'd managed to stay awake last night, but what about the next time, and the next? Without somebody watching out for him, if Perrett miraculously managed to survive a German bullet, he would end up court-martialed for dereliction of duty and face a firing squad of British bullets. Goaded by a compulsion he could not explain, Nigel felt that it was somehow his responsibility to make sure that did not happen.

But there was something that troubled him far more. It wasn't just Chips or Perrett. Nigel knew that *he* had to prove himself in combat. What if he couldn't do that? What if he was a slacker, one of the sort who, when things got really hot, cried for his mother, a coward who ran from danger, or tried to? What if he was one of the sort who made off in the dark, deserted—and got shot for it? Snoozing while on sentry duty was not the only offense that put a man in front of a firing squad.

Unsheathing his bayonet, Nigel jammed it viciously into the packed earthen wall of the trench. What troubled him went still deeper. It was what he felt when he was told to stay in the relative safety of the trench while his squad, exposed to the enemy, patrolled the barbed wire. It was the involuntary fluttering of relief, that selfish sense of being safe, at least for the moment, whatever happened to the rest of the squad. This deeply troubled him.

Minutes dragged by, agonizing minutes. Still Nigel waited. Suddenly, Nigel felt every nerve in his dog's body go rigid. Both ears at full attention, Chips' nose twitched as the animal scoured the darkness for something—or someone.

Nigel bent low, his mouth close to the dog's left ear. "What is it, boy? What do you hear?" Pulling off his Tin hat, he ran his fingers through his close-cropped hair and strained his ears. Though he couldn't distinguish any particular sound that was worse than the rest, Nigel knew something was out there. Chips persisted in rigid alert. Nigel felt frantic. He was under orders, strict orders, to stay in the trench, to keep his dog from making a sound. But if Chips knew something, had detected some threat, and Nigel didn't warn Sergeant Ayres and the others, they could be in grave danger.

And Chips was rarely wrong.

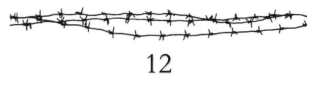

12

NIGHT RAID

"Sir?" Nigel hissed into the vast darkness. He had
hesitated as long as he dared. How could he just
sit in the trench and wait? Whatever it was, Chips
knew something was afoot, and it wasn't good. Nigel
knew his dog's signs: every nerve taut to the breaking
point, eyes wide and riveted on something the dog's
infallible instincts told him was there, nose accosting the
air—grappling, sifting, collating through every intricacy
of scent. Ordering Chips to stay put, Nigel had climbed
the ladder, against orders. Now, at the lip of the trench,
he knew he had to do something.

"Sir?" Nigel hissed again into the blackness.
"Sergeant Ayres?" He waited.

"This had better be immensely important, Private."
It was Sergeant Ayres's voice, so close Nigel jumped.

"It is, Sir," said Nigel. "Something is wrong."

"Of course something's wrong," hissed Sergeant
Ayres. "There's a war on."

"No, worse than that," said Nigel.

"Worse than war?"

Spike was within earshot, corkscrewing a picket in the mud. "Poor boy's gone blighty before 'is time."

"It-It's hard to explain," stammered Nigel, "but dogs—well-tutored ones, that is—they know things."

"And your dog tells you these things?" said Sergeant Ayres.

"Whispers sweet nothings in your ear, does 'e?" growled Spike.

"Speaking one cur to another," added Lloyd, circling his finger around his ear. "This 'ere's a bad case of blighty."

Nigel ignored them. "He goes on alert. That's what my father calls it. And a good dog handler takes heed when his dog alerts. A bad one ignores it, to his peril."

"You're telling me," said Sergeant Ayres, "your dog is telling you something?"

"Yes, Sir," said Nigel.

"And you're telling me this while I am on a dangerous maneuver with my squad?" continued Sergeant Ayres, "against my orders?"

Nigel felt this wasn't going well, but it was too late now. "He knows something's wrong. Someone's out there, and my dog knows it. I couldn't sit in the trench and wait, knowing of it, Sir, for fear of what it might mean—mean for you and the men, Sir."

"Your dog's right," said Sergeant Ayres, tapping his index finger on his Tin hat.

Nigel felt relieved. "I knew you'd see things my way—"

Gripping Nigel by his collar, Sergeant Ayres said, "Of course someone's out there, Private! There's an entire

German Army out there, every man of which wants to kill us, your dog included!"

"I know, but, that's just it. But what I mean is—"

"Private Hopkins, you seem to have trouble following orders," said Sergeant Ayres. "There's one thing we do with a soldier who—"

Ploomph! His words were cut off by the sound of something being launched into the night sky. *Ploomph! Ploomph!*

"On your faces!" yelled Sergeant Ayres. "Flares! Get down!"

Peeking around the rim of his Tin hat, Nigel watched in open-mouthed wonder as the flares burst above their trench. Splaying in arching tentacles of light, three flares—in rapid succession—exploded and hovered above them, illuminating an eerie wasteland of gray mud, barbed wire, and mangled tree stumps.

The ominous, lingering light had the effect of elongating time, so that what occurred in the next flickering second felt to Nigel as if it unfolded in slow motion, every fragment of time laid bare for contemplation. And in that second, Nigel saw him. Wearing the same gray uniform as the training dummies at Étaples. Wearing the same terrifyingly efficient-looking iron battle helmet as the dummies. Nigel had seen pictures of captured German soldiers. But this was his first glimpse of a genuine, combat-hardened Hun. Yet the man's face seemed as alarmed at the sudden illumination of the battlefield as Nigel felt.

"Sergeant Ayres!" cried Nigel.

In the same instant, a burst of flames came from the opposite trench line. *Dat-dat-dat-dat-dat!* Machine gun fire, bullets rending the darkness, making divots in the mud. No sooner had it begun than a commanding German voice yelled from across the divide in the enemy trench, "*Halt! Halt!*"

In the fraction of a second when the light of the flares died into a sickly gray, there was an eerie instant when nobody seemed to know quite what to do. But the irresolute instant soon ended.

"Hold your fire!" Realizing the danger, a junior officer halted a sentry about to fire his Enfield at the German. With Sergeant Ayres, Wallace, Perrett, and the others exposed, the sentry could easily shoot one of his own men, friendly fire Nigel had heard it called. Friendly fire seemed an odd name. Bullets from friend or foe, Nigel imagined, would have the same effect on human flesh and bone, and internal organs.

Meanwhile, skulking toward their trench for a night raid and now exposed, the German soldier, to avoid getting shot by his own comrades, lunged into a crater only yards in front of the British trench line.

In the last faint glow of the flare-light, Nigel felt as much as saw one of their men scramble to his feet. Nigel knew who it was. Wallace. He winced as he watched the man hurl himself, without a qualm, into the crater after the German soldier.

Horrified, Nigel and the rest of the squad were forced to deduce from the sounds alone the scene unfolding in the crater: Two men up to their knees in mud, in a hole created by high explosives, knives drawn, facing off, hand-to-hand, in the dark. The shying of steel on steel made Nigel conclude that neither man had a firearm. It was over in less than a minute, but it was a tense, chilling moment, one that left an indelible scar on Nigel's mind.

What he heard was heavy breathing, boots sloshing in the mud as the men tried desperately to find firm footing, the thudding of fists on ribs and flesh, slashing sounds. Then their arms must have become dead-locked; straining and gnashing, teeth-grinding curses; grunts of exertion, of pain. More heavy breathing, but now more like inhalations of horror. Bitter words in German, escalating in pitch, more rapid, pleading. It was not necessary to understand the language; the doomed man's inflection alone was eloquent with meaning.

A final thrusting blow. Silence.

13

LATRINE DUTY

His spade poised and ready to strike, Nigel held his breath, eyes narrowed at the creature. Greasy black fur, begrimed with mud and filth, the creature paused on its haunches, its front paws clutching the rotting remains of some indistinct organic material; it may once have been an apple core; it was impossible to tell for sure. For this moment, Nigel cared little for the rumbling of artillery, the near-constant accompaniment to trench life, playing in the background. For this moment, there was only one enemy. His face scrunched in revulsion, Nigel made his move. *Sploosh!* His aim was true, and the spade came down on the creature like a pile driver.

"We got us another rat!" cried Nigel, wiping splattered filth from his face. "This one's huge, the size of a cat." He took another final swing. "Take that!" Heaving a sigh, Nigel leaned on his spade and nodded at Chips. "Finish him off."

Chips dove on the rat, his jaws locked around its throat. With a swift wrenching of his head, Chips broke the rat's neck. The dog dropped the dead rat back into the grime swirling around Nigel's tattered puttees; beneath them his boots were entirely immersed in a slurry of filth.

"Good boy," said Nigel, pulling off his Tin hat and wiping a grimy sleeve across his forehead. "Best get back at it."

After the foiled night raid, the night Wallace killed the German in the crater, for three back-breaking days Nigel had barely touched his Enfield rifle. In its place was a spade. "Latrine duty," Sergeant Ayres had ordered, not unkindly, but no less firmly. So for three hand-blistering days Nigel had dug latrines, killed rats, and breathed through his mouth.

Latrine duty for the necessities of several thousand men living in holes in the ground, in close quarters, was a task proportionate to feeding the 5,000 but without the five loaves and two fishes—or the supernatural enabling. Nigel had grown up on a farm. He had shoveled his fair share of animal waste. Three days of latrine duty at the Front, however, was altogether of another order, an undertaking akin to baling a sinking battleship with a teaspoon. Worse than the never-ending nature of the task, worse than the smell, worse even than the rats, was the grinding humiliation.

"Any good conversations with your dog lately?" It was Spike. He had taken shelter under a sheet of corrugated iron for a smoke. "Say, you missed that bit, just there," he continued, blowing blue smoke in Nigel's direction. "They say that a man takes on the character of what he does, that's what they say. I say, this 'ere private's blending in with 'is duties so well a body can't tell where one ends and the other begins. This new duty, don't you reckon, Lloyd, it suits 'im."

"May suit *'im*," said Lloyd, "but not much good for the dog, now, is it?"

"Waste of a good dog, if you ask me," said Spike. "Now, if you ask me that there dog would make a good show in the pit—"

"Nobody's asking you." It was Wallace. Nigel hadn't seen him come. But that was nothing; the trenches were laid out by design in short zig-zags. That way the explosive impact of a shell that hit its mark was limited to a short section of trench, did less damage, maimed or killed fewer men. It also meant that a man could suddenly appear around a corner, seemingly out of nowhere, unexpected.

"Clear out," said Wallace, his words like well-aimed thrusts with a trench knife.

"Don't go and get testy about it," whined Spike, taking a deep and final drag on his stub of a cigarette. "Was just saying."

"Aye, 'e was just saying," said Lloyd.

"A fella offers a few encouraging words to 'is mate," said Spike, flicking the butt of his cigarette into the slurry at Nigel's feet, "and we gets told off." Grumbling, he and Lloyd mounted the duckboards, heading back to their dugout.

Nigel eyed Wallace. He wasn't sure what to make of the big man. Sometimes he wondered if he really was a man, a human being. Nigel shuddered as he recalled Wallace, without hesitation, jumping into the crater after the German soldier.

"Thanks," he murmured to Wallace, "for clearing them out." Nigel took up his spade and resumed shoveling.

"Don't mention it," said Wallace with a nod. He resumed whistling.

Hearing it but not seeing it, somehow, had left a deeper impression on Nigel's mind. He'd had a nightmare about it, the deadlock scuffling of the two men, the pleading voice of the German, the final thrust of Wallace's knife. The silence. And then with a grin, Wallace had popped out of the crater, mud mingled with blood all over him, whistling snatches from, "It's a long way to Tipperary, It's a long way to go," as he vaulted one-handed over the sandbags and back into the trench. Resuming his place near the opening of the dugout, Wallace's face that night had looked exultant and eager, like he was hoping it would happen again, that he would get another chance at a German's throat before morning.

What made Wallace do it? Made him want to kill Germans with such pleasure? Nigel wondered if perhaps the man was a pathological killer. Could it be that war made him happy because only in war was there a legitimate outlet for what he did best—killing? Nigel shuddered again. Somehow this war made a man like Wallace whistle, as casually as if he were heading down a forest path, rod and tackle in hand, for a day of course fishing in his favorite brook.

Rain fell heavily as the morning ground on. His mates in his squad would be taking turns cleaning their rifles, writing letters home, preparing for inspection, waiting for what was coming. Water dripped from his Tin hat down his back. Shivering, Nigel pulled the collar of his

105

trench coat up higher around his neck. He looked at his hands, caked with filth, wrinkled from being constantly wet, wrinkled like an old lady's face. But it was his feet he was worried about. They hurt, ached, and smelled like they were rotting. How many days would it be before he'd have anything like a proper wash? The filth was inescapable and demoralizing, especially on latrine duty. When did soldiers bathe, change their underclothes, change their socks?

"Argh, Chips, my feet, they're killing me."

Chips tried to cheer up his master and even pitched in, as if to demonstrate a better digging methodology. Sergeant Ayres, though never harsh, was relentless. Nigel began to worry that latrines were his cross to bear, that he had been assigned permanent duty at the latrines, that the sum of his contribution to the war effort would be this most foul, putrid, and ignominious task. "Father, tell us what you did during the Great War?" he feared his children would someday ask—that is, if he survived to have children. "Mine was a most essential task, my dears," he would reply. "Without my labors, the entire British Army would have been overrun, dumped upon, completely subsumed in the foulest of outcomes."

Floating on its back in the putrid slurry that flowed from the latrines, the dead rat, stiff and bloating, drifted closer. With the flick of his spade, Nigel hurled the swollen corpse over his shoulder into the refuse heap behind the latrine. At this rate, he would have plenty of time to refine just how he would someday reply to his children's query.

Then came the morning of his fourth day in the latrines.

After a meagre breakfast of cold Maconochie stew and a salt biscuit made chewable by soaking it in his tea, Nigel was preparing to take up his spade and resume latrine duty when Sergeant Ayres stopped him.

"That is enough, Private," he said, smiling briefly. "This is His Majesty's army. This is the Somerset Light Infantry, a regiment with a long and decorous history." He paused. An artillery round whistled nearby. Already Nigel knew from the sound that it was poorly aimed and would fall short of their fire trench, though, by the pitch of the whistling, it could find its mark on the lads due south of their position. "In the Somerset Light Infantry," continued Sergeant Ayres, pausing as the shell erupted, "orders are orders. Do I make myself perfectly clear?"

"Yes, Sir," said Nigel. "I deeply regret—"

Sergeant Ayres stopped him with a hand gesture. "As you were, Private. We have a war to fight. Later tonight, I'd like to discuss how it works with a dog like Chips. For now, put up your spade. Clean your weapon."

That evening after a cold supper, Nigel explained to his squad sergeant how it worked with a sentry dog like Chips. How his father had trained the dog to give a silent alert rather than to bark. "By alerting only the handler and not the intruder, the handler is given an enormous advantage: advanced knowledge of the intruder but without the intruder knowing he's been discovered. It's brilliant, really."

Eyeing the dog, Sergeant Ayres stroked his moustache in thought. "An enormous advantage, indeed. And you say he can be relied upon to do this?"

"Yes, Sir."

"Every time?"

"I-I believe so, Sir," said Nigel. "Every time."

"How is he at survival?" asked Sergeant Ayres, running his hand down the head, neck, spine, and then tail of the dog.

"Survival, Sir?"

"In this 'ere war," interjected Spike from his sleeping niche, "dogs is killed by Fritz at a 'igher rate than is 'umans." Spike paused, spitting onto the floor of the dugout. "Sergeant Ayres, I'm thinking, is asking if your mongrel's smart enough to keep 'is 'ead down, not get it blowed off? I'd like to know the same."

The strap of Nigel's Tin hat seemed to tighten. "He's still here, isn't he? That makes him a survivor, so far." It was meant to be a light comment, a jest, and he tried to laugh. But his voice cracked and it came out more like a cough.

"What else can he do?" asked Sergeant Ayres.

"Carry messages, Sir," replied Nigel. "Like nobody's business, you can rely on old Chips to get through with a message. That's a problem, isn't it, Sir? Getting messages through?"

"Indeed, it is," said Sergeant Ayres. "It's a war full of problems, but communication's the biggest. Germans always cutting our telephone lines, and, to be fair, we always cutting theirs. Then when we send out a man to repair the line, their snipers take him out. Our snipers doing the same to theirs, tit for tat all around."

Halting abruptly, Sergeant Ayres held up a hand for silence. Without making a sound, he reached for his trench knife.

108

14

WRONG DUTY

Signaling for silence, Sergeant Ayres drew out his trench knife, its blade flashing in the candlelight.

Nigel's heart nearly froze. Sergeant Ayres was an old sweat; he had to have heard something. Was it a raid? Knives drawn, German soldiers infiltrating into their fire trench to slit their throats? Both sides did it. Officers wanting to keep their men in fighting trim while holed up in the trenches would send out raiding parties, and not always at night.

Eyes narrowed, Sergeant Ayres took aim with his trench knife. Nodding at the dark shape slinking in the corner of the dugout. He cocked his arm back and threw.

Thonk!

Wheezing like a punctured tire, the rat convulsed, then lay still.

"Well-aimed, Sir!" said Nigel.

Perrett chimed in. "Bravo, Sir! It were a splendid throw."

"I've killed a few myself, Sir," said Nigel, "but never with such a throw as that was."

"I've had more practice," the sergeant replied, recovering his knife. Frowning, he weighed the knife in his hand, then crammed it into its sheath. "If only we could, once and for all, do the same to the Hun, and end this."

Eyes wide, Perrett nodded in agreement, then returned his attention to a 75mm shell casing he had been sketching on with a bit of charcoal.

"Communication—it's *the* big problem," continued Sergeant Ayres. "Take the runners, for example. We depend on runners carrying dispatches from command post to the front lines." He paused, staring absently at the dead rat in the shadows. "The platoon lost two runners in the last month. The whole regiment's lost many more than that. The Germans set up snipers with a line of sight on our communication trenches. So when a lad is running a message from the main fire trenches to command post, they pick him off. Two of our boys, last month alone."

"I'm sorry, Sir," said Nigel. "What about using—" He broke off, biting his lower lip. Along with carrier pigeons, by this time in the war many other units were employing dogs for communication, the Allies as well as the Germans. But there were risks. Sure, a dog was lower down in a communication trench than a man running upright on his feet. Surely a dog wouldn't be shot by a sniper. And Chips was a survivor, that's what he was. Still, he was reluctant to say more.

"The Germans thought it'd be over like that," continued Sergeant Ayres, snapping his fingers. "'Paris for lunch,' so said Kaiser Wilhelm II back in August of 1914, 'dinner in St. Petersburg.'"

Perrett looked over the rim of the shell casing he was working on and scowled. "What?"

"Pa-ris, a ci-ty," said Spike, drawing out each syllable. "In a place called Fr-ance. I'd wager you've never 'eard of it, Fr-ance."

"Leave off, Spike," said Wallace.

Spitting onto the floor of the dugout, Spike glared, but made no reply.

"'Paris for lunch,'" continued Sergeant Ayres, "'dinner in St. Petersburg.' There may never have been a greater miscalculation by a world leader."

"Sir?"

"The Germans believed France would fall in six weeks," said Sergeant Ayres, "Six weeks! And Russia shortly thereafter. That was more than three bleeding years ago. Three years and how many millions of lives?"

Nigel didn't know what to say. Sergeant Ayres had never spoken so many words directed at him before now, and he wasn't sure how to respond.

"Word is the Kaiser has a final plan under his spiked helmet," said Sergeant Ayres. "Hindenburg-Ludendorff Offensive, they're calling it, if our intelligence gathering can be trusted, named for a couple of their big-shot generals. My guess is, our grandchildren will be reading about it in history books. It's his plan for a final desperate offensive to win the war."

"Will he do it, Sir?" asked Perrett. "W-win the war?"

Sergeant Ayres stroked his moustache pensively. "That part of the history books—it hasn't been written yet."

111

Looking up from where he was cleaning a Vickers Machine Gun, Wallace said, "It'll be over my lifeless corpse if he does."

"The Hun will spare nothing," continued the sergeant. "This war is hellish. Before it's over, if it were possible, it will feel like something worse than hell."

"But it's so quiet," said Perrett.

"Fritz does seem like 'e's losing 'is nerve," said Lloyd. "Morning hate this morning was more like morning let's-be-friends."

"Calm before the storm, I reckon," said Wallace.

"Making ready," agreed Sergeant Ayres.

In the uneasy quiet, Nigel and the squad spent the next day repairing and reinforcing portions of trench. Hefting a final sandbag in place on the lip of the trench, Nigel wiped his forehead with the sleeve of his trench coat. Though it was far better than latrine duty, it was still back breaking work. So Nigel was relieved when Sergeant Ayres dismissed them and sent them back to their dugout to prepare a meal.

Waiting till he the rest of the squad was out of earshot, Nigel hung back. Coming alongside Sergeant Ayres, he said, "Sir, there's a matter I wanted to raise with you."

"What matter?" said Sergeant Ayres.

"It's about Private Perrett, Sir."

"Again?" said Sergeant Ayres warily.

"I feel that it's my duty, somehow, Sir." Nigel hesitated.

"Your duty?"

"You've seen him, Sir," continued Nigel. "And how the others treat him."

"I make it my business," said Sergeant Ayres, "to know what is going on in my squad."

"They'd have never put him in a combat unit," said Nigel, "if we weren't so low on men. With the offensive coming on, I'm afraid for him. Ever since training. And now with what's coming. I know it doesn't really make much sense, but I feel that it's somehow my duty to watch out for Perrett, to keep him alive, Sir."

Sergeant Ayres turned slowly until he was facing Nigel. Tilting his head, his eyes narrowed as if he were trying to look deeply into Nigel's head, to figure out what made him say things like this. "You, then, must be the Almighty himself?" he said at last. "There's times I've wondered in this war if we had all been abandoned by you. Frankly, miserable lot that we are, I wouldn't blame you for doing so. We deserve as much, maybe more. But now I know otherwise. It is a pleasure to make your acquaintance."

Nigel stammered, "I-I meant no sacrilege, Sir."

"I know you didn't, young man," said Sergeant Ayres. "Commendable as is your care for your fellow soldier, you've taken on a task far too great. God alone determines the number of our days—yours, mine, the Prime Minister's, the Kaiser's, and certainly Private Perrett's. War or no war, lad, you've taken on a duty far above your pay grade. It does not belong to you."

"But Sir, Perrett, if I may say so," said Nigel, "he doesn't belong here."

Sergeant Ayres paused, his eyes sad and deliberate as he scanned the muddy labyrinth of the fire trench. "And you or I, or any man jack of us, does belong here?"

"But Perrett, he's not like Wallace, nor is he like Spike or Lloyd," persisted Nigel. "He has other strengths. I'm sure he does. But this, infantry fighting like this, it isn't one of them."

"Well, he'd better amend that," said Sergeant Ayres. "He's up for sentry duty—" he paused, checking his wrist watch. "—in ten minutes' time."

Nigel's heart sank. "Sentry duty?"

"Duty roster doesn't lie," said Sergeant Ayres. "Tonight he's up for sentry duty."

"But what if—?"

Eyeing Nigel sternly from under the rim of his Tin hat, the sergeant raised a hand for silence. "I'm well aware of the particulars of my squad, better than you know. I know that a man like Perrett will never be a man like Wallace, and, pray God, never one like others I could mention but will not." He reached out a hand and gripped Nigel's shoulder, like his father often had done. "Your camaraderie with Private Perrett, your friendship with him, is a good thing, a very good thing. But you won't help him overcome his fears and become a man capable of doing his duty, doing it within the limitations of who he is—" His grip tightened. "—if you keep trying to do it for him. Commendable as is your concern for your fellow soldier, tonight Private Perrett has sentry duty. Let him do it *without* your interference. He may surprise us all."

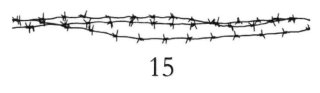

15

PRISONER

Ears ringing and head pounding, the next thing Elsie clearly remembered of the previous night and the strafing of Étaples by the German biplane was urgent talking, many incomprehensible voices, tense commands, grinding and colliding with one another, a percussion of clinking metal pans and surgical instruments, and above it all a moaning descant of human suffering.

Drawing in a hoarse breath, her stomach revolted at the smells of sodium hypochlorite, the pinching smells of bodily fluids, the metallic smells of human blood. Wincing, she managed to roll onto her side then up onto her elbow. Though her eyes smarted from smoke and particles of debris, with effort she began to focus, to take in the frantic scene. From her vantage point on a low cot set aside against a canvas wall, she surveyed the large ward, swollen with bodies, prone ones and bustling ones.

A thought suddenly struck Elsie. Why was she here, aside, alone from the rest? Was her case less urgent, less serious than the others? Wiping her forehead with the back of a hand, she tried to quell the rising panic quavering inside her. Or was it otherwise? Had she been hastily examined by an overworked, sleep-deprived surgeon, who had pronounced her case beyond recovery, and shuffled her off to be left to die?

Where was Trudy? She tried to swing her feet to the floor and sit up. Her head swirled and her stomach felt like she was back on the troopship crossing the channel.

"Trudy?" she called. "Trudy?"

"Here, I'm right here." Trudy's voice sounded hollow, distant, as if she were calling from the musty depths of a crypt.

"Why am I here?" Elsie, took hold of Trudy's blouse. "Och, have they left me to die?"

"To die?" In spite of the trauma surrounding them, Trudy couldn't help smiling. "To die, silly? You're meant to recover without treatment. Unlike several others." Shuddering, Trudy glanced over her shoulder at the activity in the hospital ward. "Somehow you managed to survive the strafing with but a scratch here and there. Mind you, the one on your left cheek's a bit deeper." Her face brightened. "Maybe it will leave a wee scar, a beauty mark, and you can wear it like a true heroine."

"A beauty mark?"

"Well, a mark, in any event," said Trudy. "'Where did you get that lovely scar?' folks will enquire. 'Oh, 'tis a mere scratch,' you will reply with aplomb. 'The wicked Boche gave it me on the Front in the war.' It will be such a tale to tell! I really do wish I had gotten such a scar."

"So, I'm unhurt? I'm fine?" asked Elsie, examining both sides of her hands and inspecting her arms.

"No, you're all there, old girl. Nothing's missing," said Trudy. "Well, you may be a bit shell shocked, perhaps. But you probably brought that with you. You were a bit blighty before you got to the war, then, weren't you?"

Managing a feeble smile, Elsie tested her weight on her feet. "I thought here at hospital in Étaples we would be mostly out of the fray."

"We are meant to be out of it here—mostly," agreed Trudy. Her effort at a reassuring smile looked more like a grimace to Elsie. "We just had—what do they call it?— a baptism by fire on our first night, that's all. Surely the last we'll see of anything so warlike." Trudy attempted a laugh, but it came out louder than it should have. She gulped it down.

"He must have been rather a novice pilot," said Elsie, shuddering with recollection at the whining engine of the biplane, the darkness, the bullets raining down on the encampment. "Is there another ward?"

"No, this is it," said Trudy.

"There's not as many as I would have thought," said Elsie, "from the noises." Scanning the hospital ward, she looped her arm in Trudy's.

"Lucky, we were, so says the forewoman." When Trudy was nervous, to quell her fears, she often became chatty. "Could have been far worse. It's the big shells that do the horrific damage, so I've heard. I suppose with the unethical Germans and their wretched Zeppelins dropping bombs, the big variety, on British cities, there's truly nowhere fully out of the fray. Then again, our boys on the home front have been gunning many Boche airships into the Channel. The more the better, I say. Elsie, do you know how they work?"

"The Germans?" said Elsie. "I believe High Command would like to know that."

"No, silly! Only the Devil himself knows that. The airships, how the Zeppelins work? I read all about it. Sort of the opposite of hot air balloons, it said, though I don't really understand what that means. But they use a sort of thing called hydrogen which is less dense—I think that means heavy, though my brother often used the word to describe me—less dense, anyway, than the ordinary variety of air, you know, what we breathe through our noses and mouths."

After being instructed curtly by the forewoman to change from their nightclothes into their nursing uniforms, Trudy led Elsie back to their room in the hotel, chatting all the way. "The enemy used to use Zeppelins simply to watch us, you know, spy from above. That was until they discovered that they were nice for dropping bombs from. But, oh the joy, our boys learned that hydrogen catches fire so very nicely."

As Trudy rambled on, Elsie breathed in the fresh air and surveyed the camp. Here and there were signs of last night's strafing raid: a mangled bit of corrugated aluminum roofing on a supply building, bullet holes riddling the metal sides of a parked transport lorry, the canvas of a tent shredded and flapping listlessly in the breeze. But on the whole, there was remarkably little damage.

Trudy broke in on her thoughts. "You know something, Elsie?"

"No, but you will tell me, I am sure," said Elsie.

"Well, as I was saying," continued Trudy, "that hydrogen thing is highly flammable, that means it burns easily. Do you know what I would like to see? I would like to see just how flammable hydrogen actually is."

"Oh, I wouldn't think about it, dear," said Elsie, with a shudder.

Ignoring her, Trudy continued, "I would like to see a German hydrogen Zeppelin fully aflame and burning in the night sky like a dying planet." Trudy's eyes narrowed at the gray clouds above, and her fingernails dug into Elsie's arm. "And the Zeppelin's animal Boche crew leaping from the airship, their bodies aflame, arms flaying the air, howls of misery sounding from their throats as they fall—sort of like Dante's *Inferno*, only German, not Italian."

Elsie halted, staring wide-eyed at her friend. She wasn't sure what had most surprised her, the grim ferocity of Trudy's wishes, or that she actually knew something about Dante's *Inferno*. But there was something else. Something almost theatrical about her words, as if they were being recited. With a quick shake of her head, Elsie reminded herself that she had just had the shock of her life and so had Trudy.

The girls quickly changed into their nursing uniforms. "How's this?" asked Trudy, twirling.

"Lovely, indeed."

Trudy snatched up Elsie's arm, pirouetting her, their white linen veils swooshing in the air behind them.

After three turns about the room, Elsie halted suddenly. "This won't do," she said. "There's injured men in the ward, and here we are dancing. Matron will place us on bedpan duty for a month. Come on!"

Moments later, back at the hospital, they were met by the forewoman. With hair the color of brick mortar, and

119

with the posture of an ancient Cleopatra's needle, the forewoman was a puzzle to Elsie. From the fixed line of her mouth, and the rigid hardness of her eyes, Elsie had concluded that the woman had not needed the war to strip her of all tender feeling. The habits and resentments of what must be nearly fifty unhappy years of life had fashioned a bone structure of bitterness, now merely reinforced by the wastefulness of war. She was strictly a woman of business, and the business at hand was war. Every word from her was a command.

So Elsie was surprised and confused when the forewoman turned in exasperation and said, "The Huns astonish me. Just when I thought I had seen them at their worst, they grow yet more monstrous." She paused, her mouth returning to its hard, lipless line.

"Yes, Matron?" stammered Elsie.

"Who needs an enemy?" continued the forewoman, her mouth now arched like the back of an angry cat. "The Hun pilot last night, with his indiscriminate strafing, wounded one of his own, one of our prisoners of war. The male orderlies grumble retaliatory threats, say they'll cut the throats of the lot of them." She had been scowling past them at a smudge on the tent canvas wall, but now she turned directly on them. "I need a detail to take food, bandages and some medicine."

"To prisoners?" asked Elsie.

"German ones?" said Trudy.

Exhaling an exasperated burst of air, the forewoman gave them a concrete stare.

Half an hour later, a basket of supplies in hand, Elsie stood with Trudy at the prison barracks. "It's not much worse than the billet for our boys," said Elsie.

Trudy said nothing as the guard checked their papers, tipped his Tin hat, and escorted them to the barbed-wire containment that was the prison.

"They're singing," said Elsie.

"Germans are great singers," said Trudy. "So I've heard," she added.

"But it seems odd," continued Elsie. "There's not much to sing about, now, is there?"

Trudy shrugged.

"Wait, I know that tune," said Elsie. "But the words, they're not the same."

"They're in German, silly," said Trudy.

"But why have I heard it before? I don't know any German."

"It's a hymn, silly. Everyone knows that. You sing it with English words. Germans, with German words, all set to the same tune."

"But why can't I place the English words, then?"

Trudy closed her eyes in thought. "It's… it's coming. I think—I think I've got it," she said. With a dozen or more prisoners, their firm martial voices singing the words in German, *Nun danket alle Gott…* Trudy joined in:

> Now thank we all our God
> With heart and hands and voices,
> Who wondrous things has done,
> In whom his world rejoices;

"Of course. I know this one," said Elsie, "in English, that is." And she too began singing:

> Who from our mothers' arms
> Has blessed us on our way

121

With countless gifts of love,
And still is ours today.

O may this bounteous God
Through all our life be near us,
With ever joyful hearts
And blessed peace to cheer us,
To keep us in his grace,
And guide us when perplexed,
And free us from all ills
In this world and the next.

All praise and thanks to God
The Father now be given,
The Son and Him who reigns,
With Him in highest heaven,
The one eternal God,
Whom heaven and earth adore;
For thus it was, is now,
And shall be evermore.

When the singing died away, Elsie broke the silence. "How can prisoners of war sing this? They can't be listening to the words they're singing. Whoever wrote them must've lived in happier times than these. All that about God doing wondrous things and blessing us on our way with cheerful peace—that doesn't seem to fit well with war and killing, and prison, do you think? Ouch, you're hurting me."

Digging her fingers into Elsie's arm, Trudy hissed, "Germans aren't stupid. Some of these men will speak English, almost certainly."

"Indeed, she speaks what is correct," said a prisoner in precise English. "On both counts," he added.

Elsie felt the color drain from her cheeks. The soldier smiled and tried to rise to his feet; grimacing in pain, he remained seated on the edge of his cot.

"Forgive my poor manners," continued the prisoner. "I am Captain Hildebrand. It seems I have become injured, and it is difficult to rise, even in the presence of ladies."

Elsie studied the man. He was in his middle twenties, she guessed, an officer, as he said, but she felt she would have known this by his bearing and initiative even if he had not given his rank. To her frustration, she was forced to admit he was rather good looking: square jaw; rugged, northern features; blue eyes that had a mischievous sparkle to them. Captain Hildebrand did not look like she thought a German officer ought to look: crazed, hard-bitten, with a violent-shouting expression welded into his features. He looked like he would have good taste in music, in art, in poetry, perhaps even an engaging and ready wit. All in all, he looked human.

While Elsie was studying the prisoner, by his smile and the look in his eyes, he appeared to be appraising her. Or was he mocking her? He was a German, after all, her enemy, the first she had seen up close. She saw that he favored his left arm and that it had been bandaged with strips torn from an undershirt. "You are wounded?" she said.

"Indeed, I am," he agreed, glancing at his arm, "but how do you English say it, 'It is nothing, a mere scratch.'"

"I am not English," said Elsie, jutting her chin. "I am Scots."

"Forgive me, Lassie," said the prisoner. "It appears I have inadvertently opened one of your wounds. I see from your accoutrements that you have come to tend mine, for which I am grateful, 'with heart and hand and voice,' am I grateful. Yet do I look for God to free me 'from all ills in this world and the next.' You see, I *was* hearing what I was singing. It was Martin Rinkhart who penned these immortal lines—a German, by the way. It has, indeed, become our unofficial national anthem. In fact, we Germans lustily sang this hymn in Berlin August 1, 1914, the day our Kaiser announced mobilization for this war."

Elsie now felt her temperature rising and the color shooting back into her cheeks. This man, this German soldier, this enemy of all goodness and civilization, this killer of British soldiers, who would be doing more killing if he were not now confined here as a prisoner of war—he was mocking her.

"Was your friend last night," retorted Elsie, "the pilot strafing people in their beds, was he doing it to free us from all ills in this world? Or perhaps he was doing it to cheer us with blessed peace."

"Touché, Lassie," said the officer with a deferential nod of his head. "Clearly the pilot was a novice, no doubt flying off course. Germans don't target hospitals and young, attractive nurses—unless, of course, they happen to be billeted in the midst of a military training camp, as here at Étaples."

"Your wound?" said Elsie, abruptly. "Where is it?"

The man pulled aside the strips of undershirt. "Truly, it is a mere scratch, a flesh wound, stray bullet grazing about in the skin of my arm. A trifle painful, but a mere scratch."

Without a word, Elsie began cleaning the wound, taking scant care for the comfort of her patient.

"Perhaps before submitting my life into your fair hands," said the officer, "I ought to have enquired as to your training. Young as you are, you are clearly little moved by the sight of blood."

Elsie looked levelly at the prisoner. "My training? Och, my father's a veterinary surgeon. I grew up doing this for horses, cows, sheep, pigs, dogs—the lot. Fact is, I'd rather treat one of your injured war dogs than the likes of you."

It was the German prisoner's turn; he clamped his mouth shut, the heat rising red on his cheeks.

Doing her best to look menacing, Elsie held up her scissors, eyeing the captain through the blades. With a loud *snip*, she cut off a length of cotton dressing and wound it roughly around the man's arm. "Now, if you please," she said, gathering up her scissors and rolls of gauze, "we're off to care for wounded *men*, real ones wounded by you Germans. Good day, to you."

Spinning on her heel, Elsie felt hot, angry tears on her cheeks as she marched back to the hospital, Trudy trotting to keep up.

"That was a merry message," said Trudy. "I suppose he deserved it. But he was rather handsome, don't you think?"

Elsie halted. "Trudy, you infuriate me! He is a German!"

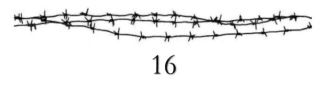

16

MORNING HATE

S tand to!" cried Sergeant Ayres.
In the split seconds before waking, dreams
lunged into action with the speed of a well-bred
race horse at the start gun. The sergeant's command
insinuated itself into Nigel's dreaming as if by Freudian
design.

"Stand to! On the double!"

At the second command, Nigel clonked his head on
the earth and timber above his sleeping niche in the
dugout. He was fully awake. This was no dream. It
happened every morning.

It was pitch dark, cold, and it must be an hour before
dawn. Nigel grimaced with pain as he pulled his boots
on over his aching feet. He and Chips had managed
somehow to survive for nearly a month, a month like no
other in his life. Grabbing his Enfield, he couldn't help
recalling his first days at the Front when he awoke to a
spade and latrine duty rather than his rifle and soldiering.

"Fixed bayonets!" It was the voice of their platoon
leader, Lieutenant Lewis.

Sergeant Ayres immediately gave the command to his squad. "Fixed!" The simultaneous echo of six other sergeants' voices rang out to their squads.

As one, every man in the platoon drew his bayonet out of its metal sheath—poised and ready, they waited. The steel-on-steel shying of bayonets always sent a tingling cataract down Nigel's spine. Adjusting his Tin hat, he wondered if it did the same for the others.

"Bayonets!"

At the command, with a chorus of a metallic clicking, forty men attached forty bayonets to the barrels of forty Enfield rifles.

Leaning against the sandbag wall of the trench, forty men waited.

This was not the first morning that had begun this way. In his early days at the Front Nigel had learned that military commanders on either side felt compelled to prepare for an attack, and what better time for an attack than before first light in the morning when most of the men in the other army might still be sleeping.

"I-I was just thinking." It was Perrett close at Nigel's left ear. "Wouldn't this be the worse time to a-attack?"

Nigel turned, inspecting Perrett from head to foot. Black circles under his eyes, he looked dog tired, but he was here. In a month, each man in the squad had had several rounds of sentry duty. Perrett was no exception and had pulled duty again last night. Nigel breathed a sigh of relief.

There had been no cry of alarm in the night, no night raid, no Boche in the trench slitting throat, no court martial in the morning, no firing squad. Maybe Sergeant Ayres was right. Maybe being thrust into a war, forced to do hard things against his nature, wasn't all bad for Perrett. Nigel couldn't help smiling.

"Wouldn't this be the worst time to a-attack?" repeated Perrett. "What are you grinning at? Wouldn't it be, when each army's expecting an attack?"

Nigel nodded. "Seems so to me." He had often thought the same. The only hope an attack across No Man's Land had of success was if the enemy was not expecting the attack. If the enemy was poised and waiting, the first men over the parapet of the trench were invariably the first casualties of the engagement. The tingling down Nigel's spine grew more intense. It was either a sharp-eyed sniper, finger poised on the trigger of his Mauser, waiting for that first head to appear, or it was a machine gunner, manning a weapon cataclysmically more efficient at reducing the first wave of attackers— and of demoralizing the next wave, forced now to clamor over the dying and newly dead corpses of their comrades.

It was senseless. Still commanders on both sides rousted their men almost every morning and put them in the defensive position to repel a potential attack. But to actually order the attack when the enemy was ready and waiting for you, machine guns poised, bayonets fixed—would be suicide. Yet commanders on both sides, far from the Front themselves, and frustrated with the stalemate, nevertheless, ordered their soldiers over the top to charge across the grim wasteland; thereby sending dozens, sometimes hundreds, of their own men to certain death.

Still they waited. Catching snatches of voices and activity from the German trenches, Nigel lifted his Tin hat, straining to hear. Officers' voices giving commands, metallic sounds of weapons and equipment, shuffling and rustling sounds of men and boots. A dog barking. Were the Germans simply doing the same thing, readying themselves for an attack if one came? Or were they preparing to attack? More waiting.

"Periscope, if you please, Sergeant Ayres," said Lieutenant Lewis.

"Our young lieutenant's learned 'is lesson," growled Spike under his breath. "It were close that first night. Nearly got 'is 'ead blowed off, 'e did."

"His wouldn't 'ave been the first," said Lloyd.

"I'll lay odds," added Spike, "it won't be the last."

Still they waited.

"What do you see, Sir?" asked Sergeant Ayres.

"A good deal of activity," replied the second lieutenant. "The lens is fogged and it's dashed blackness. Perhaps a quick peek over the parapet would be in order."

"I wouldn't advise it, Sir," said Sergeant Ayres, not a hint of condescension in his tone. "Fact is, they're hoping you'll do that, Sir."

"Let's just see," said Lewis. "Lend me your rifle, if you please."

Sergeant Ayres handed over his rifle. The second lieutenant holstered his Webley revolver, took the rifle, and reached for his Tin hat. He hesitated.

"Save your battle bowler, Sir," said Wallace, removing his Tin hat and offering it to the young officer with both hands, like it was a collection plate at church. "It'd be an honor, Sir."

Lieutenant Lewis, nodded, then placed Wallace's helmet over the bayonet. It waggled as he slowly raised it up past the last row of sandbags, over the leading edge of the trench, now in full view of the enemy.

"One shot or two?" murmured Spike. "Place your bets."

Nigel held his breath.

The snarling *Crack* of a single rifle shot rent the chill morning air.

With a penetrating clang, Wallace's Tin hat tumbled off the bayonet. Soldiers standing at the ready below hunkered as it clattered down on them.

"Look-ye 'ere!" said Lloyd, fishing Wallace's Tin hat out of the mud. "Blasted Bosch sniper plugged a 'ole in 'is Tin pot, 'e did—in one shot!"

"The h-hole, it's smoking!" said Perrett, fingering the chin strap on his own helmet.

"Good for you, Sir, your 'ead wasn't in it," said Lloyd.

Turning his Tin hat slowly in his hands, Wallace placed a finger in the fresh bullet hole. He nodded slowly, a smile spreading across his boney features.

"Dreadfully sorry about your helmet," said Lieutenant Lewis, his face paler than usual. "I'll speak to supply. They'll issue you a new one."

"Don't mention it, Sir," said Wallace, a finger still poked in the hole. "I rather prefer it this way." He crammed it on his head. Weighing his Enfield in his hands, he checked the magazine, and said, "Now, then, Sir. When do we go?"

Nigel's heart skipped a beat. And if his eyes did not deceive him, the muscles in his second lieutenant's jaw and throat constricted. "Orders are orders, Private. We have no order to charge, not this morning."

The muscles in Wallace's jaw flexed, and he exhaled heavily, making a sound that reminded Nigel of an exasperated horse.

"Your eagerness to fight for King and country is commendable, Private," said Lewis. "Your chance will come."

The lieutenant's words were interrupted by a dull thundering followed immediately by the escalating whistling of enemy artillery fire.

"In-coming!" shouted Sergeant Ayres. "Courage, lads!"

Nigel cradled his Enfield rifle and clamped his hands over his ears, keeping his mouth wide open. He'd once seen a terrified young man on his first day in the trenches forget to open wide his mouth. When the artillery rounds began erupting, under the pressure of the novice soldier's terror, blood spurted from under his hands as his ear canal burst.

It happened most mornings. Morning hate they called it. Nigel wasn't sure he would ever get used to it. When neither army was wantonly willing to sacrifice its men in an all-out charge at the other's fire trenches, the artillery went to work. Launching a thundering barrage of leaden mayhem—machine gun fire, artillery, mortars, grenades—each army intended to send a clear message to the enemy: "We are here. We hate you. We have the weaponry to kill you, but we don't want to send our boys out to die, not this morning."

Hammering with heavy ordnance at the entrenched position of the other, each army hoped, thereby, to kill as many as they could, and terrorize with shock and awe those who managed to live through morning hate—this time.

17

CAPTAINS OF OUR FATE

After an hour of morning hate, thousands of pounds of heavy ordnance hurled back and forth by each army, the thundering barrage began to exhaust itself, gradually subsiding into the irritable grumble of an occasional exploding shell, strung together with intermittent machine gun fire, and the crack of a Mauser as a sniper honed in on the head of a careless Tommy caught square in his iron sites.

After tending the wounded and seeing to the recent dead, those who had survived ate a cold breakfast. The morning meal consisted of salt biscuits so hard a man could break a tooth on them; only after soaking the biscuits in bacon drippings and tea could they be swallowed.

"Blah!" said Spike, spitting. "Dog biscuits! Worse than!" Under his breath he grumbled, "I'd get nothing if I fed this kind of rot to a prize fighting dog."

Chips fixed all his attention on Spike, staring motionless at him, both ears erect.

"What-cha staring at?" snarled Spike.

It wasn't the first time Chips had looked that way at Spike, and Nigel couldn't help being troubled by it. Spike was supposed to be on the right side of this war. So why then did Chips bristle so at him?

Mechanically, Nigel broke down his Enfield and began cleaning it. He smiled wryly. He hadn't had a good wash in weeks himself, but his rifle never missed a day. His life depended on it. Because all of their lives depended on their weapons, the squad never cleaned them at the same time, only in shifts. Sergeant Ayres was insistent: "Never more than half my squad cleaning your Enfields. I won't have the Boche descending on us with all rifles torn apart."

After the squad had oiled and reassembled their rifles, and honed their trench knives and bayonets, men were assigned various duties: repairing sections of trench hit by artillery during morning hate, filling and hefting sandbags in place, pumping water from dugouts and low places in the trench—there were always low places in the trenches. When the chores were finally completed, men had time to themselves. Some wrote letters home to parents, wives, or sweethearts. A few others, dredging up what they could remember from their grammar school days, tried their hand at writing poetry.

During the boredom of these hours some men smoked. Most men smoked, most of the time. Smoking was one of the things that the two enemies shared in common. During waking hours, when the trenches were not filled with smoke from exploding ordnance or poison gas, a blue haze of burning tobacco hung low in the trenches of both armies. Nothing else but the aroma of tobacco smoke was potent enough to cover over, at least partially, the putrid stench of mud, and waste, and death that bore down on the yet living.

"How lovely! Smokeables from my father," Nigel had once overheard Lieutenant Lewis gleefully exclaim as he opened a care package from home filled with tobacco for his pipe.

And some men occupied their free time with drinking. Strong drink and plenty of it seemed to pair well with the gamblers. The army had an official ration of rum for soldiers, but few looked forward to it. It hadn't taken men long to realize that officers issued rum as a prelude to going over the top. Rum served as an anesthetic to calm the fears, a panacea to numb the pain they were about to experience, a last alcoholic fling before the steely hand of death snatched their young lives from them forever. Nigel shuddered at the thought. No rum for him.

Hand in hand with the drinking, some men filled the hours of boredom by gambling. Betting at cards, dice, dog fights—almost anything. Spike would propose laying bets on killing rats, how many fleas made their home in a man's bunk, even on the survival of his comrades. Gambling, though not strictly forbidden, was unofficially frowned upon by officers, though there were some with the king's commission who joined in.

War brought something else out in men. Art. War seemed to Nigel to be the very antithesis to creating objects of beauty. In war, men were so intent on destroying anything of beauty and usefulness. He had never been to France before the war, but pictures he had seen of vast fields of lavender and sunflowers, muscular white cattle grazing contentedly on broad rolling pasture lands, rural lanes lined with plane trees—all this had made him long to explore the fair garden across the channel from his home in England. He looked around at the mud hole that was his billet. War had destroyed all that used to be lovely in France. Yet, perhaps it was precisely to counteract the destructive forces of war and its wasting ugliness that compelled some men to create something beautiful.

Perrett was one of these men. Hunkered over a brazier, Perrett alternately heated and tapped on a 75mm shell casing.

"Is there not something intensely ironic about him doing that," observed Lieutenant Johnson one morning after breakfast, "wresting from an object designed to destroy and obliterate, creating from it a thing of beauty? If that is not irony, I know not what is."

"Indeed, the very name 'trench art' is ironic," said Lewis.

"As an adjective, 'trench,' as we have come to know the foul ugliness of ours," said Johnson, "does not seem to go well with any meaningful understanding of the word 'art,' now does it?"

"Yet, Private Perrett tap-taps away," said Lewis, "thereby, planting his flag, taking his stand, undaunted in the face of the grinding forces of war." He hesitated, shaking his head in wonder. "Truly, his labor is a triumph of the human imagination."

"Perhaps the genuine heroes of this conflict," said Johnson, "are the artists, the poets, the ones who, in spite of the monolithic forces of destruction raining hate and devastation all about them, retain and celebrate being human by tap-tapping away at their art."

Perrett could scarcely avoid hearing every word the two officers were saying, but so intent was he on his work that he appeared to be wholly unaware of their fascination with his doing of it.

"What'll it be when you've finished?" asked Nigel.

Turning the shell critically, then holding it up to the gray light, Perrett replied, "A vase, I think—for holding flowers in."

Flowers? Looking around at the wasteland of mud and filth that was the trenches, Nigel tried to recall when he had last seen a flower or smelled the sweet aroma of one. He wondered when he would see one again. He further wondered about creating a flower vase out of a shell casing for heavy explosive ordnance and then there being nothing whatsoever to put in the vase.

"Who's it for?" he asked.

Perrett, holding the shell aloft reverently, like a priest with the chalice at the Eucharist, turned and whispered. "Mother, it's for my mother." He looked at his creation again. "That is, if—" He broke off.

"It's fine work, Perrett," said Nigel quickly. "How'd you figure out how to do it?"

Shrugging absently, Perrett bent closer to the flame of his brazier, as if to return to his tapping, but he hesitated. "Nigel, if something were to happen to me, would you—" he paused. "Would you see to it that she gets it?"

Nigel was about to laugh off the notion that something might happen to him, but the sober expression in Perrett's eyes made him halt.

"Please, would you?" said Perrett.

"If she lived in the Orkneys," said Nigel, "and I had to walk there and back on these aching feet of mine, it would be an honor."

Perrett smiled and resumed his work. *Tap-tap-tap.*

Something had begun to change for Perrett; slowly, imperceptibly at first. *Sergeant Ayres was right again,* thought Nigel. It wasn't exactly courage, and Nigel doubted if he'd ever be the gallant hero, but the shameless blubbering terror of his early months at war was melting away. He would never be a killing machine like Wallace, and he probably would never win the Victoria Cross, though who could say? Somehow Perrett had become an ordinary man who, in the face of his fears, was determined to do his duty. And to make something beautiful along the way.

Watching the glow of light rimming the hunched form of his bunk mate, Nigel wondered just what it was that compelled men to create something of beauty in the midst of war, especially the ugliness and filth of this war. Turning his hands slowly and flexing his fingers, he could not escape the compulsion to create that he also felt.

Surrounded by the teeming array of human conditions, and confronted with suffering and death like he had never experienced before in his life, Nigel felt strangely drawn to poetry. As a child in his home they had read poetry: sonnets, lyric poems, poetry from the Bible, and sometimes entire Shakespeare plays; *Henry V*, *King Lear,* and *Julius Caesar* had been favorites. Eyeing the small stack of thin blue paper on his knees, Nigel bit his pencil. The paper was government issue—it had that smell—for writing letters home. But he figured it would work just as well for poetry. He gnawed more viciously on the pencil. Perhaps he ought to write some lines about the war, verses about his hopes, about his comrades—his mother would like that; or a stanza or two about manhood and courage—his father might like that. Writing poetry worked better, however, when things were quiet and he could contemplate. Crammed in close quarters, his efforts were constantly interrupted.

Lieutenant Johnson's words broke in on Nigel's thoughts. "For Private Perrett, here, his medium is trench art," he continued. "And we commend him for applying his creative genius so relentlessly to such a chillingly violent medium. But yours, Jack? Yours is poetry." He laughed. "Now, none of that, no wafture of your hand, feigning to deny it. I have observed you, straining at your candle, your own kind of violence as you grind your teeth and furrow your brow at the lines taking shape on the page before you. I've been watching. The results of Perrett's labors, however, lie before us to observe, but you are far too stingy with yours. Let us hear some of it."

"I fear mine is not so, how shall I say it," said Jack, "so uplifting, so useful, so beautiful as is the private's trench art. But how's this?"

It matters not how strait the gate,
How charged with punishments the scroll.
I am the master of my fate:
I am the captain of my soul.

"That's cheating!" said Johnson, with a laugh. "Unvarnished plagiarism, that's what that is. It's Hensley penned those lines, and you know it. And if I may say so, for all his clever use of poetic convention and subtle biblical allusions—Hensley's lines are all rubbish."

"You think so?" said Jack.

"Look around you, man," said Johnson. "Look in the mirror. Who of us actually is master of our fate, the captain of our soul? If this intractable war has revealed anything about the human condition, it's that such a grandiose claim applies to none of us. No more Hensley. I want to hear a Lewis, Jack Lewis, or whatever dashed Irish name it is your mother christened you with."

Lewis laughed. "All right, then. You shall hear. But I promise, you will not like it."

Though Nigel strained to hear, it was no good. Perhaps shy about reading his poetry aloud, the young second lieutenant lowered his voice. Though he only caught a whole stanza here and there, it was impossible to miss the bitter, accusatory tone of the lines.

Come let us curse our Master ere we die,

For all our hopes in endless ruin lie.

The good is dead. Let us curse God most High…

"Wait," broke in Johnson. "What do you call it?"

"*De Profundis*," said Lewis. "Now, may I continue?"

Nigel, afraid he may not have heard the opening lines correctly, moved closer to the doorway of the dugout. The second lieutenant's voice continued:

O universal strength, I know it well,

It is but froth of folly to rebel;

For thou art Lord and hast the keys of Hell.

Yet I will not bow down to thee nor love thee,

For looking in my own heart I can prove thee,

140

And know this frail, bruised being is above thee.

Laugh then and slay. Shatter all things of worth,
Heap torment still on torment for thy mirth—
Thou art not Lord while there are Men on earth.

"Jack? This is blasphemy, nothing short thereof!" said Johnson when he found his voice. "You've managed to give yourself credit for all the good, all the beauty, all the triumphs of millenniums of civilization— and then you've turned and blamed God for using his universal strength to shatter anything good. You give yourself credit for all the progress and turn and blame God for all murder, vice, and war—this war, in particular."

"I did say you would not like it," said Jack.

"Indeed, yet there's more *not* to like than I anticipated," said Johnson. "In your verses, Jack, all that is evil comes by 'heavenly compulsion… a divine thrusting-on,' as the Bard has it. 'An admirable evasion of whoremaster man.' Nonsense, Jack! And that puerile line about you being above God—Jack, you can't be that naïve, or is it god-deluded arrogance? Surely this is some kind of parody, and you don't mean a word of it."

"Of course, it is parody," said Lewis. "Surely you know it from the liturgy, your Anglican one. Psalm 130, 'Out of the depths I cry to thee, O Lord.'"

"Yes, yes, hence, your title, *De Profundis*," said Johnson, with a dismissive wave of a hand. "'Out of the depths.'"

"And, make no mistake," continued Lewis, "I mean every word of it."

"How could you?" said Johnson. "You seem to think it clever, but I believe you have gone badly off the rails with this, this *poetry*, as you call it. Poetry for the ancients was about many things, but in the big picture it was about making us less self-referential, not more so, as you have so blatantly done here. The Greeks have a name for this, Jack. Hubris! When a mere man thinks he's god. I'd cook my bully beef over it if I were you. Or leave it conveniently in the latrine!"

"Not on your life," retorted Lewis. "I mean to submit it for publication."

"One can only pray," said Johnson, laughing and slapping his comrade on the back, "that there'll be no self-respecting publisher desperate enough to set it to type."

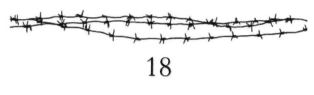

18

QUARRELLING

G ive it me!" shouted Perrett. "That's my shell casing!"

"Is it, now?" said Spike, looking from the 75 mm shell to Perrett. "It's just trench clutter, lying about the dugout. Bloke could trip and fall on the likes of this rubbish. Who says it yours? Strictly speaking, it belongs to the French government, now, don't it?"

"You know it's mine!" said Perrett, lunging for it.

In a well-timed maneuver, Spike drew it away just out of reach. Perrett's boots slipped on the duckboards. With a *splat* he was face-down in the mud.

"Leave off," said Wallace. He knelt on the duckboards and helped Perrett to his feet. "Give him back his shell, Spike. We all know it's his. He's been at it with that infernal tapping for days. Why take his? There's plenty more where that came from."

Spike, tossing the trench art into the mud, laughed. "As you wish, Prime Minister."

Perrett, heedless of the mud, scrambled after his shell casing, feeling beneath the ooze until he found it. "I've got it!" he said, shaking out the mud and water and wiping the brass with his sleeve.

Sergeant Ayres emerged from a dugout. "What's going on here?"

Spike had a way of feigning innocence by whistling softly, pretending to be preoccupied with reading from a notebook he kept near to hand. Looking up wide-eyed and innocent at his sergeant, he shrugged.

Scratching between Chips' ears, Nigel felt the heat rising on his cheeks. He'd had about enough. "Sir, what's going on here is—"

"—Nothing, Sir," broke in Wallace, his eyes steady on Nigel. "Nothing."

Sergeant Ayres looked from Wallace to Spike then back to Nigel. "Good, then," he said. "Private Hopkins?"

"Yes, Sir."

"The lieutenant's asking for you," said Ayres. "You and the dog, on the double."

"Yes, Sir. Come along, Chips."

In the labyrinth of the fire trenches on the front line, a platoon was billeted in short quarters; every dugout within earshot of another; there was little privacy to be had. A few yards scuffling on the duckboards and Nigel winced as his boots nearly slipped on the mud in front of the officer's dugout.

"Ah, here he is," said Lieutenant Johnson, "the man and his extraordinary dog. We were just speaking about what went on there."

"You heard, Sir?"

"Indeed, the tussle over the shell casing, the trench art," replied Johnson. "Yes, we try not to miss much."

"At it hammer-and-tongs," said Lieutenant Lewis, lighting a cigarette and exhaling a plume of blue smoke. "Like a couple of dogs."

"I would say very much *not* like a couple of dogs," said Johnson.

"I beg your pardon?" said Lewis, rubbing his hands together. "Are we now to enjoy the stimulation of a good quarrel ourselves, is that it?"

Johnson laughed. "Quarrelling is a curious thing. But it's essentially different when dogs do it. Animals just act on instinct. Put two of them in the room with one bone, and they'll go at it." He paused, patting Chips' head. "Except Nigel's dog. Remarkably well-mannered animal, is he. Far better than many men, if this war is any indicator."

"A fight's a fight," said Lewis. "Dog or human, it's all the same."

"That's where we differ," said Johnson, nodding slowly. "When two men, or two countries quarrel, each side is trying to show that the other side is in the wrong, hence all the propaganda. When they do that, when they quarrel, both sides, perhaps unwittingly, are demonstrating that they believe in a law of decent behavior, one that applies to every human being."

"O, but I do agree," said Lewis, "if you mean the Laws of Nature, that is to say, gravity, heredity, chemistry, mathematics. I agree about all that."

"Yes, there's that," said Johnson. "But the ancients taught that there was a Law of Human Nature, a moral law. But unlike the law of gravity, or the rest, which operates whether we choose to believe it or not, the Law of Human Nature governs above all; it gives everyone the gold standard of what is right and wrong—even for you, Jack. Whatever the applied variations of this law, human beings quarrel precisely because we all know there is a right and there is a wrong."

"Have you gone daft?" said Lewis. He turned to Nigel. "Private Hopkins, you seem a chap of good sense. Surely you cannot agree with such nonsense?"

Johnson smiled. "But don't you see? We're doing it, quarrelling, that is, like gentlemen, of course. But in our very doing of it you and I are demonstrating the very point I am attempting to make. Don't you see it, Jack? In the quintessence of irony, you are arguing with me—about there being nothing to argue about."

Nigel smiled, looking quickly away, busying himself inspecting Chips' paws; trench foot could fester in animals as well as men.

"What are you grinning at, Private?" snapped Lewis.

"Nothing, Sir," said Nigel. "That is to say, I agree that by your reasoning there is nothing to argue about, Sir."

"Yet, he is arguing, is he not?" said Johnson, slapping his knee triumphantly.

Mouth agape, Lewis seemed about to make a reply. Blinking rapidly, he clamped his mouth shut.

"Ah, methinks I detect a flicker there," said Johnson. "I know, I know, it flies in the face of every preferred assumption of modernity, but facts are stubborn things, Jack, stubborn, indeed."

Lewis flicked ash from his cigarette; it hissed in the mud. He made no reply.

"Well, then, enough of this for now," said Johnson. "Jack, you look like you need a spot of tea. I'll be mother."

"Tea?" said Lewis. "After encircling me as you have? I feel like a lion in a den of Daniels. Make it whiskey, straight."

"We've only just finished our breakfast, Jack. One cannot drink whiskey after breakfast; it might quarrel with the bacon. But I'll make an extra strong pot of tea. Have a cup with us, Private." He glanced at his watch. "Ah, but duty calls. First we have a dispatch for your dog to carry to HQ. Sergeant Ayres is convinced he can handle it."

Nigel felt a sudden sinking in his stomach, as if he was riding too fast in a motor lorry down a steep hill. "He can, Sir," he said.

Johnson handed Nigel a small sealed envelope. Nigel rolled it tightly into a small metal tube fitted under Chips' collar.

Stroking his dog's head, his hand lingering for an instant, Nigel gave the word, "Off you go."

Grinning up at his master, Chips placed a paw on Nigel's trouser leg. Nigel knew what it meant. He bent down. Chips licked him on the cheek, turned, leapt onto the duckboards and, in a scruffy flash, disappeared around a zig-zag in the trench. Nigel touched the moisture on his cheek as he watched him go.

"He'll be fine," said Lieutenant Johnson, placing a hand on Nigel's sleeve.

No sooner was the dog out of sight and Nigel heard it. Immediately forward of their trench line a rocket burst, splaying into three red balls of light.

"Fritz is signaling range to their artillery," said Johnson. He hollered the order, "In-coming! Take cover!"

An instant later, a shell hovered at the apex of its trajectory, then bore down on them, shrieking louder, more furiously than Nigel had heard before.

"That one'll be close!" yelled Lewis, ducking into the dugout.

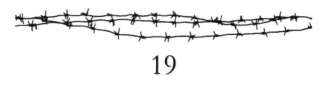

19

COSMIC SADIST

Hellish though things had been in his months at the Front, Nigel had not yet experienced anything as terrifying as the sustained bombardment that followed. So prolonged and deafening was this artillery barrage, it made the daily patterings of morning or evening hate seem like boyish training exercises by comparison.

When Lieutenant Johnson shouted "Take cover!" Nigel had followed the two junior officers deep into their dugout. Every man in their sector scrambled for cover in other dugouts. It was pitch black. Though the mud and earth surrounding them muffled the full force of the deafening explosions, so intense were they, that Nigel felt each eruption deep inside him. Somehow, though they were seven or eight meters below the surface, the acrid stench of exploding ordnance filled his lungs. The gut churning was from more than the bombardment. What would become of Chips? There had been little time. Then again, he was fast. He only hoped that his dog had made it to the communication trench and then safely out of range before the full force of it hit.

With every blasting detonation, Nigel wondered just how long the walls of a dugout could survive the violence of the shaking. They were made largely of mud and timbers, timbers that swayed and creaked, earth and mud showering down with each new explosion.

What if the dugout collapsed entirely? Nigel shuddered at the thought. There were stories. Not a few. It was common, far more common than any soldier hunkered in the pretended safety of a subterranean dugout cared to dwell on. The entire Western Front was a network of burrows, dug ostensibly for protection against bombardment. A fresh hailing of earth thudded on Nigel's Tin hat, and with it, he felt the irony. A direct hit could send tons of mud and earth crashing down, burying the soldiers alive in the very place they came hoping for shelter.

"Well, here we are," said Johnson, striking a match, "alive, for the moment. Efficient, really, isn't it?" he continued, glancing up at the dugout shaft. "If this mound of earth doesn't hold up, it's burial for us, gratis. We dug it, that is, we and the French dug it. We put ourselves in it under our own steam. Remarkably efficient—and saves the family a bit of quid in funeral costs."

Nigel failed to appreciate the attempt at humor in Lieutenant Johnson's morbid observation. As near as he could tell in the dark, Lewis wasn't amused either.

"Fritz's is really at it this morning," said Lewis, changing the subject, "like nothing I've ever seen before. Does he never stop for tea?"

"Flinging everything they've got at us," said Johnson, striking another match.

"As if the floodgates of hell have been flung wide open." There was awe in Lewis's tone, and on his face, dimly visible in the flickering match light.

"Hell? So you do believe in hell?" said Johnson.

Lewis groaned. "We're for it, then? Another quarrel, is it?"

"No better time to discuss hell," said Johnson, "than in the hellish duress under which we find ourselves at the present, don't you think?"

"All right, then. Metaphorically speaking, yes, I believe in hell," said Lewis. "Hearing all that up there, fighting a war like this one, how could one not believe in hell?"

"'…thou art Lord and hast the keys of Hell,'" recited Johnson. "Wasn't that how you put it in your poetic screed?"

"Yes, and God, if he is there, is fumbling with those keys. Dropped them in the mud, for all I know, and can't find them. Either way, we're stuck with what he's left us, hell."

"But only as a metaphor, you say," said Johnson. "So how about heaven? Do you believe in heaven? Oh, I know—

"—Strictly as a metaphor," they said in unison, laughing companionably.

Nigel tried to join in, but another barrage shook the walls. If his father were there, he would be praying. There would be no light theoretical banter about the existence of hell or heaven, or God. He would simply be crying out to God in prayer. Not wanting to wish such a predicament on his father, nevertheless, Nigel wished his father was there to pray with them—with him.

"Jack, why are you so intent on unbelief?" continued Johnson. "It's so much extra work to be an unbeliever. It requires such early rising, 'all those fasts and vigils,' constant propping up of the cold, tottering walls of unbelief."

From other arguments Nigel had overheard, he braced himself. His platoon leader would fire back a retort challenging his friend, something along the lines of, "Nonsense! It's *belief* that requires all the extra effort. One has to suspend all rational thought, for starters, then strain every nerve to focus one's attention on—nothing at all." Nigel was caught off guard at what his platoon leader actually did say.

"Oh, officially, I am a believer, card-carrying," said Lewis, though it sounded flippantly said to Nigel's ear.

"You, a believer in Jesus Christ?" said Johnson. "I am all astonishment."

"Well, that would be overstating," said Lewis, "considerably so. But I did allow myself to be prepared for confirmation. One of the worst acts of my life, but my father was persistent."

"So, let me get this straight," said Johnson. "You were confirmed in the Church, in the C of E?"

"Indeed, I was, and as such am eligible for burial in consecrated ground," said Lewis. "Though if Fritz has his way that won't be necessary."

"So just what is it you were confirmed in believing about Jesus Christ?" asked Johnson. "Surely you don't deny that he existed?"

"That there was a real man called Jesus Christ?" said Lewis, "born in the ancient near-east long ago? Of course I believe that. But I don't accept his claim to be God. All that about being born of a virgin—ridiculous! Humanly impossible! That he was somehow the Son of God? Certainly not. A great moral teacher, perhaps. But not God."

"Jack, whatever you say about him," said Johnson, "what is ridiculous is to say the really foolish thing—I realize, people often say this about him—but it's utter foolishness to say that he was a great moral teacher. Don't you see, Jack, that is the one thing we must not say? A man who was merely a man and said the sort of things Jesus said would not be a great moral teacher, now would he? He would either be a lunatic—on a level with the man who says he is a poached egg—or else he would be the Devil of Hell. Jack, you must make your choice. Either this man was, and is, the Son of God; or else a madman or something worse. You can shut him up for a fool, you can spit at him and kill him as a demon, or you can fall at his feet and call him Lord and God. But, Jack, *Jack*, let us not come with any patronizing nonsense about his being a great human teacher. He has not left that open to us. He did not intend to."

"You sound like Chesterton," said Lewis.

"Yes, I had observed you reading Chesterton," said Johnson with a laugh. "In a paroxysm of smiling with pleasure and scowling with rage, there you sat feasting on his essays."

"Scowling with rage, nonsense," said Lewis. "But, I admit it, here in the dark, with artillery descending, Chesterton made an immediate conquest of me. Not his theism, mind you. I am an experienced enough reader to know the difference between liking an author and agreeing with him. And I like Chesterton, if not agreeing with him."

"What is it about him you like?"

"His humor, but still more I like him for his goodness."

"You may not know what you are letting yourself in for, Jack. I predict this is Providence quite over-ruling your previous tastes and prejudices."

"Providence, bosh," said Lewis.

"Let me give you a piece of advice," said Johnson. "A young man who wishes to remain a sound atheist cannot be too careful of his reading. Jack, if you persist in reading Milton, Donne, Spenser, even Shakespeare and his beloved Sophocles—your atheism will get blown to smithereens. It worked for me. I guarantee it. But tell me more about your confirmation?"

"Not much to tell, really. I dutifully attended the propaganda classes and was, forthwith, confirmed at St. Mark's on December 6, 1914, if memory serves. And there made my first communion, in total disbelief, I might add, acting a part, eating and drinking my own condemnation."

"December, 1914," mused Johnson. "You confirmed just weeks before the Christmas Truce, as it is now called. One of the greatest moments of fraternization of enemies in the history of warfare. Surely, even a confirmed unbeliever like you, you've heard of it. Men on either side, laying down their arms, clasping hands in No Man's Land. Dibbing up teams and playing a round of football in the snow. Exchanging small gifts, peppermint sticks, chocolate bars, tobacco, showing pictures of wives or best girls. Enemies companionably laughing together. Remarkable moment. And what did it, Jack? Singing *Silent Night*, one trench line in German, and the other in our English. That's what started it, Jack, Christmas. 'Round yon virgin… Holy Infant so tender and mild."

"Sentimental rubbish," snorted Lewis. "You and your hymns. Judging from most of them, obviously good taste in poetry and in music are not essential for salvation. But remember, all was not calm and bright a few hours later that Christmas, 1914, was it now? Bombs bursting in air again, like up there just now. The same men exchanging chocolate bars were slitting each other's throats hours later. You cannot deny it. And here we are, still at it more than three years later. Your Christmas didn't work so well, now, did it?"

"I despair of you, Jack," said Johnson. "Unbelief, it tends to make one such a killjoy—at Christmas, to be sure—but all the year through."

"Not a killjoy," said Lewis. "A rational realist."

"And what part of rationality," retorted Johnson, "believes that a man who goes about insisting he is God, God-deluded though he is, yet is, at one and the same time, a good moral teacher? Logic will not allow you to say that. You can't have it both ways, Jack. No, I have become convinced. Unpopular as it makes me in the current climate of academia, I am convinced that there's only one road leads home. All the rest lead into the wilderness."

Nigel couldn't help smiling; he was glad that it was dark; he couldn't be seen doing it. The two young second lieutenants going at it again. It was like the war. In their war, he had to admit, Johnson had just won another engagement, so it seemed to him.

"Ah ha, do I detect a falling off?" said Johnson, striking another match.

"You've just grown accustomed to it," said Lewis. "Whew, it's hot down here."

"Hot? I was thinking how chilly it is down here, like the grave," said Johnson. "We must have the medic check you over. Could be Pyrexia."

"Nonsense," said Lewis.

"I don't know. I believe Fritz may have exhausted himself," said Johnson. "They may be running low on munitions. After that barrage, nothing is more likely."

"There! Listen to that," said Lewis, bitterly. "Just cooling gun barrels. Now back at it in force."

The match burned out. For several moments, listening to the continuing barrage, sitting in total darkness, no one said anything.

Lewis broke the silence, his tone sober, brooding, almost simmering. "My mother was a rock, the fortress of our existence. When she died our fortress crumbled."

"I am so terribly sorry," said Johnson softly. "You were how old?"

"Nine. Almost Ten."

"Tender age," said Johnson. "Such a pity. How did you cope?"

"I became an atheist."

"Why an atheist?"

"Why not? I had prayed—nobody could have prayed more earnestly than I. She died, my praying notwithstanding. God did not answer."

"I am truly sorry for you," said Johnson.

"You need not be," said Lewis. "It's just the facts. Facing them is the same as growing up, leaving childish ways behind."

"'God did not answer,' you say," said Johnson, picking his way cautiously, so it seemed to Nigel. "*Ergo*, he does not exist? It sounds to me as if you do believe in God, but you want him on a leash, dutifully at your side, a tame lion, coming when you call, doing your bidding."

"Balderdash," said Lewis.

"'Facing the facts,' as you call it," continued Johnson. "I'm rather fond of facts myself. Enlighten me. Did you decide not to believe in God because you had grappled with the evidence and had concluded that no such divine being existed? Or did you—I mean no offense, mind you—did you decide not to believe in such a being because you were angry with him for not healing your mother? Put simply, was your unbelief in God to spite him?"

"That's more balderdash. It was—" Lewis broke off, saved by a rapid staccato of exploding ordnance above them.

After another uncomfortable silence, Johnson cleared his throat and began again. "One wonders if it makes rational sense to organize one's metaphysics around the notion that by simply choosing not to believe in someone that that someone, thereby, no longer exists. If that actually worked, I'd commence not believing in the Kaiser—*Poof!* Away with him. *Poof!* Away with the Boche firing their ordnance at us right now. *Poof!* Away with the whole dashed war."

"All right, all right. Perhaps, strictly speaking," said Lewis. "Perhaps, I did not become an atheist. I do not know."

"I used to think I was one," said Johnson, striking another match. "But at the end of the day, Jack, atheism is too simple, wholly inadequate to explain the complexities of life, a boy's philosophy. That's what it is."

Lewis, mesmerized by the flickering match light, sat brooding, seeming not to hear him. "Perhaps, I had become something worse." As he proceeded, his voice was a strained monotone, each word coming like a lash. "Perhaps it was then that I began to think of God, if he exists at all, as malevolent, a cosmic sadist, inflicting pain on his creatures for his sport. Or an eternal vivisector, toying with his human rats merely for his curiosity or amusement."

It was pitch dark again. Listening to the exploding artillery rounds above them, no one said anything for several minutes. Nigel concluded that, furious as it yet was, clearly the main force of the bombardment was winding down. He wondered if one of the German howitzers jammed, or if the British counterbattery fire had managed to take out some of the enemy's big guns.

It was Lieutenant Lewis who broke the silence. His voice was barely audible in the dark. "I wish I could remember her face."

20

TRENCH FOOT

Y ou've contracted P.U.O., I am afraid," said the regimental medic. "Hence, your fever."

Whenever there was a sufficient lull in bombardment at the Front, regimental medics were ordered to perform inspections of all troops, officers and the enlisted. When the fury of the latest artillery barrage had at last exhausted itself, survivors began to emerge from dugouts and trenches. In a flurry of activity, officers ordered damage and casualty reports: Where were the direct hits? What trenches needed repairing or rebuilding? How many wounded? How many dead or missing? Everything came under inspection, everything from scalp to sole.

"Definitely P.U.O.," repeated the medic cheerily.

"And what precisely is P.U.O.?" asked the young lieutenant, scratching the back of his neck.

"Pyrexia of unknown origin," said the medic. "P.U.O. There's no precisely about it." Nodding, he yanked his stethoscope from his ears. "Definitely pyrexia."

"Pyrexia?" said Lieutenant Lewis. "Why must modernity abuse classical language by employing Greek for all of her diseases?"

"For non-Greek-speaking roughs," said the medic, "we just call it 'trench fever.' I know, as a name it's not very original—you have a fever; you contracted it whilst in a trench, hence, 'trench fever.' But there's a war on; what more can I say? We mostly come up with highfalutin, classical names for illnesses during our leisure in peace time." Glancing left and right, he leaned closer and added, "But trench fever, my good fellow, is your ticket to hospital and out of all this."

"Is it... well, is it...?" began Lewis with poorly executed nonchalance.

"Trench fever?" said the medic with a bitter laugh. "Look around you, man. There's plenty of other things far more likely to take you off in this war." He licked the tip of his pencil and scribbled something in a notebook. "But for the moment, you're out of the fray—doctor's orders."

Nodding at Nigel, the medic called, "Next!"

Nigel winced as he stepped toward the medic's examination station.

"Uh-oh, don't like the looks of that," said the medic. "Off with your boots."

Clenching his teeth, Nigel unwound his frayed puttees, unlaced his boots, and peeled them gingerly off his feet.

The medic scrunched up his face. "Argh! Foul stinking feet you have here, young man. Be thankful you still have them. You're making my job too easy, aren't you? Any quack could diagnose this."

"W-what is it?" stammered Nigel.

"Lad, you have what they call 'trench foot.' Now, in your specific case it would be best called 'trench feet,' being as how you still have both of yours—for the time being, that is. "

"Can you give me something to fix it?" asked Nigel, reaching for his boots.

"No, not your boots. You'll not be putting those back on for a bit," said the medic. "Though you're a strong young lad, if I leave you here, *you* may possibly recover—but your feet will not. You get my meaning? Let me be blunt. As I read it, you're only hours away from gangrene. It's hospital for you, post haste."

Nigel, as the medic field dressed his feet, looked anxiously toward the communication trench. Where was Chips? "Sergeant Ayres, Sir, is there anything you can do? I mean, I'm needed here, with my dog, aren't I? Shouldn't Chips be back by now, Sir?"

Sergeant Ayres, narrowing his eyes at the communication trench, drew air through his teeth. "They may hold him for a return communique. It's more than likely they'll do so."

"For how long?" asked Nigel, his throat constricting.

"There's no telling how long. An hour, maybe two."

"Can you do anything, Sir?"

"I don't think you understand, Private," said Sergeant Ayres. "It's HQ. Command headquarters *gives* orders. They don't take them, not from the likes of a sergeant."

From the set to the sergeant's jaw, and the agitated way he combed his moustache with his fingernails, Nigel felt that this might be a time when the man wished it were otherwise.

"No, there's nothing I can do," concluded Sergeant Ayres.

Meanwhile, coiling his stethoscope and returning it to his bag, the medic completed his morning inspection. "Now then, lads," he said. "You're today's lucky ones. Failed your medical, so you're off to transport and hospital."

Forming a human chair out of their arms and clenched hands, two of the medic's assistants hoisted Nigel between them.

Nigel felt a wave of panic. He yanked off his Tin hat and ran his fingers through his hair. This couldn't be happening.

As the ambulance detail formed a line and began its hobbling retreat away from the Front, Sergeant Ayres called after, "We'll carry on best we can without you."

Nigel twisted in his human chair, trying to look back. "None of that," grunted one of the ambulance carriers, "or we'll plant you face-down in the mud."

Ayres touched a knuckle to his Tin hat and added, "And, lad, we'll do our very best to take good care of the dog, be sure of it."

Just loud enough to be heard by Nigel, Spike murmured, "We will, indeed."

21

WHISPERS IN THE NIGHT

L et's us run away together, just you and me." It was a male voice, hushed and gravelly, in the darkness.

Drifting deliciously off into sleep his first night in the field hospital in Étaples, Nigel was dredged back by the whispered voices and now fully awake.

"Run away?" replied a breathy female whisper. "We're already far from home, silly, here in France."

"When we're finally out of all this," came the male voice in reply.

"Is this a proposal?" asked the female voice.

"Ah… a proposal? Of marriage, you mean?" stammered the male voice. "Darling, that's all outmoded conventions, isn't it, concocted legalities? Let's not worry about all that, not just now."

"So it's not a proposal, then?" The female voice had a pouting tone to it.

Besides the occasional flickering of torchlight muted through the canvas walls, Nigel could see almost nothing in the dark field hospital; they were phantoms, whispered voices in the night; ineffectively whispered, so it seemed to him, audible to any wakeful patient.

"I didn't say it wasn't a proposal," came the whispered retort. "It's a proposal, of sorts." In a crooning tone that made Nigel think of the purring of a predatory cat at Regents Park, the male voice tried another tack. "Let's us not quarrel. There's plenty of that back at the Front. There's only one thing that'll fix this war—and that's love."

"Love?" replied the female voice. "You call it love, silly, but I wonder if it isn't merely—"

"Shush!" hissed the male voice. "What's that?"

Nigel heard it too, the stern footfalls of a VAD forewoman, torchlight sweeping ominously on the canvas walls, making midnight inspection of the ward, and bearing down closer with every thick-soled clip-clop.

"I must go!" hissed the female voice.

Next morning, with a yawn, Lieutenant Lewis observed, "The human whisper is a very tedious and unmusical noise." He yawned again. "Especially so at night. How they expect us to recover with all that amorous hissing through the night disturbing our rest, is beyond me. But it's a small price to pay, wouldn't you agree Private Hopkins, for cleanliness, hot food, and a warm bed far from the Front?"

Nigel surveyed the handprints staining the tent canvas of the ward, the rows of low cots, the sick and wounded lying prostrate on them, the poor fellow to his left murmuring deliriously as the blissful effects of anesthesia wore off and the grinding reality of pain and loss returned in its place. Judging from the clean white bandages where his feet ought to have been, Nigel decided the man must have just survived life-saving, and life-altering, surgery. Frowning at his own bandaged feet, he shuddered at the thought.

"A small price to pay," repeated Lewis, "wouldn't you agree Private Hopkins?"

With effort, Nigel murmured vague agreement.

His second lieutenant seemed in a chatty mood and continued. "Since my childhood, I have learned to make a minor illness into one of life's pleasures, something akin to heaven—if there was such a place."

Nigel sat up and looked at him. Could he be serious? He wondered how Lewis managed to go from intensely sober reflection to an almost giddy flippancy. "I-I've always thought it a good policy to stay far away from sickness and hospital," said Nigel. "But I'll grant you, it is a bit cleaner here."

"A bit? It's infinitely so," said Lewis. "Admittedly it may fall a tad below the bar when compared with the spit-and-polish of a peace-time hospital back in England, after what we've been living in at the Front, it is the epitome of warmth and cleanliness. Inhale deeply, Private."

Dutifully, Nigel breathed in the hospital smells. And coughed.

"Oh, all right, all right, a bit too strongly flavored with medicine powders and bedpans," admitted Lewis, "but a world apart from the bad food, unwashed bodies, open latrines, and the decomposition of the unfortunates—I'll say nothing of the bullets and the bombs. But think of it, man! Our new duty, yours and mine, fleeting duty though it be, our duty is to lie about on a warm bed with clean sheets, being waited on hand and foot by England's best. Aha, here comes one of them now."

Elsie had just consulted the duty roster and was making her way to the patients she had been assigned to care for that day. Halting before two cots side by side, she glanced from the chart to the faces of the two soldiers lying in them. The one the chart labeled as a second lieutenant was looking at her appraisingly. His face was pale with blotches of red on his cheeks, and his eyes looked bright and intelligent, but with more than a hint of arrogance, Elsie thought. He smiled at her as if he were enjoying being in hospital. Furrows crinkled the brow of the other soldier, the younger of the two. She couldn't tell for sure if he was in pain or if he was simply unhappy about being in hospital—or about something else. It could be all of the above.

"Good morning," she greeted them. "I am to attend to your needs today. How are you feeling?"

"I'm feeling better and better," said Lieutenant Lewis. "Hospital suits me. Anything is better than rats, fleas, and mud to the knees in the trenches."

"And you?" said Elsie to Nigel.

Nigel tried to smile. "Most of me feels fine."

"Ah, yes, it says here your feet might be giving you a wee bit of grief."

"And how are you this morning?" asked Lewis conversationally.

Elsie eyed the second lieutenant. Her father had told her about the ways of men in wartime, far from home. She would never forget that conversation. Finding it easier to talk with his daughter about such things while doing the chores, he had invited her to come along with him to the pig sty. Scratching at Bertha's ears, the sow grunting contentedly, he had cautioned his daughter, even with tears in his eyes. Three months surrounded by 100,000 Tommies, far from home, had made Elsie appreciate the wisdom and foresight of her father's tender warnings and urgings. She had thought it uncanny the way her father knew such things about men.

"There's a war on," she said shortly, "as you know better than I, but, all things considered, I am well, thank you. Now then, as to your treatment."

Biting her lower lip and flipping through the pages of their charts, she continued. "Now then, Sir, it says here I am to take your temperature. And you, Sir, I am to examine your feet and change the dressing." She laughed. "I must confess, I'm best with dogs and sheep," she said, "being as how my father's a veterinary surgeon and I've had most of my experience with animals. Mind you, I can manage just fine with humans, when they're not ornery, that is, and behave themselves." She glanced significantly at Lewis.

Nigel sat up, studying the young woman more closely.

Setting to work, Elsie fell silent. There it was again. That dull ache in her chest. She could never so much as mention her father without feeling it. She blinked rapidly. Her father was a humble, quiet man, and she missed him a great deal. She wanted to make him proud of her, but deep down she felt it was something more. She wanted to prove herself to her father, to show him that she could do something big, something important, something that would make life meaningful.

There were times in the last three months when Elsie wondered about her father's life, an ordinary country veterinarian, no ambition to do or be anything else. Why couldn't he be more enthusiastic about the war? She had urged him to volunteer. Thousands of horses and dogs serving in the war needed his care; he could do veterinary work for the war effort. But, no, he was perfectly content to stay back on their little hillside holding in Scotland, treating local sheep, stitching up the gash in a dog's paw, delivering calves, drenching lambs—all such frightfully ordinary things. But with a little gumption, he could be saving the life of a gallant horse wounded in combat, stitching the wound of a fearless sentry dog, mending the wing of an indomitable carrier pigeon mangled by a German goshawk trained to cut off the line of feathered communication. But, no, her father insisted on remaining home in Scotland—with the pigs.

"Your father's a veterinary surgeon, you say," said Lewis. His words brought her back to the present. "And where might that be?"

"A wee village, up to the north, in Mid-Lothian Scotland," replied Elsie. "But I must insist that you not speak whilst I'm doing my best to take your temperature."

"North, uh-hmm," grunted Lewis, nodding, but keeping his eyes on the young woman.

"Now, about those feet of yours," said Elsie, trying her best not to let her face betray her revulsion. "Och, they must be hurting you a wee bit, I'm thinking." Fanning at her face with one hand, she stifled a cough with the other.

"Like the dickens," said Nigel, "for more than a week." He hesitated. "I-I apologize for the odor."

"Not to worry," said Elsie, unwinding the old bandage. "But doctor says—it's right there in the chart—that you're like to recover with both feet staying put, proper like where they belong, firmly attached to both legs." Taking a hasty glance toward the moaning patient next to Nigel, she continued, "A prognosis such as that ought to put a smile on your grim features."

Nigel tried to smile. An idea suddenly occurred to him. "You say you're good with animals." He paused, watching her work. A patient three beds down was cursing the Germans and calling for his boots; an orderly attempted to quiet the man. "Being as you have experience with animals," he continued, "I'm a bit worried about my dog. Can dogs get trench foot like we humans?" He winced.

"Oh, did I hurt you?"

Nigel shook his head. "I'll be fine."

"If you mean can a dog get infections in his feet from long exposure to mud and filth—foot rot, we call it with sheep—indeed, a dog can, just like a man. We've treated plenty of war dogs for it here at hospital, and for other ailments and wounds." She looked around the room. "But where is he?"

Nigel ground his teeth together. "Back at the Front."

"You left your dog at the Front?" Elsie looked fiercely at him. "What kind of a handler leaves his dog untended at the Front?"

22

VILLAINS BY NECESSITY

Nigel frowned. "Do you think I wanted to leave my dog at the Front? I had no choice. A soldier's job is to take orders, do what he's told. Believe me, I've heard that over and again for months now. Medic's orders. I was to be immediately transported to hospital."

"And your dog?"

"On a mission, carrying dispatches from HQ," said Nigel miserably. "They do lots of that with dogs now."

"Why not use men?" asked Elsie, reaching for the thermometer in Lewis's mouth.

"Snipers," said Nigel shortly. "Germans target runners, draw a bead on them in the communication trench and *Blam!* communication cut off with a bullet, message undelivered."

"So, they use dogs?" said Elsie.

"They're lower to the ground," said Nigel defensively, "less of a target."

"But a target, nevertheless," said Elsie, frowning at the thermometer.

"Lieutenant," she said, turning to Lewis, "the mercury says you've a fine fever roaring away on your insides, Sir."

With a dismissive wave of a hand, Lewis said, "From near Edinburgh, you say?"

"I beg your pardon?"

"Your wee village, as you term it," said Lewis, "is it nearby Edinburgh?"

"Not so near if you're walking," replied Elsie, "farther if you're walking on feet like his. But we go by train to the big city from time to time."

"Now there's a coincidence," said Lewis. "The exquisite Artemis has relations in Edinburgh. As do I."

Elsie looked at Lewis before replying. "Och, no. Our people are mostly humble country folk." She rose to her full height and put her hands on her hips. "And, just so you ken, our people are Scots not Greeks. The name's Elsie, if you please, not Artemis."

She turned to go. Lewis stopped her. "All right! All right! Elsie it is. Now then, fair Elsie, do you have any good reading material here in hospital?"

"I'll see what I can find," she said, turning to go.

"Something Greek would do nicely," called Lewis after her.

Later that afternoon she returned. "I managed to find this wee volume for you, Sir." She handed Lewis a book thick as a loaf of bread.

"Shakespeare," said Lewis reverently, caressing the spine. "Veterinary surgeon's daughter from Mid-Lothian Scotland, you are a goddess." Holding the book up so Nigel could see it, he added, "Private Hopkins, we've landed on our feet, and no mistake."

"Speaking of feet," said Elsie, turning to Nigel. "Let's have another look at yours." After removing the bandages, she said, "We'll just let them air out a wee bit, whilst I fetch a bowl of warm water and some powder.

"Can you sit up?" she asked moments later. "There's a good fellow. Swing your legs over the edge of the bed. That's it."

Though Nigel tried to conceal the tingling pleasure as his toes entered that warm foot bath, it was no good. "Ah-ooh," he grunted. Since his conscription in the army, he had become so accustomed to a life almost entirely devoid of comforts or pleasures—even basic necessities were in short supply—Elsie's warm foot bath felt like it was transporting him to another world. Nothing had felt so soothing and comfortable for months.

"There, now," said Lewis, grinning at Nigel. "You see what I was telling you about minor illnesses and life's simple pleasures?"

Nigel nodded. "I do, Sir. I do now."

Smiling, Elsie ladled more warm water into the bowl.

"How long?" asked Nigel, watching her work.

"Ah, feels so good, you want it to last forever, now don't you?" said Elsie. "But there's other patients needing attention. Another ten minutes, give or take."

"No, I mean, how long before my feet are well?"

"Och, aye, you're one of the ardent ones, are you?" She nodded knowingly, wiping her hands on a towel. "Can't wait to be back with your mates at the Front, is that it?"

"Private Hopkins is in my platoon," said Lewis, glancing up from the volume of Shakespeare on his lap. "He's a fine soldier, a gentleman, really."

Nigel bit his lower lip.

Taking his pulse, her white fingers on his wrist, Elsie studied Nigel. "It's your dog, isn't it?"

Nigel nodded.

"Amazing animal, is Private Hopkins's dog," said Lewis. "I've observed him with my own eyes—" He launched into a recounting of Chips discovering the spy at the wharf, fetching the Testament, and alerting the platoon of a German night raid. "You think I am 'remembering with advantages what feats he did that day.' But I am not. Remarkably gallant animal, indeed," he concluded.

"What's his name?" asked Elsie.

Nigel looked at her. She seemed truly interested in his dog. "Chips."

"Is that short for something?"

"No, just Chips."

Over the next two weeks, Elsie or Trudy were often assigned duty to care for Lewis and Nigel's ward. Both men slept a good deal, ate hot food, read sonnets and plays from Shakespeare, and discussed companionably what it all meant. There were moments in those conversations when Nigel felt, in spite of the disparity of rank, that if things were different he and this young Oxford second lieutenant might have become companions, even friends.

One evening, after finishing the tragic conclusion of Shakespeare's *King Lear*, Lewis closed the volume carefully, smiling with satisfaction. "A remarkable gift

173

had the Bard. As I see it, he managed to combine two species of excellence like no other: the imaginative splendor of the highest type of lyric and the realistic presentation of human life and character—remarkable gift, indeed."

Nigel nodded in agreement.

"Do you have a favorite part?" asked Lewis, handing the volume to Nigel. "This war brings to my mind that bit about the gods, 'They kill us for their sport,' and we Allies would heartily agree that we're 'more sinned against than sinning.' But what's your favorite? I know, it's difficult to narrow down, rather like trying to find a favorite painting at the National Gallery, or a favorite brush stroke of Botticelli in his *Birth of Venus*. Nevertheless, give it a go. Do you have one?"

Thumbing through the pages, Nigel replied, "As a matter of fact, I do. My father often quoted these lines when things weren't going so well on the farm—or when one of his offspring had given him grief. Ah, here it is."

"Read it out," said Lewis.

"I have heard it so often, Sir," said Nigel, handing him back the book, "I believe I have no need of the words."

"Well, then, my literary private," said Lewis, but without condescension, "give it to me from memory— no, better yet—from your heart."

Leaning back on his pillow and clasping his hands behind his head, Nigel studied the mildew blotches on the tent canvas above him and began: "'This is the excellent foppery of the world that when we are sick in fortune—often the surfeit of our own behavior—we make guilty of our disasters the sun, the moon, and the stars, as if we were villains by necessity, fools by heavenly compulsion, knaves, thieves, and treacherers by spherical predominance, drunkards, liars, and adulterers by an enforced obedience of planetary influence, and all that we are evil in by a divine thrusting-on. An admirable evasion of whoremaster man, to lay his goatish disposition to the charge of a star!'"

Ordinarily appreciative and enthusiastic in literary matters, Lewis at first said nothing when Nigel finished his recitation, no applause, no "Bravo!" Nigel glanced at him. Had he done it poorly, inflections all wrong, weight on the unstressed syllable? His second lieutenant, brows furrowed, seemed deep in thought, almost pouting. Refusing to meet Nigel's eye, it was he who now seemed engrossed in the mildew blotches on the canvas ceiling.

A little alarm began going off in Nigel's head. With a groan, he remembered. Lieutenant Johnson, when critiquing Lewis's own poetry back in the dugout, had quoted lines from this very passage. Clutching a wad of bedsheet in his fist, Nigel wondered how he could have been such a clod.

Clearing his throat awkwardly, Nigel tried to explain. "Sir, I never meant—" He broke off. "That is to say, I never intended to imply, Sir, that your own lines of verse were 'an admirable evasion.'"

Clenching his teeth, Nigel hesitated. But Johnson had, he was forced to admit, made a very good point. It did rather seem like his second lieutenant's poem was 'excellent foppery.' He stole a glance at Lewis. How could he say so to the man who had written the poem, his platoon leader? Nigel's father had explained this passage from Shakespeare many times. "It's the fool that says there is no God but then credits a 'divine thrusting-on' for all the evil in the world, 'an admirable evasion,' indeed." Nigel couldn't get around it: Lieutenant Lewis's poem epitomized the fallacious evasion.

"Not to worry, Private," said Lewis at last, closing the volume with a thud. "It's just what it is." The barrier of rank was restored and the conversation over.

"Get some sleep."

23

BACKS TO THE WALL

As the field medic had predicted, Nigel was young and otherwise healthy, and, thanks to Elsie's ministrations, his feet began feeling better and smelling better within days. During his time in hospital, surrounded by other men recovering from illness or injury, with time on their hands, it was impossible not to hear news about the war. There was no avoiding it. Patients and hospital staff often speculated about the war, about what the Germans would do next, about the outcome, about when it would all be over.

"In short, the Huns are desperate," said a junior officer two cots on Nigel's left. "Depleted and demoralized as the war grinds on, Germany finds the glorious Fatherland plagued with mutinies, civilian and military."

"And just how do you know that?" said another patient, leaning on an elbow "Hey, my guess is, the bloke's a German spy, planted right here in hospital to learn all our dirty little secrets."

"It's all there in the newspapers," retorted the junior officer. "When German sailors on board the battleship *Prinzregent Luitpold* mutinied in August 1917, it set off a chain reaction. But then, perhaps you don't read newspapers. Perhaps you don't read at all. In any event, like gangrene, mutinies spread to near revolutionary proportions throughout Germany. Starving civilians at home, weary of war, want their sons and husbands back, don't they?"

"So will they surrender?"

"Surrender? Zhey are Germans," said another patient, feigning a German accent. "Germans don't surrender lightly. No, my guess is, they're building up to a massive offensive. Defensive warfare, sitting back, waiting for their enemy to wear itself out, never suited the Hun. Mark my words, things are about to change in this war."

"No more trenches, then?" said another patient. "After all that work we done digging of 'em."

But it wasn't only patients speculating about the war. Nigel and Lewis and most of the other men in their tent overheard a conversation through the canvas; though the substance of that conversation was not altogether a surprise, it sent a chill down Nigel's spine. It had been a late winter storm, a day of torrential rainfall, the tent canvas above them saturated and bulging, strained to the breaking point, a slurry of mud running between the two rows of cots. At dusk the clouds parted, and as night fell, eerie blue moonlight shone through the canvas of the ward. It was then that Nigel heard them.

"If our intelligence can be trusted, and I, for one, believe it can be, First Quartermaster General

Ludendorff plans an all-out offensive, a last-card, do-or-die strategy."

"I know that voice," whispered Lewis, leaning close, his words barely audible. "The colonel, camp commander." Feigning a terrified grimace, he pointed at the thin canvas wall, the only thing separating the colonel and his staff officer from them. He mouthed more than said, "It's him, right there."

"He's a clever Bosch, is Ludendorff," said the colonel, drawing on his cigarette. Nigel heard the indrawing and saw the ash glowing orange, then fading. The two officers were so close, he caught the scent of burning tobacco as the men smoked. Moonlight coming from behind the two officers cast up their shadowy silhouettes, bigger than life, on the canvas tent walls.

"He plans to drive a wedge between the Allies, the French and we British," continued the colonel, "not a difficult task, mind you. They have their intelligence sources as well. The French generals care far more about protecting their beloved Paris than they do about supporting their Allies, don't they? Ludendorff knows this and will use it."

"He will, and word is," said the colonel's staff officer, "Ludendorff has specially trained shock troops to lead the push."

"Formidable as the Hun has been in this war," said the colonel, "we are about to face the worst kind of enemy. A desperate one. An enemy that knows that if they do not succeed in this one final aggressive offensive, they are finished. The war is over, and they will have lost it."

"But we now have the AEF on our side," said the staff officer, another orange glow showing through the canvas. "The American forces are joining the fight—at long last." His voice was low and raspy. Nigel wondered if he had had a near miss in a gas attack, or if he just smoked too much.

"The Germans keep telling themselves it is the 'American bluff,' that Yank soldiers are soft," said the colonel. "But deep down, I think they believe otherwise. Proof comes in battle, and if they are wrong, it will be too late to correct the myth. For our part, we can only hope there is no bluff. Either way, more manpower means that Ludendorff must act now," continued the colonel. "German High Command knows that they have to make their move before the American Expeditionary Force arrives on a large scale. Ludendorff is counting on it taking a year before the AEF will have sufficient men trained and in combat to tip the scales against Germany. Let's hope he's wrong about that. Nevertheless, this is their last card; they must act now."

Clearing his throat, the colonel raised his voice just above a whisper. "We are about to face," he said, pausing for dramatic effect, so it seemed to Nigel, "the greatest military offensive in the modern world, perhaps of all time. The German Army will come on like a vengeance. We must stop them—or die in the attempt." With his words, a gust sent a ripple along the tent canvas wall; his silhouette quavered.

"Indeed," agreed the staff officer.

Nigel, his face close to Lewis's, as they strained to hear, wondered. Surely these officers intended to be overheard, but why?

"Since powerful German trade unions will not allow their women to work in factories, many otherwise able-bodied men, needed for building war machinery at home, cannot be used for fighting."

"Germany is rapidly approaching a crisis of manpower," agreed the colonel. "They cannot hold out for long. Lose too many men in this offensive, they will not be able to replace them. Though we might be tempted to feel smug about our chances against a depleted enemy, beware. Men fighting for their lives, for their cause and country, for the very existence of the Teutonic race—such men will be a formidable enemy in the extreme. Make no mistake."

"And our counter strategy?" said the staff officer.

"It's all men to the Front," said the colonel no longer in a whisper. "We have our orders from HQ. 'Send back every man to his regiment—every man not dead or dying.' Those are our orders. The outcome of the war may very well depend upon it. It's no more hunkering in the dugout for any of our lads. And no more prolonged recoveries from minor illnesses in the comparative comfort of hospital. It's up and out, backs to the wall. Face the Hun like men, and be done with them—or they will be done with us."

Their voices drifted into a murmur and then faded altogether as they walked on to the next hospital tent.

"They wanted us hearing that," said Lewis. "Every word of it. Just like setting up Beatrice and Benedick in *Much Ado About Nothing*. If Spike were here, he'd be taking wagers on the number of days before we're all shipped back to the Front, able-bodied or otherwise."

"Spike and his infernal wagering," said Nigel.

The next three days passed quickly. Nigel was torn. If the colonel was correct, every hour brought him closer to the inevitable. And the German offensive, had the massive bombardment been its opening salvo? Had it already begun? What were Sergeant Ayres and his squad going through? And what had become of Perrett?

With each passing hour, Nigel felt more guilty about the cooked meals, soft bed, and the leisure hours of lounging at hospital. More than any of that, he worried about Chips. He knew Sergeant Ayres would do his best to take care of his dog. But there was a war on, a war, if the colonel could be trusted, about to become more hellish than it already was, hard as that was to imagine.

When the day finally came, and he and Lieutenant Lewis, along with several hundred other men, were deemed well enough and ordered to return to the Front, Nigel's sense of dread intensified, his stomach churning like the wheels of a locomotive pulling troop cars crammed with men to the Front.

They had their orders. Looking east, he listened to the low, faraway grumbling of the big guns. While at hospital, he'd tried to forget how cataclysmically different artillery sounded and felt at the Front. Here it was merely a soft, harmless, bass line.

Dozens of men, back in uniform, boots on their feet, reported, as ordered, to the parade ground adjoining the hospital. Nigel studied the other faces, grim and pale in the dusky light as daylight faded. They were men from various regiments, now patched up from their various wounds and ailments, called to form a line and return to the Front.

Ranking officers conferred with the colonel over the paperwork, their faces glowing eerily in the lamplight reflecting off the dispatches as they sorted through the lists of names, regiments, and companies.

Nigel knew it was coming, the order to fall in, the final roll call, the call to turn about face to the east, and march back to the Front. Unlike his experiential ignorance in that first march to the Front, this time he knew precisely the world that awaited him there.

Only moments before the order came, Elsie approached. "Take this," she said, slipping him a small package. "For your dog. For Chips."

"What is it?" asked Nigel.

"Antiseptic. The Matron knows. I got permission," she added. "If Chips has the canine version of what you had, trench foot—" She nodded as she had seen young surgeons trained at Cambridge do. "This'll cure him."

A gust of wind caught at Elsie's white veil, and she pulled her caplet closer about her shoulders. "Write me, won't you?" A soft blush reddening her cheeks, she added hastily, "And tell me how Chips gets on."

Nigel thanked her. Watching Elsie disappear into the labyrinth of tent canvas and make-shift barracks, he was torn. What lay ahead? He desperately hoped Chips had survived the last three weeks without him. But he knew the Front: fire trenches were not conducive to survival for men, let alone a dog—a dog without his handler. He weighed the small bottle of sodium hypochlorite in his hand. He hoped it would work.

It was fully dark. It would come any minute now. The officer in charge, a major with a limp in his right leg, stepped in front of the two long columns of men.

"Company! Attention!"

The major paused as a rapid succession of erupting shells rumbled miles away at the Front, louder than usual, the repercussions enduring longer. Nigel watched as a halo of light flared and lingered on the dim horizon, silhouetting the dilapidated skeleton of a barn and the cold, stone ruins of church.

When it died away, the major gave the command. "Company will advance! Left turn!"

24

CONSCIENCE ROUND

I am pleased that you've recovered, Sir," said Sergeant Ayres. "You as well, Private Hopkins."

It was nearly dark when they at last arrived at the Front. After three grueling days, marching mostly through the night, Nigel felt about to collapse. Coming off the comparative leisure of hospital life, abruptly boots on, and a sixty mile march on feet barely recovered from trench foot, had made him deliriously exhausted. But even his weariness could not prevent him from feeling the tension. Something was afoot. Sergeant Ayres seemed distracted, preoccupied, and judging from the dark circles under his eyes, he had not slept well.

"But I regret to inform you, Sir," continued the sergeant, addressing Lieutenant Lewis. "You've come at an awkward moment to resume your duties."

"The German offensive?" said Lewis. "We heard talk of it. So it's not battlefield rumor. It begins?"

Sergeant Ayres took off his Tin hat and wiped his forehead. "Yes, there's that. But, I regret to inform you, Sir, there's a more pressing matter, a regimental housekeeping matter."

"Go on," said Lewis.

"Man fell asleep while on duty," continued the sergeant, passing a hand across his face and replacing his Tin hat. "Sentry duty, Sir."

"One of ours?"

"Yes, Sir," replied Sergeant Ayres, his voice a dull monotone. Nigel had never seen the man so agitated. "Imagine a Somerset Light Infantry man sleeping on duty and leaving his mates to the mercy of a Boche night raid. No need to imagine it."

Lieutenant Lewis flinched as a shell exploded down the line to the south. He looked grim. "Lieutenant Johnson, I was given to understand, has had command of my platoon."

"He sends his regards," said Sergeant Ayres. "His company's come under heavy enemy shelling, on our right, with the Canadians. Our officer corps, Sir, it's badly depleted."

"Depleted?" said Lewis slowly.

"From casualties," said Ayres. "Junior officers, Sir, with respect, have stopped more than their share of bullets in this war. So much so, there's privates leading squads, privates leading whole platoons. Lieutenant Johnson was sorely needed down the line. I am to convey, Sir, that you are to resume command immediately," he hesitated, handing Lewis a folded piece of paper. "The official court-martial. Military justice, Sir, and the honor of the regiment are at stake."

"I am to give an order," said Lewis, his voice strained and low.

"*The* order, Sir," said Sergeant Ayres. "For dereliction of duty, there is only one order."

"One of ours, you say?"

"Yes, Sir. From the platoon. Worse yet, one of my own squad, for which I take full responsibility."

Nigel felt sick. "Don't let it be, O Lord," he murmured, "don't let it be—"

"My quarters, Sergeant," ordered Lewis, ducking into the low timber doorway of the officers' dugout.

Nigel entered the dugout that had previously been his billet at the Front. It was smaller and muddier than he remembered, and its foul odor assaulted his nostrils worse than he remembered. It felt like a place remote. There would be no hot foot baths here, no tender ministrations of a smartly uniformed WAAC. Elsie's clean pinafore and gown, sky-blue and neatly pressed; her white veil, the lilting cadence of her words, her smile—it was a vague dream, a world apart. Wiping a hand across his face, he felt he ought to detach himself from such thoughts. They would make him soft. It would only make things worse.

Here, unlike the leisure of hospital, with the offensive underway, there would be scant free time for Shakespeare. He looked around at the men in his squad; their faces were grim, like someone had died. They acknowledged him with brief nods but their eyes were diverted. Only Perrett looked him in the eye and seemed genuinely pleased to see him. Nigel breathed a sigh of relief at sight of him. But even Perrett hastily looked away.

"Why so glum?" asked Nigel, studying their faces. Someone was missing.

No one said a word.

"Where's Spike?" said Nigel. "Lloyd, where is he?" Lloyd was lying on his side, back to Nigel. No reply. He didn't move.

"Wallace? What's going on?"

"Detained," said Wallace. "Spike's been tried and court-martialed, now awaiting his sentence."

"Detained? Court-martialed?" said Nigel. "For what?"

Heaving a sigh, Wallace said, "He snoozed off. Slept—on sentry duty." Wallace looked unblinking at Nigel. "We all know the penalty. Fusillading, so the Frenchies call it. Call it what you will, we all know how it works."

"Spike went to sleep?" said Nigel his voice a bewildered whisper. "He could stay up all night gambling. He fell asleep on duty? How did that happen?"

Nigel had never liked Spike. Few people did. But he was in their regiment, in their company, in their platoon. Spike was part of their squad. In spite of his meanness, that made him like family.

Looking around the dim light of the dugout, something else wasn't right. The hair on Nigel's neck began feeling as if an army of fleas were marching up and down his spine. "W-where's my dog?" Feeling in his pocket, he fingered the vial of antiseptic Elsie had given him.

"Ask Spike," said Wallace. "But since he ain't here to answer for it, ask Lloyd. He was in on it."

Nigel could scarcely form the words. "In on what?"

"I didn't mean for none of it to 'appen." Lloyd's voice sounded like an eight-year-old caught stealing a steak pie from his mother's pantry. He rolled over. Candlelight made shadowy crevasses on his pale features. He continued. "We'd rigged things up just so. It wasn't supposed to end that way, 'onest it wasn't."

"End what way?"

Wallace turned to Perrett. "You tell 'im."

"I wish it weren't so," began Perrett. "But after Chips returned from HQ with dispatches, Spike pipes up and says he'd take care of him while you was in hospital. Sergeant Ayres told him that if anything happened, he would hold Spike responsible."

"But something happened?" Nigel barely recognized his own voice.

"It's all my fault," said Perrett. "I should've taken charge of him."

"What did he do to him?" asked Nigel.

No one wanted to speak.

"Dog fight," said Wallace.

"The pit, it were," said Lloyd, "you know, gambling. Spike's always gambling. Spike would put 'is own grandmother's lap dog in the pit and lay odds against it. But 'e assured me, things was rigged in Chips' favor. I'd a never taken part in it if I'd a known 'ow it would end. You gotta believe me."

"How did it end?" asked Nigel. His own voice sounded calmer to him than he felt, but it was the rigid calm of blunt, tempered steel.

"Up and out! Squad, up and out! On the double!" It was Sergeant Ayres.

"That'd be us," said Wallace, with an ominous lilt. He vaulted from his sleeping niche and snatched up his Enfield.

Nigel felt numb as he grabbed his rifle and followed the squad into the fire trench. He fell in line between Wallace and Perrett.

"Solemn duty lies before us," began Sergeant Ayres, his blood-shot eyes just visible under the rim of his Tin hat. "Unwelcome as it is, we all know the penalty." He paused, scanning each one of their faces. "And we all know why."

As long as he lived, Nigel would never get clear of what transpired next. A military constable dragged Spike from a makeshift holding cell in a dugout. Though he had pulled a black hood over Spike's head and secured it with a rope around his neck, they all knew it was Spike; the slouched shoulders, the swagger, it was him. It occurred to Nigel that the black shroud served two purposes: the condemned man would not have to see the faces of the men in his squad, and they would not have to see his eyes as they performed their grim duty.

Nigel wanted to hate the man. He deserved it. He felt perfectly just in hating such a reprehensible creature. Every sinew in his body revolted against him. He felt numb as he watched Spike being tied to a vertical post supporting a wide spot in the sandbag wall of the trench.

"Camaraderie," said Sergeant Ayres, his voice strained and weary. "Each man acting in the greater interest of the squad, nothing's more important in combat than camaraderie. When a man violates that camaraderie, flagrantly betraying the squad by neglect of duty—he gives the squad no other choice."

Facing Spike, Ayres continued. "For you, it's come to this: military justice in wartime. I wish it were otherwise. I wish there was no war on. I wish the German Army would go home. I wish every man in our army did his duty. But there's a war on, and there are men who choose to be derelict in their duty and, thereby, place their mates in peril. 'What's done is done, and cannot be undone.' And justice must be served for it. May God have mercy on your soul."

Grimly, Sergeant Ayres turned about face and looked at his squad. Like a priest, the sergeant handed each man, not a wafer of bread, but a .303 bullet. "For the sake of conscience," he said, his voice low, fatherly in tone, "one of you has been given a blank round, the conscience round. I don't know which one of you is holding it— and neither do you." Taking a step back, his boots squelching in the mud, he gave the order, "Squad! One round in the breach."

Mechanically, Nigel chambered the bullet along with the rest of the squad. He scowled darkly at the hooded figure. For what Spike did to his dog, Nigel hoped someone else had just chambered the conscience round. He wanted to take careful aim at the man's vital organs; he wanted to squeeze the trigger; he wanted to feel the recoil and watch a real bullet pierce into the inner circle of the target, and smash into the man's heart; he wanted to see the man's body stiffen at the impact of the lead; he wanted to watch the body go limp in death; he wanted to rid the world of a reprehensibly bad man.

But, unwelcome as it was, another war waged in Nigel's conscience. Something felt profoundly wrong. He and his mates in the squad, they had trained to level their guns at another enemy. Gray-uniformed Germans, they were the bad men Nigel had been trained to kill, not

191

a man wearing British khaki, the same uniform he was wearing.

Clenching his teeth till his jaw ached, he knew something yet deeper troubled him. The barrier between where Spike now stood and where Nigel stood was a thread, a hair, a mere breath. It could be him.

"On my signal." Sergeant Ayres's voice brought him back to the present. "On my signal, each of you will aim for the target affixed to the offender's chest. Aim nowhere but at that target. On my signal, you will fire one bullet. Understood?"

They nodded.

"Ready!"

Nigel, holding his breath, heard Perrett on his left gulping for air as if he was about to suffocate.

"Aim!"

Positioning his rifle butt at his shoulder, Nigel squinted down the iron sites of his Enfield. Here he was, under orders, taking aim at a British soldier, a man from his own squad. It felt wrong. It was not supposed to be like this. Next to him he heard Wallace exhale, his breath controlled, resolved, and steady. Nigel released the pent-up air in his lungs.

"Fire!"

25

VICKERS MACHINE GUN

Pitched to be heard above the cacophony of battle, the tuneless shrilling of the trench whistle that morning would be louder, more penetrating than Nigel could have anticipated. When the whistle trilled, he knew the routine: Fixed bayonets. Up and out. Crossing the wastes of No Man's Land. Hurling oneself at the enemy, ready and waiting in their trenches.

"Bring 'em on!" It was Wallace, resolute and eager, at his side. "Go ahead, I say. Let 'em make their final bid. Just try to break through our lines. Ain't going to happen in my sector, mine and Mr. Vickers' here."

Whistling tunelessly, Wallace inspected his Vickers Machine Gun. Ever the stickler for cleaning and maintaining weapons, three times in the night he had broken down, oiled, and reassembled the machine gun that he and Nigel would man should the Germans attack that morning.

"Mr. Vickers is good enough," continued Wallace, "when them Germans is charging at us across No Man's Land. From a fixed position, it'll mow down enough of 'em. But, see, here's the problem. It's only good defensively. Too bulky and heavy."

Rubbing his hands together and narrowing his eyes toward the German trench line, he continued. "But, the Lewis Machine Gun, on the other hand, lighter, more portable, circular magazine easier to load under fire, the Lewis Gun lets us take the fight to the Boche. Cowering in their trench, yonder, we can advance with the Lewis Gun cutting a bloody pathway for us right to their doorstep."

"Dugout step, that'd be, wouldn't it?" interjected Lloyd. He'd said little after the news about Chips and the firing squad. Done his duty but said little. Nigel wondered if his comment might be an initial effort to try and make his way back into the life of the squad.

"The Lewis Gun," continued Wallace, "it'll put Mr. Vickers here out of a job by war's end. Mark my words." He scanned the enemy trench line. "But if the Boche want to come for a visit this morning—my innards tell me they will do—Mr. Vickers here will serve us just fine."

Gnawing the inside of his cheek, Nigel felt he would never understand Wallace. An imminent German attack, and here Wallace was chit-chatting about the comparative virtues of machine guns.

"We've done defensive warfare long enough," continued Wallace, now checking the action on his rifle and propping it ready-to-hand. "Too long, I say. Hunkered in these foul trenches, this war, it'd stretch on till doomsday. Give me a hand, here, mate."

Nigel joined Wallace on the fire-step, assisting him as he positioned the tripod legs and mounted their gun.

Lieutenant Lewis squinted through the periscope on their left. Sergeant Ayres and Perrett readied another machine gun on their right. The sounds of well-oiled, metallic efficiency surrounded them. Nigel listened to the clicking and sliding as hundreds of precisely machined weapon parts snapped into their proper places. For an instant it reminded him of the percussion section of an orchestra, but no mellow strings or melodic woodwinds here. On cue down the trench line, cold steel shied against cold steel in iron-hard anticipation of the conductor's whistle.

Raising himself above the lip of the trench, Wallace murmured, "'Up and out,' I say. You first, Kaiser Wilhelm. Go on, then. Play your last card!"

Then it blew. The penetrating trilling of a trench whistle, an enemy trench whistle.

"Courage, men!" called Sergeant Ayres.

What Nigel saw next made him grind his teeth until his jaw ached. With that whistled command, scores of coal-scuttle helmets rose up from the enemy trench line, then faces, then whole bodies, iron-gray, uniformed bodies, with hands clutching Mausers, bayonets fixed. Like a timpani of thunder, Hun warriors, in full defiant battle cry, charged into No Man's Land, a Teutonic wave of death coming on directly towards them.

"The Valkyries have chosen." Nigel heard Lieutenant Lewis murmur, awe in his voice. "Their next billet— Valhalla."

"Here they come," said Wallace, his voice matter-of-fact and steady. "Better them than us. Easy pickings." Nodding to Nigel, he said, "Load for me. Keep it coming!"

In spite of the cotton wadding in his ears, Nigel pressed his hands over them as Wallace, his face contorted in defiance, commenced firing, spent cartridges spewing hotly from the weapon.

An entire German platoon. They didn't stand a chance. A man might stumble over a strand of barbed wire and land in a crater, out of the line of fire, his life saved, for the moment, by his clumsiness. One in a dozen, maybe fewer, while the rest of his comrades are mowed down by 500 rounds per minute discharging from Wallace's machine gun.

"Load! Load!" cried Wallace.

Another shrill trilling of the whistle in the German trench. Another wave of enemy soldiers, following orders from officers safely behind the front line. For an instant, Nigel was distracted; several attack dogs bound from the trench and ran alongside this wave of soldiers. It didn't seem right, man's best friend trained to attack and kill other men, all for a cause that had nothing to do with a dog. *Dogs don't have a dog in this fight*, he thought, his teeth clenched. But there was no time for such thoughts, not now.

Another wave, another platoon, husbands and fathers, sons and brothers, their terrifying advance abruptly halted by lead from bullets that Nigel, a mere instant ago, had loaded. German arms flailing the air, weapons dropping from German hands, German heads thrown back—the grotesque, rag-doll collapse in the mud. The scene played over and over, like the chattering of a moving-picture projector at the cinema—only this was real, brutally real. Numbly Nigel watched as Wallace cut down wave after wave of the enemy, spent shell casings hissing in the mud at his side.

"The barrel!" cried Wallace. "Too hot! Need a new barrel!" Grabbing his Enfield, Wallace fired single rounds at the advancing wave.

Nigel had changed the barrels of Vickers Machine Guns dozens of times in training. The intense heat from thousands of rounds was too much for the steel. Next to them on the fire-step, Perrett had been loading for Sergeant Ayres. Why weren't they firing? This was no time for both machine guns to be silent.

Glancing at the next wave of advancing Germans, Nigel shuddered. They would almost certainly make it to their trench. His hands felt stiff. His fingers refused to work as fast as in training. The oil on the new barrel felt slippery in his hands. Two minutes to change a Vickers Gun barrel? Two minutes in the heat of battle, the Boche hoard pouring in—it felt like an eternity. If the enemy made it into their trenches—he shuddered again. He knew what that meant. Hand-to-hand combat, face-to-face with the enemy, feeling their hot breath, their sweat, their blood—or his own.

Nigel glanced up. He could see their eyes now, under the leading edge of their helmets, their mouths open wide, yelling—white teeth, lips curled in defiance. He could see the cold steel of their bayonets. There was no time.

"Ready!" he cried. Had he done it right? Was there time? Clutching his bayonet in his left hand, and his trench knife in his right, Nigel readied himself for the German leading the charge.

Wallace dropped his rifle and grabbed for the trigger of the machine gun.

Nigel learned something that day: it was far easier seeing men die from a distance. He wasn't sure he would ever be able to get clear of the images seared into his mind and conscience: German soldiers, blue-eyed young men his own age, defiant eyes now blanching into sheer terror, only yards from the lip of the trench—fellow human beings cut down by high caliber machine gun fire at close range.

26

FUSILLADING

When at last the screaming of German trench whistles halted, the British machine guns frittered into silence, their barrels cooling. The killing was over. At first sight of the white rag rising out of the trench tied to the bayonet of a German Mauser, Nigel's heart leapt with excitement. A truce? After the day's slaughter of hundreds of men, were the Germans signaling for a truce? Or something more? Was it over at last?

Surveying the wasteland of carnage, his ears pulsing and ringing, Nigel found himself, against his will, weeping, the tears streaming down his cheeks, as when his father opened a weir gate to water pastureland on their farm. There was no stopping it. Like a bewildered geyser—hot with rage, cold with despair—there was no staunching this torrent. War had made its masterpiece in the killing fields of that day, and it was too much for any man to bear. In the immediate aftermath, there were no enemies, only the living and the newly dead. All the pent up horror, the incessant gut-lurching fear, the unyielding reality of mortality and human suffering—the strain was too great; it had to find its way out of him.

Paralyzed with emotion, Nigel was not alone. Perrett's hunched body at his side rocked with cathartic sobs. Placing an arm across Perrett's shoulders, Nigel found himself, as if in a cradle, rocking with him. Numb with shattered exhaustion, he felt that if he tried to stand, he would crumple like a broken toy, and the globe beneath his feet would collapse into a wrinkled mound like a deflated balloon after a carnival.

The iron-gray daylight that had illuminated the field now covered its face and was fleeing to the west, darkness hot on its heels. Launched from a mortar with a dull *Ploomph!* a flare burst and hovered over the field.

"Burial truce," said Sergeant Ayres, his voice hollow. "Temporary. Long enough to transport their wounded, bury their dead." He sighed heavily. "It'll be a silent night." He nodded toward the prone figures, rigid in death, scattered like tin soldiers dumped from a bucket by a careless boy across the bleeding wastes of No Man's Land. "Leastwise, silent for them."

Ploomph! Another flare rose and hovered over the field. Slowly, stiffly, arms spread wide to show they were unarmed, German medics and stretcher bearers, detailed for burial duty, rose from the trenches and began their grim work.

"Not all are silent," said Wallace, staring unblinking at the field. "There's some of them poor blokes still moving, smashed like half-crushed beetles, but still moving."

"May God have mercy on us all," murmured Sergeant Ayres. There was a catch in his voice, and a quaver on the final word.

In the green glow of flare light, Nigel watched as a lone tear made a rivulet in the mud on his sergeant's face. Old sweat that Sergeant Ayres was, he refused to be hardened, to be made less than human by his unwelcome duty. It seemed to Nigel that his sergeant was one of the few human beings who wanted to feel, knew he must feel, the tragedy of the day's battle. Hardening was easier. It would be easier to revel in victory, mock the dead, laugh at one's enemy's fate, but this was not Sergeant Ayres. Whelming from inside his chest and radiating to the tips of his extremities, Nigel felt an incomprehensible reverence for the man, as if he were above the common order of humanity.

After assigning sentries to keep a vigilant watch on the Germans collecting their dead, Lieutenant Lewis turned and faced the men in his platoon. It seemed to Nigel that their young second lieutenant looked at them as if he were seeing them for the first time.

"You men, 'you noblest English,' and Irish, and Welsh, and Scots—the lot of you! For King and country, you did good service today. I know you feel, as real men ought to feel, the weight of what we had to do this day, of the tragic waste and loss that it is." He paused, his eyes scanning slowly over the field. A bursting flare cast a rim of light on his profile. Turning back to his men, he continued, "But you also saved lives today, British lives. You stopped an all-out German advance, one that would have surely overrun our line, one that could have turned the course of the entire war in Germany's favor. You, each one of you, have 'noble luster in your eyes.'"

Nigel recognized the Shakespeare allusions. "Battle-weary that you are," continued Lewis, "you are dismissed. Rest, recover your strength."

Picking his way through the mud and the mounds of machine gun shell casings, Nigel felt that something was missing. If Sergeant Ayres had dismissed them, he would have said something more: "And may God have mercy on your souls." Or something like that. And, what's more, he would have meant it.

Back in their dugout, Sergeant Ayres fired up the brazier and began preparing food for his men. Nigel had never felt less disposed to eating a meal than he did that night. He handed the pan of Maconochie Stew to Perrett. Eyes still wide and glazed with shock, Perrett merely shook his head. "It's okay," said Nigel. "Neither can I." Wallace, studying his hands, didn't even acknowledge that the food had been extended to him.

Later that night, when it seemed that the rest of the squad had escaped into sleep—or into silence, Nigel heard Wallace moving, a match being struck. A flicker of candlelight shone in the dugout. He sat up. Wallace, elbows on his knees, hands clasped, sat staring unblinking at the flame, its light reflecting on the orbs of his eyes, making them look watery and pensive.

"Seems all wrong," said Wallace, his voice a husky whisper in the night. "But it had to be."

Nigel had never heard Wallace show remorse at killing Germans before. It had seemed wrong to Nigel to cut men down like that, advancing under orders, and knowing they'd be cut down by British machine guns for doing it.

Nigel grimaced. It could all be switched around tomorrow, Germans emptying their machine guns on British soldiers advancing under orders, knowingly going to certain death. A stroke of the pen from HQ, Lieutenant Lewis blowing his trench whistle, Sergeant Ayres and his squad over the top, advancing into No Man's Land with bayonets fixed, facing the death-spewing mouths of German machine guns. A numb sensation tingled on his neck. It could be their disfigured bodies up there face-down in the mud.

"Cutting down the Boche today," said Nigel, "was wrong?"

Wallace frowned at him. "Nothing so wrong with doing that. Though it do seem so wasteful sending those boys at us like that. Took more courage for them doing what they had to do today, than for our lot. But the Boche started this bleeding war. It's our job, killing as many of them as we can—before they get us. It's kill or be killed. No, nothing wrong with killing the enemy, not when there's a war on." He heaved a sigh. "What seems wrong though is fusillading one of our own. Scoundrel that he was, it don't seem right."

Nigel nodded agreement but said nothing. Deep down, he knew that he had not felt it was so wrong pulling the trigger on his Enfield, his bullet crashing into Spike's cold heart. Wrong? After what he had done to Chips, there was nothing wrong about it, so he wanted to feel. Military justice, that's what Sergeant Ayres had called it.

"Though it had to be," continued Wallace, "you and me—we don't have to like fusillading one of our own, such as he was."

Nigel felt like he might be at a threshold, Wallace about to open the door a crack, and let him peer inside. What else was there to see of Wallace, this indomitable soldier, this enigmatic killing machine? Yet, here he was, showing more regret at ending a human life than Nigel had felt.

"Fusillading." Wallace wiped a hand across his eyes and took up his Tin hat. Passing a finger through the bullet hole in it, he continued, "I've got my reasons for hating of it. And for hating them. Oh, I've got my reasons, and no mistake." Putting his Tin hat down, he blew into his clasped hands. He sat brooding and silent.

"Some think you're so good at killing Germans," ventured Nigel, "just because you like killing. There's some I've heard say that."

Wallace turned slowly, fixing his steel-gray eyes on him. Nigel tried clearing his throat. He wasn't exactly afraid of the big soldier; nevertheless, Nigel couldn't help feeling uneasy around him. He'd seen the eager glint in his eyes moments before engaging the enemy. Though it was the worst, today wasn't the only day. He'd seen him at the trigger of a machine gun, unloading the magazine on an advancing company of German troops, the hard set to his features breaking into something close to a grin as dozens of the enemy were cut down. It was no surprise that a Vickers Gun, when Wallace was at the trigger, needed a new barrel every hour.

"You tell 'em for me, they got it all wrong," said Wallace. "It's because I *hate* killing so. That's why I do it.

I hate their kind of killing, so I'm forced to do my kind. It's the only way to stop 'em. It's the only thing the Hun understands, a bullet right here, or here." He said the words pointing with his index finger at Nigel's forehead and then at his chest.

"She was in this war before it was a war," continued Wallace.

"She?"

Wallace looked at Nigel as if he should already know about her. "My sister. All my sister ever cared about was helping other folks, sick people, and unfortunates. She worked in a hospital for crook children, you know, ones that can't walk, will never walk, ones who are simple, can't read, will never read. That was fine by my sister. I never saw nobody love little ones who were like that more than she did. But on August 4, 1914 the filthy Boche began pouring into Belgium, didn't they?" Wallace clenched his teeth at the recollection.

"The Kaiser, after overrunning the country, he wanted the hospital," continued Wallace. "Wanted it for his army. No place for crook kids in an army hospital. The little ones had to go. Well, that wouldn't do for my sister, would it? She took her stand. She could be like that, stubborn like that." He smiled as if he were seeing happy episodes in his life, ones before the grinding wasteland of trenches, war, and killing that surrounded him now. "She would ha' took her stand in front of the Kaiser himself."

"What happened?" asked Nigel.

"Led her out like she'd committed some awful crime," said Wallace, his voice low and hard, "like she'd done some dishonorable deed, like she'd been court-martialed for dereliction of duty. Lined her up against a wall. That's what they done to my sister." He clenched his hands until his knuckles shone white. "It don't seem right they fusilladed one such as my sister was, and we done the same to one of ours, such as he was. It don't seem right."

Nigel wondered if using the French derived term for firing squad made what the Germans did to his sister somehow a bit easier for Wallace to bear.

"I was fourteen when they done it to her," continued Wallace. "Being big for my age—always have been—I begged my father to let me join up, so I could avenge my sister. He said he couldn't bear to lose his son too. He made me wait. Every day I waited made me more resolved. I lived for one thing, killing Germans. I kill Germans because I hate killing, the Hun kind of killing, the kind they done to my sister."

Toying idly with the hole in his Tin hat, Wallace fell silent for several minutes. The candle flickered and went out. Just when he thought Wallace had run out of words, he heard his voice in the darkness, gravelly and hoarse with emotion.

"I kill," he said, "because I hate killing. I want to stop it. But, Nigel—Nigel? Are you awake?—Sometimes I'm afraid when this war is finally done with, I'm afraid I won't want to stop. Worse yet, that I won't be able to stop."

27

DON'T SHOOT

Next morning there was no morning hate, no predawn bombardment, no trench whistle, no over the top from the German trench line. All was quiet—somber, cold, and deathly quiet.

While a murder of crows circled low over the last of the still forms in No Man's Land, Lieutenant Lewis studied the German line through the periscope.

"Anything, Sir?" asked Sergeant Ayres.

"Foul mists," replied Lewis, "and some patches of low fog. Nothing more, not that I can observe. Not a Hun in sight—not a living one."

"They took heavy losses, Sir," said Sergeant Ayres. "Up burying their dead much of the night, they may be spent—for the moment." He hesitated. "They would have lost much of their junior officer corps."

"No one alive to give commands," said Nigel.

"They're all dead?" said Perrett.

"I wish," said Wallace. "But I doubt it. More than likely it's a Boche bluff. Trying to lure us out of our trenches then give us something back."

"What the dickens!" said Lewis. He pulled back from the lens of the periscope as if it were a viper. "Ayres, what do you make of this?"

Sergeant Ayres squinted through the periscope. "Man your weapons! On the double!"

Heart racing, Nigel chambered a round in his Enfield.

"What do you make of it?" asked Lewis. "A trick? Some new Hun stratagem?"

"If I may say so, Sir," said Wallace. "Don't trust 'em. I say we gives 'em what for with Mr. Vickers and Mr. Lewis—begging your pardon, Sir. Vickers Machine Gun and Lewis Machine Gun, was my meaning. No disrespect meant to your surname, Sir."

"It appears," said Ayres, squinting through the periscope. "They appear to be unarmed. Their hands are held aloft. There must be more than sixty of them—and several war dogs."

Lewis took another turn at the periscope.

"If I am not mistaken," said Sergeant Ayres, "they are surrendering to you, Sir. It would appear that what is left of this Boche company has had enough. I congratulate you, Sir."

"What do I do with them?" stammered Lewis. "What are we to do with sixty German prisoners here at the Front? We have no way to detain them, not that many of them, or their dogs."

"We could—" began Wallace, patting the barrel of his Lewis Gun.

"We will do no such thing," said Lieutenant Lewis. "Where's our nearest officer, above a second lieutenant, that is?"

"Lieutenant Johnson, Sir, commands a company next to the Canadians, on our right."

"Are there no captains, majors, or lieutenant colonels in this army?"

"None that I know of, not here at the Front," said Sergeant Ayres. "Most of the junior officers are dead or wounded, out of the fight. To my knowledge, Sir, you are the ranking officer in this sector."

"*Bitte, bitte!*" one of the Germans called, his voice strained. "*Nicht schießen! Nicht schießen! Wir geben auf!*"

"What's he saying?" asked Nigel.

"Don't like it," said Wallace. "Too German sounding."

"He's pleading with us not to shoot them," said Lewis. "They are surrendering."

"Sir, you speak German?" said Nigel.

Without taking his eyes from the periscope, Lewis shrugged. "*Ein kleiner, aber nicht sehr gut.* Not very good at all, but enough to read a bit of Goethe and get something out of the libretto in Wagner." To Sergeant Ayres Lewis said, "How can we be sure?"

"Sure?" said Sergeant Ayres. "They took heavy losses. They appear to be unarmed. They say they're surrendering. And, Sir, observe the look on their faces, hollow-eyed, shell-shocked. They have the look of dejected men, men who are beaten."

"I don't like it, Sir," said Wallace, pressing a circular magazine into his Lewis Gun. "They're Boche. There's only one way to be sure with Boche."

Sergeant Ayres at his side, Lieutenant Lewis drew his Webley revolver from his holster. "We'll just have to find out," he said. "Have the men stand to at the ready."

"Ten rounds in the magazine," said Sergeant Ayres. "Cover us. Shoot only on my command—or if it's otherwise obviously a ruse."

"H-how would it be obvious?" stammered Perrett, loading his Enfield.

Wallace looked at him incredulously. Pointing a finger like a revolver, he said, "*Pa-kew! Pa-kew!*"

"Oh, that," said Perrett, nodding slowly. Eyes narrowed, he set his rifle on the lip of the trench at the ready.

"Cover us!" Lieutenant Lewis called over his shoulder. He and Sergeant Ayres climbed out of the trench.

Clutching his Enfield until his joints ached, Nigel held his breath and watched. The second lieutenant looked younger than his nineteen years and his face was the color of old paper. Leaning toward Sergeant Ayres, he was speaking out of the corner of his mouth, the sergeant replying close at Lewis's ear. Negotiating the barbed wire barricades, their boots made sucking noises in the mud. Again Sergeant Ayres spoke close in Lewis's ear. The second lieutenant shouted in German. Though his voice was higher pitched, less commanding than Nigel, under the circumstances, would have liked it to sound; nevertheless, the German soldiers immediately clasped their hands behind their heads.

Facing sixty German soldiers advancing toward them, Lieutenant Lewis and Sergeant Ayres looked like two boys taking on a herd of Sudanese elephants.

Wallace nodded toward the two men. "What would our Oxford second lieutenant be without him? Almost old enough to be his father—to be father to all of us. The best of men, is he."

"The very best," agreed Nigel. "It'd be doomsday," he added, "if something happened to Sergeant Ayres."

"War'd be over, we lose," agreed Wallace. Teeth clenched, he squinted down the sights of his Lewis Gun. "Boche captain," he murmured, "you so much as scratch at a flea, and you're a dead man."

Tense moments followed. But one thing became abundantly clear. It was no Boche stratagem. After yesterday's slaughter, these Germans had, in fact, had enough. They were through. But there was a problem, a big problem. They had taken casualties, nothing close to as many as the Germans, but the platoon was depleted. What were they to do with sixty German prisoners? There were too many.

"If we stop and play nursemaid to sixty prisoners," said Lewis, "and handler to their animals, we're *hors de combat*, out of the fray, as good as casualties ourselves. What are we to do?"

"Get word to HQ, Sir," said Sergeant Ayres.

"But how?" said Lewis. "Boche cut our telephone communication long ago. And our pigeon handler was shot and killed yesterday, birds with him. If only we had—" He glanced at Nigel and broke off.

"Sir, with respect," said Ayres. "We must send a runner."

Lewis eyed him, pulling him aside. "Runners get shot. My platoon has lost five runners since I took command. You know the statistics. That's below average. Runners lasts two weeks in this war."

"High-casualty duty, I realize, Sir," said Ayres.

"Next only to second lieutenant," said Lewis, trying to laugh. "Dashed pickle we're in here. If only we had—a better alternative."

Nigel was never sure why he did what he did next. "Sir, allow me." He heard his voice speaking but he felt like it was someone else's. "I-I volunteer. And I'll do my best."

Sergeant Ayres looked levelly at Nigel. "You'll keep your head down?"

"Yes, Sir. At your order." Nigel attempted a smile. "And you know I always follow orders, Sir."

Lieutenant Lewis and Sergeant Ayres briefed him on his duty. "We must have a detail, reinforcements to take this lot off our hands, and before nightfall. We can't feed and bed down sixty prisoners in our dugouts through the night. Who knows, it would only take a few of them to have second thoughts and go to work on our men with trench knives—or their bare hands."

"I can't tell you how important this is," said Sergeant Ayres, pushing his helmet back and looking intently at Nigel. "Make it through and back before nightfall—alive. That's an order."

28

SNIPER

Nigel lived a year in the next hour. He tried not to think about the statistics. *Run like the lives of your mates depend upon it,* so he kept telling himself. But zig-zagging through standing water and mud, or on soggy duckboards, his boots skittering beneath him, was far more like staggering than running.

Wherever he was able, he ran as fast and hard as he could, his lungs screaming for air. Rounding a zig-zag in the trench, he groaned. Ahead he saw a dense line of hunched shoulders and Tin hats. Several dozen men, men who were not running, plodding was more like it, creating an impassable trench bottle neck. Halting at the end of the backup, he could see that it was an ambulance detail. Walking wounded, walking very slowly, Nigel thought, and stretcher bearers carrying the wounded, blocking the way, and moving at a snail's pace.

"Communiqué for HQ!" he called. "Urgent dispatch for HQ. I really must pass! Pardon me. Excuse me. Good of you, Sir. Thanks so much."

"Watch yourself, laddie," said one of the stretcher bearers, as Nigel squeezed past. "Or you'll end up stopping one with your noggin." He nodded toward the prone figure on his stretcher, the man's head entirely covered in stained bandages.

"Yes, thanks," said Nigel. "Thanks for the advice," he called over his shoulder.

When he finally left the stretcher detail behind, for the next quarter of a mile the trench began a steady incline. It was better drained. Feet pounding the packed earth, Nigel tried to make up for lost time. He shuddered to think what lay ahead that night for his platoon if he didn't reach Command Post before dark—and back again.

Hesitating at a fork in the trench, Nigel studied the arrows on the signage. It was like country road markers back in rural England.

"You're needing a bit of tourist information?" The voice came from a niche in the earth wall of the trench just to the right of the signs.

"I suppose I am," said Nigel. "Which way to HQ?"

"That depends," said the man philosophically. "Take the right fork and, on those feet of yours, you'll get there in less than an hour."

"That won't do," said Nigel. "It'll be dark in an hour. How about the left fork? How long if I take it?"

"Now, you see, laddie," said the man. "That's the tricky bit. Left fork, you'll be there in ten."

"Got to be off, then," said Nigel, spinning on his heel.

"*If*—and, laddie, it's a big *if*," said the soldier. "You'll be there in less than ten, *if* you don't go and gets yourself shot."

"Shot?"

"German snipers love this stretch of trench just here," he continued. "They really love it. Did you notice the slight incline?"

"I did."

"So have the Germans. From there—see it through that barricade of barbed-wire? That's where they wait. There's a sniper there right now, laddie, chambering a round with your name on it—two or three of 'em, I'd guess."

Nigel had been breathing heavily from running, but now his throat constricted, and he felt his heart thundering in his chest, but from more than exertion.

"How long will I be exposed?" he asked hoarsely.

"Not long—fifty feet—if you make it that far. Then there's a zig-zag and you're safe. Boche snipers can't get a bead on you in the next section of trench. After that, you'll be at HQ in five minutes, or—" He leaned closer, tapping his index finger in the middle of his forehead, "or you'll be dead."

Frustrated with losing time, Nigel felt there was really no choice to make. He had to get through. An hour would be too late. Sixty German prisoners guarded only by Lieutenant Lewis, Sergeant Ayres, Wallace, Perrett and the rest of the platoon through a long night? Sixty German prisoners was more than three times the men left in their platoon. They could wreak havoc, overpower and kill every man. Sniper or no sniper, he had to get through. "Please God, help me." It wasn't much of a prayer. His mother, now, she could pray. He desperately hoped she was doing it right then.

Crouching low, his breath coming in hot blasts, Nigel bolted down the left fork in the trench.

"Young fella that came tearing through here two days ago," the soldier called after Nigel, "didn't last ten feet."

Nigel wondered what it would feel like if he were hit. Would it be a shot to the head and instantaneous oblivion? Or would he be hit and wounded, conscious, fully aware: the bullet plowing its way through his vital organs, searing pain, his blood flowing, his life ebbing out with it?

Ka-blam!

Nigel had heard Mauser gunfire before—hard, impersonal as a pile driver—he'd heard it often. But it had never before felt quite like this. His heart thundering in his chest, he ran faster. This was precise. Some German sniper was, at that instant, zeroing in his sights, squeezing the trigger, not just to kill any Tommy—but to kill Private Nigel Hopkins. Ten yards ahead, a slight curve in the trench. He had to slow to make the corner.

Ka-blam!

This time Nigel felt it—zinging past his head, grazing a timber support in the wall of the trench, splinters flying. It ricocheted off a piece of corrugated iron and, with a metallic clatter, sploshed into the mud. He ran faster. Twenty yards to go. Would the next bullet hit its mark?

Ka-blam!

Closer. So close his ears rang. Had it shied off his Tin hat? Too close. Had to be more than one shooter. Ten yards and he'd be clear.

Ka-blam!

Nigel felt himself falling, his feet slipping from under him. *I'm hit*, he thought. *This is it—I'm hit! Is this death?* His face burned, his chin and nose. And the forward rim of his Tin hat bent, a rakish turn downward, blocked his vision. On his hands, there was blood. Something surged within him. Ahead he could see it—no more than five yards—the last turn. If only he could reach that final bend, he would be safe, clear of the sniper, HQ only minutes away. Hugging the far side of the trench, he scrambled on the ground like a crab, then rolling right, he dove around the final bend in the trench.

Ka-blam!

The sniper was too late. Nigel felt a pounding thrill, relief and exhilaration. But there was blood—on his hands, on his face, on his tunic. Hands trembling, he adjusted the strap on his Tin hat so he could see under the bent rim. There was no time to inspect his injuries. He ran.

Moments later, gasping for breath, Nigel nearly collapsed before the HQ dugout.

"Young man, you are a mess," said a captain.

"Dispatch, Sir. Urgent," Nigel managed to say.

Things began moving fast. While a medic cleaned Nigel up, he learned—to his relief—that the blood was from planting his face in the dirt when he fell. There were no bullet holes in him. A lieutenant colonel telephoned a relief detail in the sector where the prisoners were being held by Nigel's platoon.

"By the time you return to your unit," said the lieutenant colonel, "if all goes as planned, the prisoners will be in custody, safely taken off your platoon leader's hands. Medic says you're unhurt, just a bit of grit and blood." Nodding appraisingly at Nigel, he smiled briefly. "Grit, I like that. Now, young man, I want you to return by the long route, the safer route. That's an order." He paused, consulting an aide. Handing Nigel an envelope, he continued, "Return with these, to be opened by the ranking officer in your company. Opened tonight. That's also an order. Off you go."

Iron-gray dusk was settling over the Front when Nigel arrived exhausted back at his platoon's dugouts.

"You made it," said Sergeant Ayres. "The relief detail, thanks to you, took the prisoners off our hands a quarter of an hour ago."

"Never been so relieved to be done with them," said Lewis. "I do hope the next batch of Boche prisoners decides to surrender in another sector."

"What's this?" said Sergeant Ayres, nodding at the brown envelope in Nigel's hand.

"Orders from HQ, Sir," gasped Nigel. "To open immediately."

Lewis tore open the envelope. Nigel studied his eyes as they scanned down the piece of paper. Frowning, Lewis handed the dispatch to Ayres.

Tilting the paper toward a lantern, the sergeant nodded slowly as he read.

"This is it, then," said Lewis. He fingered the trench whistle that hung around his throat.

"What, Sir, is it?" asked Nigel. "If I may ask?"

Ayres looked at the second lieutenant but did not speak. Lewis shrugged and nodded.

"Full-scale assault," said Sergeant Ayres.

"Another one?" said Nigel. "Boche learned nothing from the last one?"

"Not them." Ayres shook his head soberly. "It's a counter attack."

Nigel's knees felt like black pudding. He told himself it was from the running. "Counter attack, Sir?"

"Tomorrow morning, first light," said Sergeant Ayres. "We're for it. It's us over the top."

29

THE QUICK AND THE DEAD

I t's the bridge," said the WAAC forewoman.
"Strategic is our bridge. All our troops and
equipment on their way to the Front cross the river
on Étaples' bridge. We lose it, we lose the war. Such is
the opinion of some."

Elsie studied the bridge. In the warm glow of the
April sunshine, the bridge looked ordinary enough to
her. She squinted, sighting through the hole she made
with her hands. Since her earliest hours in war-torn
France, when she had discovered that she could block
ghastly things out by peering through her hand
telescope, she had found many things she never wanted
to see. It was possible now for her to edit out the men
engaged in bayonet training in the Bull Pen, to hide the
cramped rows of dingy canvas tents, the rows of flimsy
wooden billets for officers, the bloodied and broken
bodies of the in-coming wounded, and the relentless
rows of wooden tombstones in the cemetery. It was the
cemetery she most often cropped out of her line of sight.

In hopes of being inconspicuous, when Elsie used
her hand telescope, she practiced pretending that she

was wiping a speck from her eye, or about to stifle a sneeze. There was no fooling Trudy. "Silly, as if doing that changes anything."

Spring had brought with it whole days of sunshine and blue skies, the sea calm and sparkling, stretching toward England, and, better yet, northwest toward Scotland. Using her peep sight, Elsie felt she could block out the whole war, if only for a few minutes, and bask in the spring sunshine.

"The Germans know the importance of the bridge," continued the forewoman. "Now that they've figured out how to drop bombs from their airplanes, we are more of a target than ever before. In consequence, you are instructed to take extra precautions. Never be out and about at night. Might I remind you that it is against regulations for you to be so, in any event? But now more so than ever."

"Matron, do the Germans only do it at night?" asked Elsie. "Drop their bombs, that is?"

"Generally so, at night," said the forewoman. "Our anti-aircraft guns will, most certainly, shoot them from the sky on a clear day like this."

In the hours and days after hearing the latest threat, Elsie had been anxious. She woke with a catch in her breath, recollecting her first night in Étaples six months ago, the German biplane screaming down on them, machine gun spraying bullets, tent canvas rending, glass breaking. When would they come do it again? But as the days passed and the weather grew fairer, sunshine glittering on the blue waters of the Channel, birds flitting in the trees, here and there a small cluster of crocuses sprouting and opening their white and yellow blossoms, she thought less and less about airplanes and Germans bombing a hospital. What had that prisoner captain said? Germans don't bomb hospitals.

It must have been more than a week later at roll call that it happened. With the fine weather, roll call was outdoors, in front of the hospital tent, facing the training ground and cemetery. A breeze rippled the forewoman's veil as she glanced from the roster on her clipboard to the young women lined up before her. "Where is Trudy? Late again?"

"Not well," said Elsie. "When I attempted to rouse her this morning, she groaned and rolled over. I believe she truly is unwell."

"Again," said the forewoman, her mouth set in an exasperated line.

"I could go and see," said Elsie. "Perhaps it was just something she ate."

"Not necessary," said the forewoman with a sniff. "The war will just have to carry on without her, and we with it. Now, then, as to the day's duties—"

Her words were cut off by a high-pitched mechanical sound. At first Elsie just thought it was a motor lorry revving its engine on the opposite side of the nearest tent.

The forewoman glanced up from her clipboard. It was a biplane. Banking sharply to the left, its engine whining. Memory of her first night in Étaples and the night strafing of the camp again flashed into Elsie's mind. Then with a nervous laugh, she fingered the folds of her veil.

Planes had become more common. Surely it was one of theirs. Through her peep sight, Elsie studied the biplane: Wings stacked one on the other, struts like matchsticks holding the wings to the fuselage, the pilot visible in the cockpit.

Suddenly, Elsie heard the forewoman's clipboard clatter to the hard-packed ground.

The biplane's fuselage was painted gray, the insignia clearly visible now on the wings—an iron cross!

Whining higher and louder, the plane dove. Straight down toward the Bull Pen. With that whining Elsie's heart pounded louder and faster. She tried seeing it all through her peep sight, but it was no good. There was to be no blocking out, no escaping what happened next.

A company of several hundred men, training in a large open field alongside the cemetery, began scattering like rabbits when a fox is on the prowl in a field. The airplane dropped lower. Elsie expected to hear the *Dat-dat-dat* of its machine guns, but the pilot had other plans. Suddenly from under the fuselage of the plane three long black pod-shaped objects were released and began falling, whistling like locomotives.

When the shells hit they detonated in rapid succession, sending tons of earth and splintered debris into the air.

"Quick, girls, quick!" cried the forewoman. "The dugouts!"

Elsie did not want to watch, but she could not tear her eyes away from the horror of the scene unfolding before her. This pilot was no novice. Two of the bombs made direct hits on the company training in the field. The other fell in the adjoining cemetery.

Impossible as it seemed, Elsie watched it happen before her eyes. Bodies long dead and buried in the cemetery were instantaneously unearthed in the crater left by the erupting ordnance. These bodies mingled with the arms and legs of men instantly killed as they ran for cover from the training grounds.

Numb, Elsie felt sickened at the sight. Men, alive and hale an instant before, were now shattered to pieces by the exploding shells, their body parts commingling with the decomposing skeletal remains of men long laid to rest in the military cemetery.

"Quick, girls! The dugouts! Quick!"

Once down in the comparative safety of an underground bomb shelter, Elsie found herself laughing hysterically and crying all at the same time. "The quick and the dead!" she screamed. "The quick and the dead!" So battered by shock, Elsie's mind had collapsed what she had learned as a child about the Judgment Day and the resurrection of the living and the dead from the Bible with the forewoman's cry.

She was not alone. Packed together in the bomb-shelter, terrified sobs came from the others. When the initial flush of horror subsided, a new emotion took control. Elsie felt angry—angry at a war so vicious that mangling and destroying only once was not enough. No, this war came back to unearth men's bodies, men whom it had already killed once. What kind of war was it where there was to be no rest, not even for the already dead? How much worse for the yet living?

Lazarus, the story from the Bible her father often told, Lazarus was forced to face something like this, an exhuming like this. Her father, that faraway longing he would get in his eyes when he spoke of such things, would say, "I wonder if Lazarus didn't have the rawer deal?"

Suddenly Elsie wanted to be a little girl again, in her father's arms, breathing in the earthy scent of cattle that mingled with the wool of his sleeves, feeling the scratchy sweetness of the bits of hay that had become a part of the fabric. And hearing his voice, feeling the soothing caresses of his words, basking in the ordinariness of his presence, encircled peacefully in the aura of his contentment. Hearing his praying.

Praying. To God. That's what was missing in this war. Perhaps forgetting God was what plunged the world into this war in the first place. There, on the packed-earth floor of the bomb shelter, she dropped to her knees and prayed.

"O God, stop this war. God of peace, stop it, and let us all go home. Let me go home."

30

MEANINGLESS

It was unusually still that last night at the Front. Hunkered in their dugouts, Nigel and the rest of the platoon did their best to sleep, but in five months at the Front he had learned that anxiety is the thief of repose. Few of the men could sleep.

"As 'captains of this ruined band,'" said Johnson, "we could up and walk among our host and 'bid them good morrow, call them brothers, friends, and countrymen.'"

Lieutenant Lewis attempted a laugh. "Thawing their cold fear by giving them 'a little touch of Harry in the night' you mean?" said Lewis. Again, he attempted a lighthearted laugh.

"Jack, men like you and me, who lead men into battle, perhaps to their deaths, 'What infinite heart's-ease must we neglect that private men enjoy.'"

"That's never been my favorite part of the play," said Lewis.

"All right, how about 'We few, we happy few, we band of brothers'?"

Lewis waved his hand dismissively. "No, not that either."

"All right, then," said Johnson. "How about 'O God of battles'? "You know it, King Henry pleading for his ruined band of brothers in arms the night before facing off with a vastly superior French army at Agincourt?" He paused. "It's on the map. Agincourt is a real place, not far from here."

"Pleading for his men?" said Lewis. "Pleading for himself, more like."

"Nevertheless, he was praying."

"Prayer, humph," said Lewis. "Praying did not work for me in my greatest hour, so why should I waste my time doing it now? 'Heads I win, tails you lose,' that's how your praying works, or rather, how it doesn't work. If we can't sleep the night before battle, we're far better off dicing, or making trench art, like Private Perrett does, or writing letters home. Anything makes more sense than praying."

"'He that shall live to see old age,'" said Johnson. His voice trailed off, and they fell into a reflective silence for several minutes.

Nigel wondered if one or both of them had fallen asleep. Would any of them live to see old age?

"Living to see old age," continued Johnson, drawing out each word. "If either of us survives tomorrow, Jack, we'll have some hard letters to write, you and I."

Lewis grunted in agreement. "OTC at Keble, they always told us, regardless of how manifestly false it is, tell their families they died peacefully and without pain."

"Yes," said Johnson, "and we're never to repeat what they confess to us in their dying words. So are we instructed in the fine art of letter writing from the Front."

"Even if it's all a lie," said Lewis.

"'Now lie I like a king,'" recited Johnson.

"After this, if we survive, we'll be so good at it we could go into politics," said Lewis. "I suppose, we're obliged to keep the stiff upper lip stiff, all for the greater good. But, if folks back home really knew what it's like here. Not what the journalists and propaganda poets tell them it's like, what it's really like."

Listening to their murmured conversation, Nigel frowned up at the darkness. When attempting to write home, he'd faced the same dilemma. How could he tell his father what it was really like? His mother would read the letter. She would be more terrified for her son, if that were possible, than she already was. For an instant he felt his mother's soft caresses on his cheek, her face upturned, saw the devoted apprehension in the tears whelming in her eyes, felt her arms enfolding him in a motherly embrace.

With a convulsive shake of his head, Nigel attempted to put it out of his mind, to push her out of his mind. He had to. The war forced him to. How could he find the iron resolve to do what he must, to face what he must, when the whistle blew in the morning, if he was over-mastered by his mother's love, by his love for her, for all of them? It was why he so desperately did not want to lie to his parents, his family. So he wrote to them far less than he wanted to, believed he ought to, and felt guilty about it constantly. It was for no lack of love for them that he neglected letter writing. Precisely the reverse, or so he told himself.

"No, we simply cannot tell all," continued Lewis. "It would deeply erode morale if our families knew what it was really like: the ground gained only to be lost again, the mud, the lice, the smells, the horror of gas attack, the constant threat of violent death—senseless death—daily familiarity with corpses, long dead, and ones newly so. It's all so meaningless. It would demoralize them if they knew."

"The war, the waste of young lives," said Johnson. "It does, at first blush, seem meaningless. But what if," he continued, his voice accelerating, "what if we weren't made for all this war and conflict, for suffering and death? It would explain why we have such revulsion to it. Doesn't every man fighting want the war over, peace restored, freedom, home?"

"Even the Germans?"

"Of course, even the Germans," said Johnson, his voice hushed as if he were at evensong in a cathedral. "The enemy? The ones we've killed. They're sense of duty was no less than ours, now was it?" His voice trailed off.

In the silence, Nigel listened to a rat scurrying along the packed earth floor of the dugout. A man coughed. Another seemed to be talking in his sleep, calling out for his brother. Muffled tapping came from Perrett's bunk; he must be putting the finishing touches on his vase for his mother, and doing it under his blanket, by feel alone. Another cough.

"You wonder what his name is, where he came from," continued Johnson, his voice barely audible. "Don't you? As we kill him? Was he really evil at heart, the enemy? I wonder, often, what lies or threats compelled him to make this long march from home? Like us, wouldn't he have rather stayed there in peace?"

He paused. "The dead and the ones who manage somehow to survive, I sometimes wonder if war doesn't make corpses of us all."

"Meaningless, that's what I've been trying to say," said Lewis.

"But meaningless, implies meaning," said Johnson. "I mean, one cannot even have the word meaningless without its root, meaning."

"Rubbish!" said Lewis.

"Is it?" said Johnson.

"We've waged this battle," said Lewis, "and I'm sure I took the high ground."

Johnson laughed. "I grant you there is much that appears meaningless in this wasteland of death. But if there is no meaning, why the longing for something we don't have but so deeply want? Might it be that we were made, designed, for something else?"

"I see where you're going," said Lewis, groaning. He spoke into the darkness of the dugout. "Sergeant Ayres? Private Hopkins? Are you awake? Johnson's at it again, going up solo against settled biology. Surely, you're not going to take his part this time? Ayres, Hopkins? Are you hearing this? Am I to be a lion in a den of Daniels once again?"

"I am awake, Sir," said Ayres and Nigel in unintended unison.

"Well?" said Lewis in the dark.

"Sir, with respect," said Sergeant Ayres. "I have none of your Oxford learning. But it makes sense to a simple man, such as I am, that if there's no meaning in the world why all the fume and fret about it being meaningless?

230

Why would we ever feel such longing for something that doesn't exist?"

"Well said, Ayres!" said Johnson. Nigel heard him applauding slowly in the dark. "Settled biology, you say? Jack, you know as well as I do, Darwin notwithstanding, origins has very little to do with science and far more to do with philosophy. Though many refuse to acknowledge it, German Social Darwinianism is the intellectual philosophy fueling this great war. Surely, biologists speculate about origins, but they always do their speculating based on their philosophical presuppositions, now, don't they? Ayres? Private Hopkins? Anyone else listening in the dark? We, all of us do."

"All right, then," said Lewis. "Let's say for the sake of argument that your God designed this world." He struck a match. In its eerie glow, Lewis rose on an elbow in his bunk and gestured at the crude earth walls of the dugout. "Designed this muddy, godforsaken wasteland of a world?" He laughed bitterly. The match fizzled out. "If there is a God and he designed things, it would not be a world so frail and faulty, so full of cruelty and injustice. You see, Johnson, you and your Daniels, I'm above you in this. Your belief in God requires you to believe that your God did a very bad job of designing the world. What kind of God is that? By disbelieving in him, I am not under the obligation to believe such horrible things about him and his botched work at designing such a mess as this world is."

"I'm sure he's deeply grateful, Jack, to have you on board," laughed Johnson, "preserving his divine integrity with your unbelief. Admirable, indeed."

Lewis snorted.

"Let me get things straight. Your argument against God, as I see it," continued Johnson, "is that the universe seems too frail and faulty, too cruel and unjust for there to have been a God designing it all. Am I being fair? That's your belief, isn't it?"

"Indeed, it is, though I think it would be better called *unbelief.*"

"There you go," said Johnson, with a laugh, "attempting to conquer the high ground with your Socratic unbelief. Jack, your problem is that you are a critic precisely at the places where you ought to be a pupil."

"Critic where I ought to be a pupil—humph!"

"And it blinds you to the fallacy," said Johnson.

"Fallacy?" retorted Lewis. "What fallacy?"

"Don't you see it? Jack, where on earth have you gotten this idea in your head about what is just and unjust? You can't have one without the other. A man does not call a line crooked unless he has some idea of a straight line. What are you comparing this universe with when you call it unjust? If the whole show is bad and senseless from A to Z, why do you, who are supposed to be part of the show, why do you find yourself in such violent reaction against it?"

"Because it's so unjust," said Lewis lamely.

"It won't do, Jack," said Johnson. "A man feels wet when he falls into water precisely because man was not designed for living in the water. But plop a fish in water and he does not feel wet, now, does he? Why? Because a fish was designed for living in the water. So I return to my question: Where on earth have you gotten this idea in your head about what is just and unjust?"

Lewis sighed heavily into the darkness. "All right, my idea of justice—it's merely my own, my own private idea about what ought to be."

"Now there's another admirable evasion," said Johnson. "By privatizing justice, you've just collapsed your entire argument against God. Your argument depends on you saying that the world really is unjust, not simply that it doesn't happen to please your fancy about what you think is just. Thus in the very act of trying to prove that God does not exist you have affirmed a universal notion of injustice, and, therefore—by rigorous necessity—you have affirmed a universal notion of justice.

"As it stands, your argument against God removes the organ yet still demands its function. You want the function, a just world, but without a God of justice. To be blunt, my friend, you castrate and bid the geldings be fruitful. Lay down your arms, Jack, in the very act of caring about a just world, you declare that life has meaning."

"But how can it?" said Lewis. He sounded desperate. "The whole of reality, Johnson, it's senseless. 'Meaningless, meaningless, all is meaningless.' My favorite Bible verse, that. The war, the killing, this barren wasteland that used to be fair France—how could there be any sense in any of this?" He was almost shouting.

"How could there *not* be?" said Johnson. "If there were no sense in any of it, we wouldn't be feeling in our chests what we are feeling right now. In just over an hour, you and I will order our men over the top."

His voice dropped to a low whisper. "We will send some of them, perhaps ourselves with them, to their deaths. But if there was no meaning in this world, we would feel nothing at doing it. Living and dying would be one and the same."

The grumbling of artillery in a nearby sector momentarily interrupted his words.

"If there was no sense in any of this, Jack," he continued, "you and I would not have our endless arguments, now, would we? Your participation in this conversation forces you to believe that one part of reality—namely your idea of justice—is full of sense. Jack, *Jack!* Your professed atheism, it turns out to be too simple. If the whole universe has no meaning, you should never have found out that it has no meaning. Consider the parallel: if there were no light in the universe and therefore no creatures with eyes, we should never know it was dark. Dark would be a word without meaning."

Eyes open, gazing into the pitch blackness of the dugout, Nigel shuddered. He was not exactly afraid of the dark, but there was something cold and hard about the dark this night that set his teeth on edge and a chill clawing its way up his spine.

"All your yammering's above me," said Wallace. "But that bit about the dark, and it having meaning? I get that bit. I wish it were day."

"And why is that, Private Wallace?" asked Lewis hoarsely.

"I'd a thought that was clear enough, Sir," said Wallace. "I wish it were day because then we'd be up and out, over the top, falling on them filthy Boche, killing of 'em in their own trenches."

31

CREEPING BARRAGE

Nigel awoke with a jolt. Although his mind was restless and in turmoil, somehow he must have managed to doze off in the wee hours. It was pitch black in the dugout. The artillery barrage had begun. Beneath the inhuman chaos of noise, he heard the sounds of other men stirring, groaning, stretching, some small talk, even some jesting, but mostly there was silence, dread-filled silence.

"Behind us this time," said Wallace. Nigel listened to the metallic clicking as he pressed .303 rounds into the magazine of his Enfield. "Lobbing it right over our heads, they are."

"That's our boys," said Sergeant Ayres. "Creeping barrage, it's called. Newer strategy is creeping barrage. Our artillery will pound away on the enemy trench line, get them good and scared. Meanwhile, we up and out and advance under cover."

"Of our own artillery fire?" Nigel said the words slowly, as if weighing their meaning with great care. "While we advance across No Man's Land?"

"Under cover of our own barrage," said Sergeant Ayres, striking a match and lighting the brazier.

"So it's not like going over the top," said Nigel, "not like how the Germans did it, charging at our machine guns, ready and waiting, like they did?"

"That's the theory," replied Sergeant Ayres. "Our artillery gives us cover as we attack."

"W-what happens if they miscalculate?" asked Perrett, his eyes wide, an undulating glow from the brazier illuminating his pallid features.

Nigel was glad Perrett asked. He wondered the same thing.

"To be sure, there's pretty complicated mathematics involved," said Lieutenant Lewis. "Muzzle velocity, range, parabolic trajectory, uh, and the rest—but our artillery boys are clever lads all." Under his breath he added, "At least we can hope they are."

"It's simple really," said Johnson. "First you have to orient your guns by laying them in the horizontal plane. And then you use the target grid corrections. After you've done the calculations for the weight of the projectile, for the barometric pressure, for the wind speed and direction, for the effect of gravity on the projectile—for computing the parabolic trajectory you simply consult the site clinometer for angle of site. Then you use a periodic meteor telegram to produce a simplified 'correction of the moment' graph. Simple, really."

In the pale light, the men stared at Johnson in bewilderment.

"Simple?" said Lewis. "Perhaps to some. It does not sound simple to a brain such as mine."

"Oh, yes, I almost forgot," continued Johnson, slapping his forehead, "there's always the muzzle velocity to take into account. Oh, and then after you let fly with the thing, an observer has the task of doing a bit of mental arithmetic to make lateral and longitudinal corrections. Sort of a trial-and-error search routine, bracketing to find the exact target. You wouldn't want any short rounds hitting your own lads."

"M-mental arithmetic?" said Perrett. "Short rounds?"

"Bracketing, Sir?" said Nigel.

"Yes, bracketing, you know, firing a round, seeing where it lands, then making adjustments, and giving it another go until it lands and explodes closer to where you want it to. Then fire for effect at will. That's bracketing."

"Closer?" stammered Perrett. Propping his rifle against a rusty panel of tin, part of the trench wall, he squirmed, adjusting something in his ammunition belt.

"If I may say so," said Nigel, "'Closer' doesn't sound reassuringly precise."

"Not to fear," said Johnson, wafting a hand dismissively. "It's all old hat to our boys." He paused, listening. "Is that rain? Again?"

"Rain," said Lewis, "means more mud."

"I do say, Sergeant Ayres," said Johnson, "is that tea about ready?"

"Tea?" said Lewis, his voice barely audible. "By rights, it ought to be the rum ration."

"Tea's ready, Sir," said Ayres.

Cradling the warm mug in both hands, Nigel breathed in the comforting scent of the tea and felt its vapor condensing in his nostrils. He tried to keep his hands from trembling, but it was no good. It was the waiting, the endless uncertainty, like being suspended over a fire, knowing it was coming—waiting, more waiting. Balancing his Enfield on his knees, he reached in the pocket of his tunic and pulled out a blue sheet of stationary and the stub of a pencil. He took another sip of tea.

"My father desperately tried to get me in the artillery," said Lewis with a nervous laugh. "But I was ever dull-witted at mathematics. No infantry would want to advance under a creeping barrage I had traced out with my mathematical computations. Short rounds thundering down on my own men. No, it's the infantry for me. No mathematics needed in infantry."

"I'm of the same mind, Sir," said Wallace. "Artillery puts a man too far from the enemy. Infantry, now that puts a man face-to-face with the Boche. Man-to-man, you can see his eyes—then you kill him. None of this long distance killing for me, not on your life."

Peering over the rim of his teacup, Lewis stared at Wallace. "Yes, well, there's that," he said. "Either way, we have our orders, from the top, from General Haig himself: 'With backs to the wall and believing in the justice of our case, each must fight to the end.'"

Nigel spread the thin paper on the stock of his rifle. It would give him something hard to write on. Another sip of tea. Chewing on the butt of the pencil, he felt an idea forming in his imagination.

"The theory behind the creeping barrage," continued Sergeant Ayres, "is that it forces one's enemy to hunker, keep their heads down. Unnerved by the barrage, they won't be fit for fighting when we arrive at their line. If all goes as planned, we advance while their machine guns are silent."

Glancing up, Nigel asked, "And then what?"

"We fall on the filthy Boche in their trenches," said Wallace, "dispatch them with bayonet and trench knives—shovels work well too." He snapped his fingers. "Simple as that." Resuming his whistling, he tested the blade of his trench knife with his thumb.

"If all goes as planned," said Perrett, "a-and if they get their calculations right."

Someone coughed and cleared his throat.

"The artillery boys, you mean?" said Johnson. "Yes, well, that's where it can get a bit dicey."

With the blade of his bayonet, Nigel sharpened the tip of his pencil. Deliberately, he set the lead point on the blue paper. The poetry he had been forced to attempt in grammar school had been painfully arduous, and had never amounted to much. But this came all in a flood. He hoped that his father and mother might read it someday.

Atoms dead could never thus
Wake the human heart of us,
Unless the beauty that we see
Part of endless beauty be,
Thronged with spirits that have trod
Where the bright foot-prints of God
Lie fresh upon the heavenly sod.

Nigel glanced up, afraid that someone might have seen what he was doing. His heart skipped a beat as he saw Sergeant Ayres pull his sleeve back slowly, checking the time on his wrist watch. Ayres leaned over and whispered something in Lewis's ear.

"It's nearly time," said Lewis, his voice low.

Stuffing the piece of paper and his poem into his tunic, Nigel wondered if Lewis was wishing now that his father had managed to get him transferred to artillery.

"*Bon courage, mes amis*," said Johnson, shaking each man's hand in turn. He paused when he got to Nigel. With a wink and a toss of his head over his shoulder toward Lewis, he said, "*Bon courage*, my fellow Daniel."

"May God be with us," said Sergeant Ayres, shaking hands with each man in his squad. Pulling back his sleeve, he showed his wrist watch to Lewis.

"Give the order," said Lewis, fingering the trench whistle at his throat.

"Up and out!" cried Sergeant Ayres. "Up and out!"

32

THIS IS WAR

Rain—squally, pounding rain saturated the men of the Somerset Light Infantry as they emerged from their dugouts and formed a line. They stood motionless, like toy soldiers, waiting—waiting for the tuneless command. The prone bodies, standing rigid on either side of Nigel, softened into vague specters as he allowed his eyes to focus on the rivulets of water running off the bent rim of his Tin hat forming a translucent veil in front of his eyes. Between artillery explosions, he listened to the staccato of raindrops ping-pinging on his helmet. There was no escaping what came next.

Lieutenant Lewis fingered his trench whistle. He glanced at his wrist watch. Nigel was ever mystified by his second lieutenant. Would he prove to be a man with a chest? The next few moments would tell the tale for all of them.

"Fixed bayonets, if you please," said Lieutenant Lewis to his squad sergeants.

"Fixed!"

Nigel heard Sergeant Ayres relay the order, fixed bayonets. The weighty hesitation between the two words of the command made the blood pound so hard in his temples it nearly drowned out the thunder of artillery.

"Bayonets!"

The cacophony of shying metal as dozens of men attached their bayonets to their rifles made Nigel's flesh crawl. Then silence. Breathless waiting. But it was an odd silence, a personal, gut-ruminating silence, while all the world was assaulted by penetrating noise, the incessant thundering of the British creeping barrage, their own artillery.

"I-I hope it works," shouted Perrett at Nigel's side. "Creeping barrage, that is." He leaned close to Nigel's ear. "Are you… afraid?"

Nigel tried to smile but did not trust himself to reply. Lieutenant Lewis's whistle was poised, an inch from his lips, frozen, waiting.

"Any man who comes at you," said Wallace in a lull in the barrage, his voice raspy, "telling you he's not afeard before going over the top—he's a dashed liar."

"You too?" said Perrett, his eyes wide.

Wallace shrugged. "I think about one thing."

"What's that?"

"Making the Boche more afeard than we are."

It troubled Nigel to think that in this kind of warfare brave men and timid men, courageous men and cowards—they all die together. Machine guns don't discriminate. Exploding artillery shells, even less so. Courage was no protection in battle, not from enemy fire.

Nigel did not feel particularly courageous that morning. He glanced to his left. There was Sergeant Ayres, so unlike other men. While most powerful men he had read about in history books—kings, popes, generals—used their might to subdue others, Ayres had the singular ability of giving his inexhaustible strength away to others, as a gift. Nigel listened to his own breathing, hot and rapid. He felt it was urgent. He studied the man; he had to know what made Sergeant Ayres so unlike other men.

His mouth set in a resolute line, Sergeant Ayres lifted his left hand and kissed the gold band on his ring finger. Sergeant Ayres was married. Dedicated as he was to his squad, he was married, perhaps with children at home; his wife may have a babe in arms, one that her husband may not have met—may never meet. It had never occurred to Nigel to think of Sergeant Ayres with a wife, children, a life beyond the army. Nigel watched his sergeant kiss his wedding ring a second time. He must love her dearly, more than life itself.

Nigel felt ashamed. Being in charge was a harder condition than he had ever imagined. Up to this moment, he had only seen his sergeant as someone to help him with his own problems, his own fears, with Perrett's fears. It had never occurred to him that the man who guarded and doted over his squad, that that same man carried on his shoulders the still weightier responsibility of family, left without him back in England. Drenched fingers opening and closing on the fore stock of his rifle, Nigel felt selfish and ashamed.

But in that shame, an awakening began to occur in Nigel's mind, a realization he had always tried to avoid.

Giving the orders, when done well, was far more about giving something to others than taking something from them. Too many men cared far too much about the power and status of leadership rather than its cost. Maybe that's why there was a war like this one. It was a consideration that Nigel felt he needed to think about deeply, alone, away from all this. If he ever had the chance.

Then it began. As if frame-by-frame, Lieutenant Lewis moved his trench whistle closer to his lips. Rain water ran off the sleeve of his trench coat, drip-dripping from the elbows. The fingers holding the whistle, white with cold, trembled slightly. A stream of rain water dribbled off the rim of his Tin hat onto the whistle. The whistle and Lieutenant Lewis's lips nearly touched, like Sergeant Ayres and his ring. Nigel felt a twinge of hope; maybe the whistle, soaked with water, would fail to sound.

There it was. Trilling tunelessly, like a train nearing a crossing, a trench whistle blew. And with that blowing time seemed to fall to its belly and creep along like Nigel had once seen a sloth doing at The London Zoo.

The trench whistle, it made an odd sound. How could a single whistle sound flat, off pitch, out of tune? Out of tune with what? Beneath the thunder of the barrage suddenly it was the close sounds, the intimate ones that became distinct, penetrating: The shying of rainfall, the squelching of boots in mud, a raspy cough. And labored, intentional breathing, as men attempted to marshal courage to face the horror of what lay ahead. But there was the trench whistle.

"Why aren't we going?" asked Nigel.

"Not our platoon," said Sergeant Ayres. "Lieutenant Johnson's boys, just there."

"Why before us?" said Wallace.

Nigel watched Lieutenant Johnson, revolver in hand, whistle between his teeth, leap out of the trench, beckoning his platoon to follow him over the top. With shouts of defiance, Johnson's men hurled themselves toward the enemy.

We're for it next, thought Nigel. But still they waited. The waiting—that was the worst of it. Encircled by grinding hopelessness, by the unremitting slaughter of men, oddly Nigel did not consciously consider whether it would happen to him. It seemed so utterly inevitable that it required no consideration. All would soon be over. Nigel found a corner of his brain toying with the notion of death. Could death be worse than this? Would not a hasty obliteration, as he had witnessed to left and right of him, would it not be an escape? It required a body to feel unrelenting pain, and a brain to be numb with fear. To live each hour under the enervating anticipation of one's own violent dismemberment and dying, was it worse than death itself?

Perhaps Nigel's features betrayed his thoughts. Between erupting shells, Sergeant Ayres leaned close to Nigel's ear and said, "Courage, son."

Nigel bit his lip and nodded. "But how, Sir?"

Checking his watch, Sergeant Ayres drew breath through his teeth and said, "My good father once told me, 'Son, don't *try* to be brave, or just to *feel* brave. Feeling brave won't be enough,' said he. 'Pray God for courage, real courage.' So said my good father."

As if to punctuate Sergeant Ayres's words, the creeping barrage of the British artillery roared still more deafeningly in Nigel's ears. The ground shook, violently, like an earthquake, or the end of the world. *Are we next?* Bowing his head and pressing his Tin hat against the mud wall of the trench, Nigel attempted to pray. "Our Father which art in heaven, hallowed be thy name. Thy kingdom come. Thy will be done…"

Machine gun fire pattered in and through the roaring of the artillery barrage. It would be any minute now. The hot blasts from erupting artillery mingled oddly with the cold rain and seared Nigel's lungs. Still they waited.

"God be with you, Nigel." It was Perrett's voice at his side, almost shouting now to be heard above the artillery.

Nigel took his hand and tried to smile reassuringly. "And also with you," he shouted back.

"Remember what you promised?" said Perrett.

"I do, and I will." A thought suddenly occurred to Nigel. "Would you do the same for me, if…?"

Perrett nodded, rain water flipping off the rim of his helmet. But he looked puzzled.

"Just a poem I scribbled," said Nigel. "For my mother and father. It's not finished, but it's here in my tunic. Would you, if anything happens?"

Then, somehow above the chaos of noise he heard it. Another trench whistle. Perhaps he only saw it, Lieutenant Lewis with whistle between his teeth, his cheeks bulging, then deflating. Then he was leaping from the fire-step to the lip of the trench, revolver in hand, turning and beckoning his men.

"Courage, men!" cried Sergeant Ayres.

33

NO MAN'S LAND

Stretching before Nigel lay a smashed landscape, pocked with craters filling with gray sludge, a chaos of barbed wire and mangled debris; a lorry flipped upside down, partially submerged in the ooze; a dead horse, its decomposing body glossy with rainwater, its legs rigid and splayed heavenward.

Crouching, his bayonet in attack position, Sergeant Ayres ran just ahead of Nigel, weaving around the jagged obstacles of wire, the rims of craters, his boots seeming not to touch the ground. Nigel clambered after him, placing his boots where his squad sergeant, only a split second before, had found a way through.

Minute details of his surroundings imprinted themselves indelibly on Nigel's mind. As if these were the last moments of his life, he felt compelled to chronicle what he saw. Everything mattered a great deal.

What remained of the village of Mont-Bernenchon lay to his left. It was now a mangled ruin of medieval cottages, their skeletal remains blackened, fractured, and abandoned. Where were the occupants? Were any of them alive?

Nigel wished he could stop seeing, thinking, taking it in, but it was no good. Like an electro magnet, his mind gorged minute details—and stored them.

Choked with pity, he wondered at a war of this disposition trampling your village, smashing your home, wrenching apart your family. The road leading into the village appeared to have once been lined with leafy plane trees. Now they were shattered tentacles reaching up from the underworld, denuded of vegetation, broken and grotesque.

Miraculously the church still rose above what certainly had once been rolling pastures with cattle grazing, flower gardens—its stones pocked with bullets and shrapnel, its bell tower crumbling, but the church was still standing.

How many yards Nigel and his platoon had covered was impossible to calculate. The terrain looked so entirely alike: mud, debris, craters, new ones created instantaneously by exploding shells, molten shrapnel, mud, and water spewing upward, intermingled with twisted fragments of war debris. Erupting ordnance hurled shattered men like rag dolls—and parts of men.

Pounding in Nigel's sub-conscience were General Haig's orders, "With backs to the wall… each must fight to the end." The landscape alone looked like the end, the end of the world.

Nigel knew that every second brought him closer to the enemy line. He could see them, rain-slickened, coal-scuttle helmets just visible along the trench line. Sergeant Ayres dodged to the right, a shell erupting close—too close.

"God! Give me courage!" cried Nigel, insanely trying to overtake his squad sergeant. What if smoke had so obscured the field that the spotter could no longer convey the position of the infantry back to the artillery officer? Were they still bracketing, doing mental arithmetic for the recalibrations?

Nigel thought—he wished he could stop thinking—what would happen if the artillery ceased firing too soon? The Germans would take to their machine guns and cut down every man of them. And if the barrage was sustained too long, the Somerset Light Infantry would be caught in the barrage, obliterated by friendly fire. It was a horrific realization. There was only an instant of margin between the two deathly extremes. Which was worse? To die at the hands of the enemy or by the guns of your own army? Would it matter?

Following his squad sergeant through the smoke and fume, something screamed inside Nigel's breast. Of course it mattered! Life mattered. And Sergeant Ayres? His life mattered, to his wife and family, to his squad, to the platoon, to the regiment, to all Britain. Rare man of genuine courage that he was, Ayres's life seemed to represent something larger than that of a single man.

Then, in a thunderous flash, Nigel watched it happen, frame-by-frame. There was Sergeant Ayres, zig-zagging, like a troopship avoiding a U-boat attack. Suddenly, it came, the shrill whining of in-coming ordnance—louder, closer than all the rest, piercing and penetrating. Nigel wanted to plug his ears, fall on his face and take cover. But there was Sergeant Ayres, lunging to his right, as the shell landed, erupting in shrapnel, mud, debris, and smoke. All Nigel could see through the smoke was a new crater, a hole gaping in the ground, smoke and the absence of anything alive.

Though Nigel was close enough to the blast to feel a wall of heat press against him, to be splattered by sludge unearthed by the explosion, and pricked by hot particles emanating from it, somehow his legs continued running, his boots squelching in the mud, though his mind was not telling them to do it anymore, and seemed incapable of doing so. His eyes smarting, he scoured the terrain, clawing through the smoke, frantic, searching, hoping.

When would the chaos of the barrage end? Surely when shells stopped erupting in front of him, when he could see again, Sergeant Ayres would be there, leading his squad, with bayonet and trench knife, in hand-to-hand combat with the Bosch. That was the plan, how it was supposed to be. Surely, he would emerge upright from the smoke, his body intact, unhurt.

Nigel heard someone screaming with rage, and he felt hot tears mingling with the cold rain on his face, and a bitter, metallic taste on his tongue. How could it happen to Sergeant Ayres? Maybe he was just wounded. Nigel groped for his first aid kit. Blood, it was on his hands, diluted by the rain, dripping from his face and neck. But of Sergeant Ayres, there was nothing, no one to help, no wounds, no blood, only a reeking crater. Skirting the jagged rim of the fresh crater, just created by the shell explosion an instant before, Nigel heard the cries of defiance as Somerset men reached the German trenches. He heard his voice among theirs.

As he leapt over the lip of the enemy trench, he saw upturned, rain-slickened, German faces, white with fear. And, in direct line with his descent, the gleaming tip of a bayonet affixed to the barrel of a Mauser rushed upward at him. German soldiers, ones who still had their fighting wits about them, had set their bayonets to act as fixed pikes, to skewer the soldiers falling upon them in their own trenches.

Parry left, that's what Sergeant Ayres had taught him to do in a situation like this one. Courage, parry left, then downward thrust—withdraw the weapon. Assume attack position, at the ready, lunge. Do it again, and again. Cut down the enemy until they surrendered—or lay at your feet.

How long Nigel was in the mayhem of hand-to-hand combat, how many times he used his bayonet, his trench knife, as he had been trained, he would never know. Nor would he ever be able to piece together the grim details of that bloody engagement.

"*Kamerad! Kamerad!*" When at last the few remaining German soldiers pled for their lives, and were stripped of their weapons and made prisoner, Nigel staggered from the German trench. Removing his bayonet from his rifle, he sloshed it with his trench knife in a pool of water. A mud-red plume radiated in the pool. Sheathing his weapons, he looked numbly around at the aftermath of battle; the still forms were not all German. Where was his squad, his comrades?

Suddenly, from behind him a hand rested on his shoulder. Nigel spun around, nearly losing his balance in the mud. It was Wallace, his teeth white against the sludge and gore that blackened his face.

"Have you seen them?" asked Nigel, his voice hoarse.

Wallace shook his head. "Where did you see him last?"

Exhausted as he felt, Nigel scanned No Man's Land, then carefully began retracing his steps. Which crater was it? There were so many. Everywhere there was debris and barbed wire to contend with, and German casualties caught in the barbed wire. And others, Somerset fallen, bodies prone, their broken remains held up by coils of wire, as if reluctant to fall, as if hovering over the earth, suspended in death, too precious to be subsumed in the mud.

Khaki wool uniforms, thought Nigel, scanning the field, *—why must they all look so alike?*

"Are you sure this was it?" asked Wallace, gazing soberly into the crater.

Nodding, Nigel said, "I'd rather be wrong. There's nothing. No one here." Not trusting himself to stand, he fell to his knees in the mud. Deep down, he knew. No one could have survived a direct hit, not even a strong man like Sergeant Ayres. Courage couldn't save him. Artillery shells obliterate without discrimination.

Silent, their minds numb, they stared into the vacant mud.

"There's nothing," said Nigel at last, "nothing to bury."

Searching behind every mound of debris, turning over bodies, they slogged through the mud back toward their line.

"When did you see him last?" asked Wallace.

"Just as it hit. Right in front of me. His body shielded mine from the full force of the explosion. I so hoped he was in the smoke, alive, that he was only hurt. We could help him."

Nigel felt Wallace's big hand on his shoulder.

"Lieutenant Lewis, when did you see him last, and Johnson?"

Nigel bit his lower lip. "So much was happening at once. I wish I knew. They were on our right."

"And Perrett?" said Wallace. "When did you last see him?"

"I-I don't know." Nigel wiped a hand across his forehead. "He was behind me, not far."

"Where are you hit?" asked Wallace.

"Hit?" said Nigel. "I don't feel anything."

"Wait!" cried Wallace, lunging through the mud.

Leaning against a partially submerged hulk of a bombed-out lorry, it was Lieutenant Lewis. He was half sitting. He did not move.

"Is he—" Nigel halted.

"Sir? Are you hurt?" said Wallace, falling on his knees in the mud beside his second lieutenant.

"His face," said Nigel. "It looks bad."

"Have you seen *yours*?" said Wallace.

"Where are you hit, Sir?" asked Nigel. Hands trembling, Nigel fumbled in his pocket for his tin of bandages.

Licking his lips, Lewis winced as he moved his left arm. "My left hand, and my leg, behind the knee." He winced, his face going deathly pale. "And my side, my chest." Teeth clenched, he asked, "Is this dying?"

Frantically, Nigel pawed through the tourniquets and the rolls of celox gauze in his first aid kit.

"Medic!" cried Wallace.

"We'll get you help," said Nigel. "Medic!"

Lewis's eyes seemed to focus. "You're rather a mess yourself," he said, his face contorting as he looked up at Nigel's.

"And Lieutenant Johnson?" said Nigel. "Have you seen him?"

Lewis shook his head. "I have not. Is he—?"

"I do not know, Sir," said Nigel hastily. "It's only just ended."

The regimental medic squatted in front of Lewis. He wrenched open his kit and pulled out a large pair of scissors.

"Must you?" said Lewis, watching as the medic plied his scissors on his tunic and trousers.

"Quickest way to the wound, my boy," said the medic. "Sooner off the sooner we can get you patched up, on your feet again, eager for another go at the Boche."

"Yes, another go at them in my under garments," murmured Lewis.

After working at staunching the bleeding on Lewis's wounds for several minutes, the medic rose to his feet and stood over him, wiping his hands on his apron. "Bit more than flesh wounds, but you'll live. That is, unless you get shock from the wound, pneumonia from the rain, infection from the mud, gangrene from the infection, or if we don't get you out of here before Fritz decides to give us something back. Oh, and did I fail to mention heliotrope cyanosis, the flu plaguing hospital back in Étaples? Killer respiratory virus—nasty stuff. Turns your face the color of a field of French lavender— just before it takes you off. Dodge any one of those bullets, and you may just pull through, back at the Boche fit as a fiddle."

As the ambulance crew hefted Lewis onto a stretcher, Nigel watched helplessly as his platoon leader fainted into unconsciousness.

Gathering up his supplies, the medic halted, eyeing Nigel's face critically. "And you, my boy—are next."

Taking a step backward, Nigel's boot struck something hard; he nearly fell over. Though battlefield debris lay all about—abandoned weapons, artillery shell casings, corrugated tin, lorry parts blown to mangled bits—something made Nigel bend down and investigate. Feeling in the mud, his fingers closed around something hard and cylindrical. Drawing it out, he wiped the filth away, dread pressing hard on him. Turning it slowly in his hands, he traced the brass relief shape of a poppy. Nigel did not trust himself to speak.

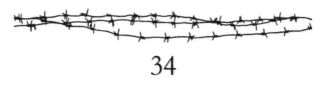

34

FLESH WOUNDS

After a hasty examination, the field medic classified Nigel as walking wounded. He ordered him to accompany the ambulance crew carrying Lewis and dozens of others from the Front to the field hospital in Étaples. "I don't care how eager you are to avenge your mates and get back at the Boche, you'll follow orders. That's an order."

So it was that Nigel found himself once again out of combat and alongside his platoon leader bound for hospital. Lewis was in and out of consciousness in the lorry that carried them from the Front. When he was conscious, gripping a fistful of Nigel's tunic, he pressed him for details of the battle, his platoon, and the casualties sustained by the regiment. Nigel did his best to deflect his questions, urging him to rest. But once settled in hospital, there was no putting him off.

"Word is, Sir," said Nigel, standing at the foot of Lewis's cot in Étaples, "we routed the Germans, many killed, several hundred taken prisoner. A great day for the regiment."

"And our losses?" said Lewis, his voice low.

"I believe they are still gathering the numbers."

"But you know something, more than you're telling me."

Nigel cleared his throat. "It's all very preliminary, Sir. The tactic has been deemed a great success."

"Creeping barrage?" said Lewis. "Success. Meaning our artillery managed to kill more Germans than our own men. Success indeed." Toying with a frayed edge of the bedsheet, he eyed Nigel levelly. "And what of my platoon? What have been our losses?"

Shifting his weight, Nigel scratched his head. "Considerable, though, we are told, not numerically so." He paused, biting his lower lip.

"Whom have we lost?"

Nigel's words were harder than he intended, more monotone than he felt they should sound. "Perrett, Sir, missing. Presumed dead."

"I am truly sorry," said Lewis.

"Thank you, Sir."

"And others?"

"War does not discriminate, does it, Sir?" continued Nigel, his words catching in his throat. "The very best of men."

"Of whom are we speaking?" Lewis's voice was taut, bitter-edged.

"Missing. Presumed dead." Nigel hesitated, pressing his lips hard together. "Sergeant Ayres, Sir."

Nodding slowly, Lieutenant Lewis said nothing for several minutes. Then he wanted every detail that Nigel could give him, what he knew, what he saw, what he did not know or see, but could speculate about.

"I believe, Sir, based on where we found you, Sergeant Ayres was killed by the same shell that wounded you." Nigel hesitated. "And that did this to my face."

"Go on," said Lewis. "There's more."

"It's speculation on my part, Sir," continued Nigel. "But it was almost as if, in that fatal instant, as if he were shielding us. It may be mere fancy, but it was as if he were stopping the shrapnel that had our names on it."

Wincing, Lieutenant Lewis attempted to reach the glass of water on the bedside stand.

"Allow me, Sir," said Nigel, holding the glass so he could drink.

Leaning back on the pillow, Lewis sighed, nodding his thanks. "I am a futile officer—they give commissions far too easily in time of war." He gave a short, bitter laugh, the kind that could catch in the throat and become something else. "I have been a puppet moved about by an infinitely superior human being. Somehow Sergeant Ayres—may he rest in peace—turned the ridiculous and painful relationship between us, me the cocky and all-inept nineteen-year-old, but the one with the commission, and he the seasoned, experienced, wise enlisted man. He turned the awkward juxtaposition of our roles into something beautiful." There was a tremor in his voice. Drawing in air through his teeth, he broke off.

For the rest of his days, Nigel could never hear that mannerism, someone drawing in breath through his teeth, without halting and coming to reverent attention—and remembering.

"He was like a father to me," continued Lewis. "Infinitely my superior in every respect, except in the mysterious arbitrament of rank. Without a trace, you say?"

"Wallace and I searched," said Nigel. "There was nothing. How I wish there was." If only he could have found something, some trace, the wedding ring. "There was nothing."

"I must write to his widow," said Lewis, "and tell her of the sad news."

"There is more," continued Nigel. "The regiment has lost 210 men. I am told it is a trifling number for the gains of such an engagement." He hesitated. "'Trifling' was the official word, Sir, not mine."

"I understand. Go on," urged Lewis.

"It falls to me to tell you the unhappiest of news, Sir." Nigel bit the edge of his lower lip. "Lieutenant L. B. Johnson is among the casualties."

"Casualties?" There was urgency in Lewis's tone. "Wounded or dead?"

"It is reported," said Nigel, "that his wounds were of the severest nature. There was nothing medics could do. They tagged him and, word is, left a comfort dog at his side. And moved on to the recoverable wounded who needed their aid. He was pronounced dead an hour after the cessation of hostilities in the battle." Nigel cleared his throat. "I am truly sorry, Sir."

Eyes unblinking at the stained canvas wall of the hospital ward, Lewis nodded in acknowledgement but said nothing.

"Can I get you anything, Sir?"

Lewis shook his head slowly.

"Very well, then. I'll come back a bit later, check in on you. Get some rest, Sir."

Ducking through the canvas flap that served as a door in and out of the ward, Nigel almost collided with a young WAAC, the medicine vials on her tray clinking precariously.

"Pardon me, miss," said Nigel.

"Och, aye!" she cried. "Let me see, trench foot, the Somerset Light Infantry. Nigel, isn't it? You liked hospital so much, you're back? How's your feet? How's your dog? And, if I may ask, though strictly speaking, we're never supposed to ask, but whatever did they do to your face?"

Nigel opened his mouth to reply, but he didn't know what to say. She seemed genuinely happy to see him, face and all. Or perhaps she greeted all Tommies this way. Though she didn't seem the type for that. Blinking rapidly, he attempted to make sense of Elsie and her questions, and to form a reply.

Studying him more closely, her shoulders sagged. She gripped his arm and said, "Forgive me. You've been through a great shock. And here I am a-yammering you with questions. I am truly sorry."

Gesturing over his shoulder back at the tent, Nigel managed to say, "I've only just had to be the bearer of a bit of bad news. To my platoon leader." He hesitated. "He'll be fine."

"I remember," said Elsie, nodding warily. "Called me Artemis, did he. That was a new one, but we see lots like him here."

"He's had a bit of a rough time," said Nigel.

"And you haven't?" said Elsie.

261

Nigel fingered the bandages on his cheeks and forehead. "I avoid mirrors just now."

Elsie smiled.

"Mine was just the outer edge of the blast," said Nigel. "Small fragments. Compared to many, mine's a light cross to bear. It's no bravado to say, it's a mere scratch—well, scratches, flesh wounds. Medic says I'll be right as rain, and back at the Boche in no time."

"No million-dollar wound for you," said Elsie soberly. "And what of Chips?"

Nigel had spent weeks trying to forget. Losing friends, human beings, extraordinary ones, had put it in perspective, to a degree. But the ache remained. There could be no replacing an animal like Chips had been.

"Did the sodium hypochlorite not work?" asked Elsie. "I thought sure it would do the trick."

"It wasn't that."

That evening, when Elsie was finally off duty, with the permission of her forewoman, she met Nigel for a stroll along a path above the beach. It being April and springtime, it was more than an hour before sunset. It had rained earlier in the day, but the late sun now glimmered like emeralds on the Channel. Nigel filled his lungs with clean sea air. Evening sunlight shone on the yellow broom bushes above the sand, and poppies bobbed in the sea breezes along the path.

"On an evening like this one," said Elsie, her veil swirling gently in the breeze, "it's as if there's no war on."

A low grumbling of artillery sounded from the Front.

"*Almost* as if," said Elsie soberly.

Nigel nodded. But the war, the Front, the recent dead—the wounds were too fresh. Thrusting his hands in his pockets, he flicked a stone from the path with the toe of his boot. He feared that the war would remain more grindingly real than any stroll on the beach in the spring sunshine could ever be, however amiable the companionship.

At hospital, Elsie only saw its dreadful effects on men, on their limbs, their lungs, their broken bodies, their minds. She was certain this wasn't all the story. At first Nigel felt like Elsie wanted him to talk about the war and the Front merely to satisfy a morbid curiosity. He resented her questions—she could ask so many questions. It felt like an invasion. What happened at the Front wasn't for sharing.

"You might try writing it down, then," said Elsie. "My father says ink is the cure to all human ills."

Unblinking, Nigel stared at the horizon. "But where to begin?"

Before he actually realized he was doing it, Nigel was telling her things. Not everything. There was so much that she could not understand, that would be a burden too great to bear for her; he felt it was a burden too great for him to bear—to bear alone.

Elsie was a good listener. Other Tommies had bored her with endless swank about killing Germans. Nigel's account was different. In his words—tender, honest, and devoid of bluster—she realized she was hearing an unvarnished account of the Front. When Nigel would fall silent, his voice trailing off in the middle of a sentence, his eyes vacant, she gently invited him to continue.

Once he began, Nigel told her more than he ever imagined telling anyone. He couldn't explain it. Elsie seemed to have known. Somehow the telling was acting as a balm, the beginnings of a cure, a healing ointment working itself deeply into the corruption of a wound.

When, at last, Nigel had no more he could say, Elsie told him about the strafing of the hospital, and the bombing raid, killing and unearthing men already dead, how terrified it had made her. With a bob of her head, she even admitted to him about her method of coping with her peep sight and how futile it had become. And she told him about her father, how he had warned her, tried to prepare her for war, how he prayed for her. Too soon, the sun set and the signal to return to quarters sounded.

"I have to go back," blurted Nigel.

"To your quarters? We all do."

Low and menacing, a barrage of shelling rumbled from the Front.

"To that," said Nigel hoarsely, nodding toward the Front, his eyes staring numbly at the dark horizon. "Without them—" He broke off.

Halting, Elsie looked up at him. "But Nigel, don't you see?" she said, the fading sunlight warm on her upturned face. "You'll not be going back alone."

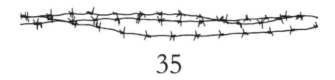

35

EXTRAORDINARY DESTINY

Next morning, after roll call, Nigel came back to check in on his platoon leader. He heard Elsie before he saw her. Through the canvas wall of the tent, it was her voice, speaking as if she were taking someone's temperature. Nigel almost turned to go. What had he said last evening? Had he told her too much? Maybe he could sneak in without her seeing him. But then he heard Lewis's voice.

"Exquisite Artemis," he heard Lewis saying, "come to heal me once again."

He sounded to Nigel as if he were in considerably better spirits than yesterday when he had left him. It was too late. She looked up and saw him.

"We really mustn't go on meeting this way," continued Lewis. "It could prove fatal. On the other hand, we could be distant cousins, you know, distant enough. My aunt married a Scot, lives in Edinburgh, she does. He died. Gave up living with his banner-waving suffragette wife."

"Elsie's the name, Sir," she said. "You've confused me with someone else—again."

"I rather doubt it," he said.

"There's a message for you," said Elsie, with a mischievous lilt, "about your brother."

The color drained from Lewis's cheeks. Wincing, he tried to sit up. "My brother? About him or from him?"

"Captain Warren Lewis," said Elsie in solemn tones. "Whilst stationed at a camp near the village of Behucourt—" she hesitated, eyeing Lewis soberly over her clipboard. With a satisfied bob of her head and a playful laugh, she continued, "—has sent word that he is coming here to see you in hospital."

Exhaling deeply, Lewis scowled at Elsie. "Dirty trick. Precisely how is he going to do that?"

"On his motor bicycle, so it says here," said Elsie, waving the telegram.

"My brother does not have a motor bicycle."

"Perhaps he's borrowed one," suggested the young WAAC nurse. "In any event, he sounds pretty cut up about the severity of your wounds, begging pardon for the pun."

"Severity of my wounds? Who told him that? Flesh wounds, nothing more. I'll be right as rain in no time."

"According to your chart, Sir," said Elsie, flipping a page on her clipboard. "It's a wee bit more than flesh wounds, if the doctor's opinion counts for anything. Shrapnel lodged in your chest—" She tucked her clipboard under her arm and scowled at Lewis. "I don't think that counts as a flesh wound, does it?"

"I'll be fine," said Lewis.

"Och, I nearly forgot," said Elsie, slapping a palm on her forehead. "I brought you this. One can only hope it will keep you entirely occupied."

"Shakespeare," said Lewis, taking the thick volume from her. "Like it or not, you are a goddess."

Ignoring him, Elsie turned to Nigel. "I have something for you, as well." She turned, calling toward the entrance to the ward, "Trudy, dear, bring him in."

Trudy entered the ward leading a dog. Nigel's jaw dropped. He bolted to his feet, his chair clattering to the ground.

"Nigel, you look like you've seen a specter," said Elsie.

Mouth agape, Nigel stared in disbelief at the dog. "He's supposed to be dead."

"I know he doesn't look like much," said Elsie.

"Where did you find him?" Nigel voice was barely above a whisper.

"He ended up here at hospital with a wounded prisoner," explained Elsie. "Nigel, are you all right?"

"With a Boche prisoner?" said Nigel, his face slack with wonder.

"Oh, it's not the first wounded dog to come in with his handler," explained Elsie, "ours or theirs."

Falling to his knees, Nigel called the dog to him. "I-it's not possible."

"Does seem a bit odd," said Trudy, frowning as the scruffy dog licked Nigel's face. "He's not really the Boche's type, is he?"

"The prisoner was pretty cut up," continued Elsie, "but the dog was worse yet. Looked like a dog my father once tried to save who had got himself caught under a harrow. They were about to shoot this one when I managed to intervene."

267

Fatigued by the trauma of battle, Nigel felt an uncontrollable escalation of feeling, as if he were about to be subsumed by a wave, as if he might collapse under a weight of insupportable joy.

"He's not much, Nigel, I ken that," said Elsie, looking anxiously at his face and biting her lower lip. "But he likes you, and he really is loveable. We don't ken his name. Oh, and there is one other thing. How's your German?"

"You see, we reckon he'll have a preference for taking commands in German," explained Trudy. "Mind you, it's not his fault."

"I'll teach you some German," said Lewis absently, from behind the volume of Shakespeare. "There's nothing to it. English with a tad more growl."

"I-I won't need German," said Nigel at last. "They were going to shoot him, you say?"

"Round in the chamber," said Trudy. "But Elsie— you should have seen her—she fairly wrestled the gun from the corporal's hand. She's like that, you know."

"It was nothing," said Elsie. "Anyone would have done the same for the poor thing."

"No, I don't think so," said Nigel, only with great effort keeping his emotions in bounds. "Don't you see? Lieutenant Lewis, don't you see?"

Lewis looked up from Shakespeare. The book slipped from his hands onto the floor. Recovering himself, he said, "It can't be? Chips, old boy. Is it really you? Word was—well, never mind about that. Chips the war dog, alive and not dead after all. I always thought he was a survivor."

268

That evening, Nigel sat up reading with his platoon leader, Chips curled in a wiry gray ball at his feet, Nigel's hand often straying to ruffle his dog's floppy left ear.

"I can only lie on my right side," said Lewis. "Would you do the honors?" He handed the volume of Shakespeare to Nigel.

"Your pleasure, Sir?"

"*Hamlet*, if you please."

Two and half hours later, the tent ward was dark and quiet. The pot of tea Elsie had brought them was long empty, and Nigel had been reading by candlelight for some time. Silhouetted against the moon shining through the tent canvas, his platoon leader lay on his back, his hands clasped behind his head. Nigel read the final lines:

Bear Hamlet like a soldier to the stage…

…and for his passage

The soldier's music and the rite of war

Speak loudly for him.

Take up the bodies. Such a sight as this

Becomes the field, but here shows much amiss.

Go, bid the soldiers shoot.

Nigel closed the volume slowly. Maybe Lewis had fallen asleep. Rising softly to his feet, Nigel snuffed the candle and turned to go. Chips stretched and yawned, and rose to follow.

Lewis stirred. "My mate, Paddy," he said in the darkness. "Been missing for over a month. Rifle Brigade, second lieutenant, like me."

Nigel sat back down. Heaving a sigh, Chips rested his chin on Nigel's knee.

"We roomed together during officer training at Keble in a carpetless little cell with two beds," continued Lewis. "Went missing in battle at Pargny. Word is he was last seen the morning of March 24, with but a handful of men, defending a position on a river bank. Overrun by infinitely superior numbers, so it was reported. But they never found Paddy, not a trace."

"I'm so very sorry, Sir," said Nigel.

"I must write his mother Mrs. Moore," continued Lewis. "'Your very gallant son was reported missing...' And so forth. I must write her. His father is gone. It will come as a heavy blow to her."

"I am sure it will," said Nigel. "But hearing it from you, his friend—that may soften it, if only a bit."

"We made a pact, Paddy and I," continued Lewis.

"A pact, Sir?"

"Since his mother was a widow," said Lewis, "and my father a widower, we made a pact that if anything happened to the other, the survivor would care for the other's parent. We took a solemn oath, gave our word." He fell into a brooding silence for several minutes. Nigel said nothing.

"At present," he continued, "it appears that I may just have managed to survive." He paused. "One does wonder. Why me? Why am I the Horatio left standing when the curtain falls? I do not pretend to know. Nigel, what do you think Johnson would have to say about it, if he were here?"

It was the first time his platoon leader had ever used his Christian name.

"I don't really know, Sir," began Nigel. Chips placed both paws on his master's lap. Nigel stroked the dog's neck.

"Call me Jack."

"Sir?"

"No, not Sir. Call me Jack."

"Is that an order, Sir?"

Lewis laughed softly. Nigel joined him. "May I call you Nigel? I would very much like you to call me Jack, if you would. That's not an order. Merely a request, one friend to another."

Nigel was glad it was dark. Military protocol was inviolable, including what enlisted men called officers. It was as if Lieutenant Lewis—Jack—wanted to shuffle off the coil of war, and with it the weight and responsibility of rank. He was glad it was dark.

"All right, Jack it is," said Nigel. "Perhaps Lieutenant Johnson would say, 'There's a divinity that shapes our ends, rough-hew them how we will.'"

"I suspect you're right," said Lewis. "Agree or disagree, LB would have said something very much like that."

"I only remembered it," said Nigel, "because I just read it here, in *Hamlet*." He thumped the volume with his knuckles. "If I may say so, Jack, it does appear that Shakespeare, like Johnson, believed in God, a God who purposefully shapes our lives. Don't you think Johnson would here press his advantage, and remind you to be more careful of your reading if you intend on remaining a sound atheist."

Lewis laughed, a sober and short laugh. "You were listening in."

"Impossible not to in close quarters," said Nigel.

"Indeed, he did say that," said Jack. "He was so good at pressing his advantage. I agree with the rough-hewing bit," he continued, sighing heavily. "This war, it's rather a ghastly monument to human rough-hewing, so Johnson would say. But as I see it, there is one advantage to war. It sets you longing for it to be over, for beauty restored. I have been the happiest in my life when I have longed the most, for the beautiful. It sets me longing, always longing. Somewhere else there must be more of it. It almost hurts me, I feel like a pigeon left in its cage at the Front when all the others are flying home. Nigel, the sweetest thing in all my life has been the longing, to reach the Mountain, to find the place where all the beauty came from, my country, the place where I ought to have been born."

Nigel nodded slowly. "Lieutenant Johnson would say 'Amen' to that. So would Sergeant Ayres. And so would Perrett." He hesitated. "I found his shell casing, after it was over. Perrett was gone. Gone with nothing to bury. But his art—in a world devoid of flowers, Perrett created his own, forged out of the violence of a shell casing." Nigel paused. "We, too, made a pact."

"What was your pact?"

"Perrett made me promise that if something happened to him I would deliver his trench art to his mother. And then I stumbled upon it in the mud, just as the stretcher bearers were carrying you off, and the medic was collaring me for hospital. Stumbled on it as if by design."

"LB would chime in, 'There's a divinity that shapes our ends,'" said Jack. "But a pact, Nigel, it has two parts."

Nigel felt in the breast pocket of his tunic. "Mine was nothing."

"I doubt that, very much."

"It does make one wonder," said Nigel.

"—why we were spared?" said Jack.

Nigel nodded. They were silent for a moment.

"'War makes corpses of us all,' dear LB put it," said Jack. He paused, frowning at Nigel. "Oh, bother. I sense a Daniel moment coming on. Nigel, what are you thinking?"

"I was just wondering, if Lieutenant Johnson were here, knowing now with clarity what's on the other side, who is on the other side, just what he might say. I wonder if it mightn't be something along the lines of what my father says."

"And what is that?"

"'Hardships often prepare ordinary people for an extraordinary destiny.' I'm no prophet, Jack, but I wonder if the God you don't now believe in has been preparing you for an extraordinary destiny."

THE END

Glossary
World War I Terms

Battle bowler: Slang for Tin hat, the helmet shaped like a washbasin worn by British soldiers in World War I.

Billet: Where soldiers are housed is their billet.

Blighty: Slang term used by the British for a soldier with Post-Traumatic Stress Disorder (PTSD), called shell shock in World War I.

Brazier: Portable cook stove used in the trenches.

Bully beef: What soldiers called corned beef.

Cantonment: A group of temporary billets for soldiers.

Counter battery fire: An artillery assault directed at knocking out the enemy's artillery.

Counter offensive: Aggressive action in response to an attack.

Carrier pigeon: Over 100,000 pigeons carried messages with a 95% success rate for the British forces in World War I.

Creeping barrage: Attack employing a curtain of shells erupting in front of advancing troops, highly dangerous, a miscalculation could wipe out your own men. The enemy would keep their heads down during the barrage, while the troops advance upon the German trench. Enemy soldiers not killed by the barrage are unnerved and speedily overcome by the advance, or taken prisoner, or bayoneted.

De Profundis: Latin for "Out of the depths," and the title of a poem written by C. S. Lewis as a teen atheist during his service in World War I.

Doughboy: American soldier wearing the washbasin British style helmet, called a Tin hat by the British. The Doughboy helmet replaced the Smokey-the-Bear campaign hat that looked like the hat worn by highway patrol troopers.

Duckboards: Planked walkways designed to provide a place to walk above the mud in the trenches.

First-step: A platform cut into the forward edge of the trench, sometimes called a fire-step, allowing soldiers to gain a higher position from which they could fire on the enemy.

Foreign entanglements: A term coined by George Washington in his Farewell Address, in which he urged future generations to avoid getting entangled in European affairs. To convince Americans to get entangled and enter the war required propaganda of various kinds.

Fusillading: French derived word for what a firing squad does to a condemned person.

Hors de combat: French term used in international law meaning out of combat.

Kit: British name for a soldier's personal equipment.

Liberty Cabbage: American name used in place of sauerkraut during World War I.

Lorry: British name for a truck with an internal combustion engine.

Malevolent: Evil.

Metaphysics: Philosophical category concerned with what is or is not above the physical, material world.

Military terminology:

 Squad: 4-12 men, led by a sergeant (i.e. Sergeant Ayres).

 Platoon: 20-50 men, or 2-12 squads, led by a junior officer, a second lieutenant or lieutenant (i.e. Lieutenant Lewis).

 Company: 100-250 men, or 5 platoons, led by a captain or a major.

Neophyte: Someone with no previous experience at doing a task.

Old Sweat: Seasoned experienced soldier.

Plonk: Anglicized name for *vin blanc*, the cheap French white wine soldiers bought from the locals.

Puerile: From Latin, meaning boyish or childish.

Puttees: Cloth gaiter wrappings around the calves of British soldiers.

Sadist: Someone who gets pleasure by inflicting pain in others.

Salient: When the front line is pushed forward into enemy territory.

Sector: A subdivision of a military front.

Slacker: A man who dodged the draft or anyone who was perceived not to support the war.

Sodium hypochlorite: A common antiseptic before Alexander Fleming discovered Penicillin ten years after World War I.

Suffragette: The name for an early feminist protesting for women's rights.

Surfeit: Excess of something.

Trench art: Sometimes elaborate and skillfully crafted brass vases and other artifacts created from shell casings by soldiers during long days, weeks, and months of waiting in the trenches. While researching for this book at the *Musée Somme 1916* in Albert, France, the author acquired a work of trench art crafted in 1915 from a 75mm artillery shell casing.

VAD: Acronym for Voluntary Aid Detachment, women volunteers who did support work in hospitals. Some British soldiers borrowed the abbreviation VAD to indicate a young woman they saw as a Very Adorable Darling.

Valkyries: Ancient Norse goddesses who are said to choose those who are slain in battle and go to Valhalla.

Vivisector: Someone who dissects animals.

WAAC: Women's Auxiliary Army Corps.

TIMELINE of World War I

1914 - June 28: Assassination of Archduke Franz Ferdinand.

August 4: Germany invades Belgium.

September: Battle of the Marne; trench warfare begins in the
    Western Front.

December 25: Christmas Truce.

1915 - January: German zeppelins bomb English cities.

February: The worst disaster in British military history begins
    at Gallipoli, orchestrated by Winston Churchill who
    was demoted to fight in the trenches.

April 22: Germany begins using poison gas at Ypres,
    Belgium.

May 7: German U-boat sinks British liner *Lusitania*.

1916 - July 1: Battle of the Somme begins, "the bloodiest day of
    the British Army."

July 14: J. R. R. Tolkien's first day in combat.

1917 - January 31: Germany declares unrestricted U-boat attacks
    on civilian shipping.

April 6: The United States declares war on Germany.

November 7: The Bolshevik Revolution.

November 29: C. S. Lewis's nineteenth birthday, his first day
    of trench warfare.

1918 - April 12: General Douglas Haig issues his "backs to the
    wall," do-or-die order to repel Ludendorff's offensive.

April 15: Battle of Arras; Lewis wounded, Johnson and
    Sergeant Ayres killed.

October: Corporal Adolph Hitler wounded by gas attack
    near Ypres.

May 28: American forces first victory at Battle of Cantigny.

August 8: The "Black Day" of the German Army.

October 29: Revolution breaks out in Germany; Kaiser
    Wilhelm II flees for his life to Holland.

November 11: Armistice signed in a rail car (near the
    birthplace of John Calvin).

1919 - June 28: Treaty of Versailles signed.

ACKNOWLEDGEMENTS

Though this book is a work of historical fiction, the author has created several of the characters from the writings of C. S. Lewis, including *Mere Christianity*, *Screwtape Letters*, his *Collected Letters, Vol. I* (in which he mentions Perrett who was killed), and especially his spiritual autobiography *Surprised by Joy*, in which he speaks reverently about "dear Sergeant Ayres," and 2/Lt. Johnson, who was "moving toward theism," with whom Lewis had "endless arguments," both of whom were killed when Lewis was wounded. Still other dialogue was created from J. R. R. Tolkien's reflections on his time in the war. The study guide, available at www.bondbooks.net, directs readers to many passages from Lewis's works for further investigation. The impact of World War I on the human beings involved was created from eyewitness memoirs.

Douglas Bond, blessed husband and father of six, is author of twenty-five books, a hymn writer, and an award-winning teacher. He speaks at churches, schools, and conferences, directs the Oxford Creative Writing Master Class, and leads Church history tours, including an Armistice tour of the Western Front. Find out more at www.bondbooks.net.

MORE DOUGLAS BOND

Neil Perkins, a student at Haltwhistle Grammar School in England, unearths an ancient Roman manuscript. After dedicating himself to studying Latin, he uncovers a story of treachery and betrayal from the third century.

"Enjoyable reading for anyone who likes a gripping, fast-paced adventure story, **Hostage Lands** will especially delight young students of Latin and Roman history."
        Starr Meade, author of *Grandpa's Box*

Half-Saxon, half-Dane, misfit Cynwulf lives apart from the world in a salvaged Viking ship, dreaming of spending his life with the fair Haeddi. When he is accused of murder, he must clear his name before he loses everything to the vengeance of the community that has already rejected him.

"In **Hand of Vengeance** Douglas Bond shines a light on the past in a way that's as entertaining as it is informative."
        Janie B. Cheaney, senior writer, WORLD Magazine

CROWN & COVENANT TRILOGY

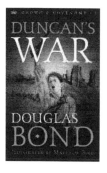 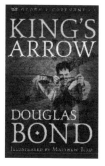 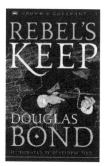

The Crown & Covenant trilogy follows the lives of the M'Kethe family as they endure persecution in 17th–century Scotland and later flee to colonial America. Douglas Bond weaves together fictional characters and historical figures from Scottish Covenanting history.

"Unleashes the reader's imagination—a rip-roaring good yarn."

George Grant, author, teacher, pastor at Parish Presbyterian Church

"Douglas Bond has introduced a new generation to the heroics of the Scottish Covenanters, and he has done it in a delightful way."

Ligon Duncan, First Presbyterian Church, Jackson, Mississippi

FAITH & FREEDOM TRILOGY

  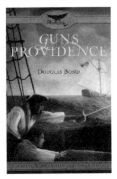

The Faith & Freedom trilogy, sequel to the Crown & Covenant trilogy, chronicles new generations of the M'Kethe family who find freedom in 18th-century America. Adventure is afoot as Old World tyrannies clash with New World freedoms. Douglas Bond seamlessly weaves together fictional characters with historical figures from Scottish and American history.

"Action from beginning to end. I wish I'd had this kind of book to read when I was a kid."
Joel Belz, founder, WORLD Magazine

"A tale of America's revolutionary beginning, told with strength and truth. . . . Take up and read!"
Peter A. Lillback, author, *Sacred Fire*